NEVER TRUST AN EARL

The Never Series
Book Three

By Maggi Andersen

ARE YOU SIGNED UP FOR DRAGONBLADE'S BLOG?

You'll get the latest news and information on exclusive giveaways, exclusive excerpts, coming releases, sales, free books, cover reveals and more.

Check out our complete list of authors, too!

No spam, no junk. That's a promise!

Sign Up Here

www.dragonbladepublishing.com

Dearest Reader;

Thank you for your support of a small press. At Dragonblade Publishing, we strive to bring you the highest quality Historical Romance from some of the best authors in the business. Without your support, there is no 'us', so we sincerely hope you adore these stories and find some new favorite authors along the way.

Happy Reading!

CEO, Dragonblade Publishing

No other love
Can warm my heart
Now that I've known the comfort of your arms

No Other Love

Bob Russell
Sidney Russell
Paul Weston
Music by Chopin

PROLOGUE

T WO HOURS BEFORE dawn on a warm summer night, Dominic Thorne, Earl of Redcliffe, entered Berkley Square on foot. A full moon rode the cloudless sky and lit his way from the hackney he'd left at the corner. The streets around the square were quiet, the carriages and link boys gone.

A suspicious shadow moved among the trees in the garden in the center of the square. Ruing the snug fit of his evening coat, Dominic took a good hold of his cane. He'd imbibed a gallon of champagne during the evening and was too mellow to search for footpads bold enough to enter Mayfair and rob a gentleman. Not entirely in his cups, apparently, for his gait was steady and his thoughts clear. Fortunately, when he had taken another few steps, a man vaulted the fence and emerged onto the moonlit road.

Dominic held his cane in both hands. "Who goes there?"

"I'll have your watch and wallet if you wish to live, me lord," came the coarse reply, as he crossed the distance between them.

He looked gaunt and hungry. Dominic slid the sheath of steel from its bed within his cane. "And if I don't wish to give them to you?"

The thief hesitated, then he advanced, the knife flashing silver. No match for Dominic's blade unless he threw it at him, but Dominic was ready for it. Years in the army had taught him some useful skills.

As the thief raised his arm, Dominic was already moving. His cane deflected the knife, which missed him by a whisker and clattered to the ground.

Dominic took a step closer, sheathing his swordstick. "Want to take your chance? I'm happy to oblige. I haven't had a good fight since I returned from the war."

Taking in Dominic's pugilist stance, his attacker's eyes widened with sudden awareness. He backed away, then turned and ran. The slap of his shoes echoed around the square for several minutes, then nothing.

"A fellow isn't even safe in his own street," Dominic muttered. He snatched up the man's knife and mounted the steps to his front door, then fished the key out of his waistcoat pocket, having instructed the staff to go to bed.

Lord and Lady Crompton's ball, being the last of the summer before the heat drove the *ton* from the city, inevitably ended close to dawn. And, as usual, it was still in full swing when he and his cousin, George Yardley, bade goodnight to their hosts.

Dominic had spent the evening trying to cheer George up, who was in despair because the lady's father had refused his offer of marriage. "It's bloody when a fellow's judged by his bank balance," he'd said gloomily. "And by a fellow who makes his money in trade."

"Did you love her, George?"

"No, but Miss Willingdale loved me, and her dowry was splendid," George said regrettably. He glanced at Dominic, anger and disappointment darkening his brown eyes. "I would have done my duty by her."

"I'm sorry, George." Dominic had expected it. Willingdale would never have agreed to the suit. George had a reputation as a gambler. Dominic had given him money in the past and knew if he did so again, it would go the way of the rest at the gaming tables.

"If only I'd inherited the earldom," George murmured into

his wineglass.

Dominic chuckled. "I would have had to die for it to happen."

George looked stricken. "Lord! Sorry, old fellow. Didn't mean it."

"Apparently, the estate comprises an old house and lands miles from anywhere. I dread traveling such a distance in the coach."

"Dashed unpleasant on a horse," George remarked. He threw back the last of his drink and put the empty glass down.

"Best we go to our beds, George." Alarmed at his friend's despondency, Dominic took his arm.

"Watch out for highwaymen when you go." George staggered and slurred his words. To Dominic's knowledge, there hadn't been highwaymen on the Great North Road for years.

George leaned against Dominic as he assisted him into a hackney. He tipped the jarvey to ensure George reached his digs safely.

It had shocked Dominic when the family solicitor advised him his father's elder brother, Uncle Alberic, had passed away, and he was now the Earl of Redcliffe. Alberic's two sons assured the lineage. But all that changed with startling swiftness. His heir, Miles, succumbed to a fever, and then, not more than a year later, the younger son, Adrian, died during a duel on Hampstead Heath. Now, George Yardley, although a remote connection, stood next in line after Dominic.

The change of rank and the resulting Redcliffe estate meant little to Dominic. His carefree existence in London after the grueling years of war satisfied him, and he'd been happy to continue living it. But as the Earl of Redcliffe, his life was altered in ways he couldn't ignore. At balls, debutantes' mothers went to outlandish lengths to throw their daughters his way. Shopkeepers and tailors, bootmakers and hatters sought his patronage. Doors previously only slightly ajar, opened wide to him. While his new position made no difference to old friends because they knew him for who he was, fair-weather friends now invited him to all manner of affairs, as if being in his company might improve their position in society.

Life became intolerable when an article in a scandal sheet mentioned how many women the new earl had squired around London and speculated on his choice of bride. Another, far worse, followed, written in more lurid and inaccurate detail. They accused him of being a rakehell, and produced the testimony of three women, only one of whom Dominic had met but declined to bed, who declared they'd engaged in a night of riotous lovemaking.

A caricature of him as the new earl wearing his coronet and carousing naked in a bed with the three women was displayed in a print shop window, where people gathered to look. Friends spoke out in his defense, and one or two laughed and slapped him on the back. But there were also some who cut him. And as a bachelor who was seen to enjoy the company of women, it was impossible to defend. He disliked that the image of him as a rakehell tarnished his reputation, when only a few years previously, Wellington had hailed him as a hero after the battle of Waterloo. He'd been proud of that, as had his father, and he was glad his parents were no longer here to learn of this slander.

Dominic groaned. And now, attacked by some cutthroat a few steps from his house. London had lost its charm for him. It made him wish he could conjure up a magic carpet and fly away.

As he passed the hall table, he picked up the post awaiting his perusal from the silver salver and went into the library. Candlelight from the hall sconces guided his way to the desk. He put the knife in a drawer, noting it was expensive and finely made. The thief had likely stolen it. Lighting a candle, he picked up the pearl-handled letter opener and slit the missive from his sister, Evelyn, Lady Trelawny, a keen correspondent. Their three-year-old son, Gerald, had developed hives, but the doctor assured them it wasn't serious. Was her beloved brother in good health and spirits? Could they expect him at Christmas? How fortunate that their neighbor, Viscount Gillingham's delightful daughter,

Marianne, had not yet become engaged. She was pretty and excelled at the pianoforte. Evelyn felt sure Dominic would approve of her.

His sister's persistence made him smile. She'd come to the entirely erroneous conclusion that he was lonely. That marriage would serve him better than the life of a bachelor. She was wrong, but her concern touched him. He tossed the letter on the leather desktop. Sifting through the rest, he discarded all but one from Williams, the estate manager Dominic had recently employed to take care of matters pertaining to Redcliffe Hall.

Until now, the unoccupied mansion and estate grounds in Northumberland held little interest, as it still eked out a small subsistence, enough to keep it functioning. Ignoring its existence for months, he was now forced to make a decision. He'd hoped to rent the house and sell some of the land, but Williams's letter deplored the state of it. He urged something must be done. Could his lordship come to Redcliffe Hall to advise him?

Days of travel in the coach, which Dominic detested, and a forestalling of his intention to take a new mistress. Lady Anne Cranston had been at her loveliest tonight, her assets on display in the plunging crimson silk gown, and she left him in no doubt that she was available. He yawned, picked up the candle, and made his way to bed.

Right now, he grasped at the chance to leave London. While away, hopefully, another scandal would engage the *ton*. Prinny, for instance, could be relied upon to set tongues wagging.

Dominic supposed the house was moderately comfortable. Williams's description had been brief, but he assumed some of his uncle's staff remained in service. All would be revealed in time. Now all he wanted to do was go to bed.

CHAPTER ONE

Northumberland, Summer 1819

THE EARL OF Redcliffe was jolted from the seat when his carriage struck a deep pothole and lurched into a ditch. The vehicle tilted at a precarious angle. He shoved open the door and leapt onto the bank beside a small stream and gazed with concern at his coachman, who bent forward on the box, a hand to his head.

"Are you hurt, Grimsby?"

Grimsby rubbed his forehead and climbed gingerly down. "A bit of a banged noddle is all, milord."

Dominic's groom appeared to be hopping as he hastened to calm the skittish horses.

"What about you, Fellows?"

"Merely twisted me ankle, milord." As the chestnuts whickered and strained in their harness, Fellows ran experienced hands over their legs. He shook his head. "No sign of injury."

Dominic and Grimsby squatted down to examine the undercarriage.

"That front right wheel's broken'n two, milord," Grimsby said, stating the obvious.

Dominic stood and brushed his trousers. "We passed a sign a way back saying it was three miles to the village. I'll fetch the wheelwright. You and Fellows stay with the carriage."

"No need, milord," Grimsby said, shocked. "I'm well able to walk."

He eyed the man's pale face and the bruise forming on his forehead. "No. I relish a stroll after hours spent in the carriage."

Dominic left them and strode up the road, breathing in fresh air tinged with damp foliage and wet earth. The trees bordering the route dripped from an early rain shower, but above him, the summer sky was almost cloudless and a clear, bright blue. In the distance, the drying fields shimmered. Since he'd sold out of the army after the Battle of Waterloo, he preferred not to stray far from London, and yet here he was, miles from anywhere.

Surprisingly, after a few days on the road, with the ever-changing view of peat bogs, moorland, and hay meadows, so different from anything he'd seen before, Dominic found he gained some perspective on the last disappointing year. While he didn't consider himself a rakehell, because he would never coerce a woman, he feared the gossip worried his sister. But even for Evelyn's sake, he had no intention of marrying until well into his thirties.

As the last mile passed, he considered this trip to be an excellent idea. To leave the sooty gray skies and crammed streets of London for a short spell, not to mention the gossip swirling about seemed exactly what was needed. He hailed a pair of black-and-white cows standing in a field. They remained like statues, staring at him while they chewed. Dominic chuckled. The silence here was positively deafening. He felt untethered from his London life, floating free. It was a good feeling.

He considered it unwise to leave the men and the horses for too long, and careless of the mud sticking to his top boots, he jumped a puddle and broke into a run. Rounding a bend in the road, a few thatched-roofed cottages came into view. A sign welcomed him to Redcliffe Village. It gave him a jolt as reality struck. He was the fifth earl in a family whose history reached back to William the Conqueror.

By the look of the small, quiet village, he feared it could prove grindingly dull. A week or two at most would be enough with Williams's help to prepare the estate for leasing or sale. Then back to London, refreshed.

The church spire came into view. He walked past the water-mill, crossed a stone bridge over the River Tyne, and entered the village.

There were few people about, but it was still early. The coach had departed the last coaching inn at first light. Once the wheel was mended, breakfast would be in order. An inn, the Plough, was farther along the street. After a hearty meal, he could face the neglected estate his uncle had shut himself away in for decades.

He passed a few shops and businesses overlooking the green, not yet open, and approached a barn with the wheelwright's sign affixed above the door. As he drew near, a young woman, her skirts gathered high to reveal a trim ankle, bolted out the barn door. Her eyes on the path, she cannoned into his chest.

She stared up at him, her bonnet shoved back on her head, saved from falling by its blue ribbons, while Dominic steadied her, his hands on her shoulders. He gazed down into a pair of stunning, violet-blue eyes. "May I be of help?"

She stepped away to a safer distance. "No, thank you, sir." Something akin to recognition dawned in those wonderful eyes. A frown creased the smooth skin between straight, dark brows.

Dominic swept off his hat. He'd enjoyed the brief moment her fragrant, slim body rested against his chest. Amused, he observed her. From her bonnet to her shoes she was a decidedly fetching woman. "Are you sure?"

"I am quite sure, Lord Redcliffe." Her voice crisp, she settled her straw hat over her disordered dusky curls. Knew him, did she? He cocked an eyebrow.

"There's an article in the local paper," she explained. "They mentioned your visit."

But why the distrustful attitude? Had London gossip traveled this far? Surely not the print shop caricature? *Lord, no.* His estate manager, Williams, would likely have spread about Dominic's intention to visit. "And you are?"

"Miss Jenner, my lord."

She spoke well for a country lass. Some years past twenty, and still unmarried, judging by the lack of rings on her slender fingers. He was pleased to find a pretty woman here, miles from a big town. Not a good welcome, however, for her eyes remained wary. "My carriage ended up in a ditch, and I have need of the wheelwright," he said affably. "Is the fellow inside?"

"I... er... yes... he is." After an annoyed shake of her head, she said, "He's busy."

Rendered curious by the flush creeping over her cheeks, he hesitated, then replaced his hat. "I must have a word with him. Good day to you."

"Good day, milord." With a bob, she hurried away.

When Dominic reached the door, he turned. But she'd disappeared from view down the street. She must have almost run. He stepped into the dim interior, breathed in the smells of sawdust and sweat. The wheelwright stood buck naked, a towel in his hands, a bucket of water at his feet.

Dominic thought of Miss Jenner's reaction and grinned. "Bickle, I believe."

Naked, Bickle paused from vigorously drying his hair and turned, displaying a broad chest covered in a matt of black hair. He was quick to perceive Dominic as a gentleman, and snatched up his breeches, pulling them on. "I won't be but a moment, sir."

Dominic introduced himself. It was possible Bickle knew who he was, for he calmly nodded.

"Take your time. I don't wish to interrupt your ablutions."

As Bickle slipped his feet into his boots, Dominic explained his situation.

While the wheelwright readied the trap, he wondered who Miss Jenner was. He would expect a farmer's daughter to have an earthier attitude to nudity.

The trap ready, Dominic joined Bickle on the seat.

As Bickle drove the carthorse along the road, Dominic wondered whether he would see Miss Jenner again. Bound to—it was a small place. Although she'd hardly been welcoming, once she got to know what a genial fellow he was, she might change her mind. If by some unseen circumstance he was stuck here for weeks while he worked out what to do with this property left in his unwilling hands, any feminine company—and most particularly someone as attractive as Miss Jenner—would certainly while away the hours.

EVERYONE IN THE village would know him on sight, dressed in his superbly tailored Bond Street clothes. Never in her memory had such a well-dressed, highborn gentleman visited the village. The former earl didn't count. On the rare occasions he ventured out, he dressed like a pauper.

Olivia picked up a long stick and used it as a switch to batter away the leafy fronds encroaching on the path. The heat had only now left her cheeks. She had wanted to meet him, but not in that fashion. The drawing in the local newspaper hadn't quite captured him. They'd made him appear sober and steely-eyed, and while his features were rugged and his jaw hard, when he smiled, he looked more like the rake they'd heard about. His arrogant, green gaze flickered over her, from her head to her feet, making her quiver. Yes, definitely a rake.

Entirely too attractive with smile lines radiating from his compelling eyes, a lean muscled body, and skin of an olive tone. His wavy, dark brown hair invited a woman's touch. That last bit made her frown. Was she to act like a silly girl? But when she recalled his amused smile at her recognizing him, and his even white teeth, her heart gave a strange flutter.

Olivia continued along the road, increasingly annoyed at her foolishness. She needed to keep a cool head about Lord Redcliffe and not allow the embarrassment of their first meeting to spoil her plans. This was her chance to right a wrong, and she was determined to seize it with both hands.

She often walked the few miles to Redcliffe Hall along the road bounded by the estate's high stone wall, to see if anything had changed since the old man died. From her limited vision through the tall, padlocked gates, nothing had. The ancient gatehouse deserted, the avenue of gnarled trees unchecked by any gardener still formed a dark tunnel over the driveway, the grounds overgrown, and the lawns past thigh-high. What must once have been a magnificent Elizabethan mansion now sad and neglected, with broken panes in the cobwebbed, mullioned windows.

Haunted, many believed, by the old earl guarding his money, which rumor claimed he'd hidden somewhere in the house. Olivia didn't know if that was true, but he certainly didn't spend any of it paying his bills. If he still lived, her poor father could attest to that.

Olivia entered through the side gate of Lady Lowry's establishment and followed the path to the servants' entrance. Her mistress had sent her to Bickle to arrange for him to fix the broken axle on her cabriolet. Before Lady Lowry questioned her, she must find an excuse for why she hadn't seen him. Although she certainly had, much more than she ever wished to see. As it was, she loathed having to speak to him because he leered at her and made improper suggestions. Fortunately, Bickle had a towel over his head, and she made her escape without him seeing her. Then in her haste to get away from the man, she'd run into Lord Redcliffe. Literally. Smack bang against his hard chest. *Heavens.* He'd caught hold of her. Held for a moment while she breathed in his clean male smell.

He'd be very different to Bickle when stripped. She batted that thought away. She'd been tongue-tied with embarrassment, and he must think her an idiot. But then her absolute distrust of all Redcliffes took hold, and she'd had to take herself in hand not to reveal it.

Olivia entered through the servants' door of the manor house, a solid two-story brick edifice built in the last century, where Lady Lowry employed her as housekeeper. Her mistress, the widow of Sir Hubert Lowry, could be difficult, at times quite horrid to her servants. As she entered the breakfast room, Olivia wondered what mood she would be in this morning. She hoped the young maid, Emily, hadn't served her mistress cold porridge again.

In a dressing gown of pale pink, lavishly trimmed with ribbons and bows, Lady Lowry looked up from buttering her roll. "There you are. You've been gone a long time." She gazed suspiciously at Olivia. "Did you tarry to flirt with the fellow?"

Olivia suppressed a shudder. "I had no chance to speak to Bickle. He was busy."

"I'll send the footman. He will not be turned away."

"As I left," Olivia said, aware this would draw her mistress's attention from herself, "I saw Lord Redcliffe."

Lady Lowry put down her roll. "The earl has arrived?"

"Yes."

She tucked strands of fair hair beneath her cap. "I must get busy. Such a lot to organize. Of course, he will want to meet those in society equal to his rank. Whom shall I invite?" She frowned. "So few to choose from. Mr. and Mrs. Crompton of the Pastures, and the widow, Mrs. Herrington, and of course, Mr. Lancaster, the squire at Northoaks..." She drifted off for a moment in thought.

Olivia's cheeks warmed. She told herself she was immune to her mistress's callous disregard for her feelings but feared she wasn't. Would never be.

Impervious to any hurt she might have caused at the mention of the squire, Lady Lowry stared up at her. "Don't daydream, girl. The reception rooms need to be cleaned. Thoroughly. Take up the rugs and make sure the piano is properly dusted and polished. The servants always make a poor job of it." She tapped her chin.

"We might have some music. And see they are careful with my china ornaments. Any chips, and the girl will find herself out in the street. Tell Cook to come here. I wish to discuss the menu."

Lord Redcliffe's arrival had stirred Lady Lowry into a frenzy. Relieved to escape, Olivia hurried from the room. In the kitchen, Cook sat with her morning cup of tea, something delicious baking in the oven. "Sit down and have a bite to eat before you fade away," she said, eyeing Olivia. "Is Madam in one of her moods?"

"She wishes to discuss the menu for the party she plans for the Earl of Redcliffe. He has arrived in the village"

"Oh?" Cook pushed her cap on straight. "Well, his nibs will have to take what he's given, won't he. I'm not one of the Prince of Wales's fancy chefs."

Olivia laughed as she poured herself a cup of tea. When free of her duties, she would call on Lord Redcliffe. As soon as she learned of his expected visit, she had given this considerable thought, for she feared he may not remain here long. If he planned to restore the house with even a skeleton staff for further visits, he would soon see what a pickle he found himself in and could hardly refuse her offer. She rubbed her aching temples. The success of her endeavor rested on his acceptance of her proposal.

CHAPTER TWO

JAMES WILLIAMS, DOMINIC'S estate manager, unlocked the Redcliffe Hall gates, and Grimsby drove the coach onto the grounds. The vehicle bumped and rattled along the ill-kept gravel drive through an avenue of ancient elms.

Reeling from the state of the gardens, Dominic's spirits sank further at the daunting sight of the Elizabethan house, built centuries ago by courtiers in the hope of the queen staying there when she traveled north. As far as he knew, she never did. Ivy grew rampant over the pale stone walls. He anticipated smoking chimneys and a leaking slate roof.

The coach stopped outside the front doors, set in a recessed stone archway above a short flight of steps, where he alighted with Williams.

Williams produced a large key and unlocked the solid oak doors.

"No servants stayed on?" Dominic asked in despair.

"Not a one, milord."

The entry, with a cedar settle, led into an echoing great hall, the ribbed ceiling two stories high, a mammoth stone fireplace at each end. A refectory table and a few straight-backed chairs were the only furnishings. Portraits of the family's ancestors still hung on the walls, along with massive tapestries depicting battle and hunting scenes, getting ragged. The air smelled thickly of dust.

It was odd to imagine his father spending his childhood here before he went to boarding school and on to Cambridge. He'd spoken often of the beauty of the Northumbrian landscape, and its history, but to Dominic's knowledge, he'd never visited again after he married.

He removed his hat and gloves, then flicked the dirty table with his handkerchief before he laid them down. The vast hall was cold as a tomb. He should turn around and go back to London. Leave it to Williams to find a tenant, or failing that, sell it. He sighed. "How many bedchambers are there, Williams?"

"Not sure, my lord. All but a few, shut up for years. Shall I have them counted?"

A widower of some fifty-five years with dark hair graying at the temples, Williams had a reassuring manner Dominic appreciated. Especially now. He had taken to him immediately, finding wisdom in his hazel eyes.

"Leave it for now."

"Servants' quarters are up near the attics."

They crossed the slate floor to the carved timber staircase rising to the floors above.

More portraits of his ancestors hung in gilt frames in the long gallery, which ran the length of the house. Dominic paused before a gentleman on horseback, his riding clothes in the style of the last century.

"Your uncle," Williams said at his elbow.

"He would have sat for this in his middle years, well before his riding accident." The portrait differed from the idea he'd formed of his uncle. Alberic was a big man with a powerful build and keen green eyes, uncomfortably similar to his own. Astride a magnificent jet-black horse, a riding crop resting in a large, capable-looking hand, he appeared in control and confident, every inch the earl.

They entered through a stone arched doorway into the drawing room, paneled in dark oak, and crossed the boards covered by an Aubusson carpet. Beautifully proportioned, the room still displayed a shabby elegance. Slender columns framed the white marble fireplace, the mantel reaching up to the ceiling, from which hung twin chandeliers of Italian crystal, dulled by neglect, as were the cherrywood Queen Anne sideboards, gate-leg tables, and needlepoint covered chairs. The silk curtains were threadbare, and the damask upholstery on the sofas, faded.

Dominic eyed the blank patches on the walls. "Some paintings are gone."

"Before I came and made an inventory. Your uncle may have sold them."

"May have?"

"Or they were stolen."

Dominic frowned as he studied a large cobweb swinging in the draft from a heavy dark beam. "Can we hire back some of my uncle's staff?"

"I doubt it. The house servants left well before the old earl died. The home farm is still worked, and Clough, the gamekeeper, lives in a tied cottage. Your uncle's will stated they were to be kept on. He left funds for the purpose." He shook his head. "But not enough is produced here to warrant it continuing."

Dominic found his uncle's generosity surprising. He had doubted his uncle was capable of such benevolence. His father rarely mentioned his brother, but when he did, it was with a decided lack of warmth. They parted over some argument before Dominic was born, and he never came to visit or attend family celebrations. He would have liked to know more about Alberic, but there was no one to ask, as his mother and father died of fever, a month apart a few years ago. His younger sister, Evelyn, had remained at home until her debut at eighteen and her marriage the same year. She might be better informed than he.

"I'm surprised the gamekeeper has been kept on."

"It's at your uncle's directive. Clough culls some birds to feed the poor. You'll find the woods in better order than the house, milord."

Again, that baffling view of his uncle. But one didn't live in the woods. Dominic rubbed his chin. "I'll need an army of servants to make this livable."

Williams raised his eyebrows. "I thought..."

He smiled. "That I'd sell it and scurry back to London? I might yet." What made him question his early decision? His uncle had begun to interest him. The family portraits certainly stirred his curiosity. But might it be the once beautiful, now unloved house steeped in history, which remained a mystery? It certainly appealed that by improving the estate, he might change some people's lives for the better. Money spent in the right quarters to make the estate more productive, and he would rarely need to come here.

He wasn't sure why he'd decided to prolong his stay. "I'd be loath to spend more than a couple of days at the inn," Dominic said as they left the room. "I'll move in here as soon as we have a few servants. Surely there are some in the area in need of employment?"

Williams led the way to the stairs. "The locals won't come here after the caretaker left. Spooked by the place. Candlelight's been seen flickering through the windows at night since the old man died."

"Any idea who's behind it?"

The estate manager shrugged. "Someone searching for the supposed treasure? I discovered a jimmied window, rooms in disarray, drawers open, and cupboards searched. Books scattered over the library carpet. Even some of the oak wainscotting ripped off the reception room walls."

Dominic raised his eyebrows. "Strange business."

"The rumor persists of a cache of money hidden somewhere in the house. The old earl certainly thought someone wished to rob him."

Dominic swung around from studying the bleak view of overgrown lawns through the long staircase window. Smoke rose from a distant cottage chimney. "Do you think there's any truth in it?"

"Seems unlikely, but who knows?" He shrugged. "The old gentleman was known to be a bit…" He tapped his forehead with a finger. "His health declined after a fall riding to hounds some years ago. As for the servants, we might have better luck in Gateshead," Williams added.

"Then I'll leave you to deal with that. I would like to speak to the former steward. Is he still living in these parts?"

"Yes, he works for the squire now, at Northoaks."

Dominic walked to the door. "Show me the earl's suite."

On the upper floor, Williams threw open the door to the musty smelling suite of rooms. "In the last few years, your uncle didn't sleep here. He'd made a bed in the butler's pantry. I've heard he kept a loaded shotgun at hand."

Dominic suffered a swift tug of sympathy for the old man. He disliked the walls papered in such a dark green, himself. Above the oak, four-poster bed, blood-red curtains spilled from the earl's coat of arms. Dominic crossed the rug patterned in crimson, green, and gold arabesques to the windows. He pulled aside the velvet curtains, raising a cloud of dust, and opened a window, which overlooked a moss-covered fountain filled with dead leaves, centered in a weedy forecourt bordered by shapeless hedges.

He turned away, growing increasingly disheartened by the task ahead. Not somewhere he cared to sleep. He chided himself. He'd slept in far worse places during his years in the army.

So far north, even in summer, the nights could turn cold here. He crouched down and peered up the chimney flue. He rose, slapping his hands together. "Needs sweeping. Will you see to it?"

"That I can do, milord. And I have a young fellow in mind who might serve as footman."

Dominic pushed his hair off his forehead with impatient hands. "Well, that's a start. Any chance of a few housemaids, a cook, and a housekeeper?"

Williams stroked his chin. "A cook and a couple of house-maids maybe, but a housekeeper will be difficult to find. The gentry hereabouts employ the best on offer or else send abroad as far as Newcastle for them."

Dominic grimaced. "Best see what shape the stables are in. I'll need to purchase a horse. As soon as I can, I'll ride over the estate, meet the tenant farmers." He thought regretfully of Firefly, his gelding stabled in London. It would be impractical to send for him for such a short period.

"The squire of Northoaks keeps an excellent stable. He might sell you one of his thoroughbreds," Williams replied. "He stables a few hunters for foxhunting."

When they reached the stables, the coach stood on the cobbles in the quadrangle while Grimsby cleaned it.

"Quarters all right, Grimsby?"

Grimsby nodded toward the rooms in the stable block. "Comfortable enough, milord."

"That's something to be grateful for. We'll eat at the inn for now. But return here tonight for the horses. Any concerns, have a word with Williams. Tell him what you need."

Within the dim interior, Fellows tended the carriage horses resting in their new stalls.

"No injuries to the horses, Fellows?" Dominic asked, coming to stand beside his groom.

"No. None the worse for their experience, milord."

"A good-sized stable."

"Yes, and a decent tack room."

Dominic wandered the other buildings with his groom. He chuckled when he found his uncle's high-perch phaeton stored in a corner, partly covered in straw. "Take it out and clean it. If it's still sound, I'll use it."

He returned to the house, pleased that much could be salvaged from his uncle's sad neglect. Impossible to stay long without a minimum number of servants. He debated sending for his valet, Cushing, then decided against it. While an excellent valet, he was not a man who would lend a hand beyond his own duties. And Dominic was more than capable of dressing himself after years in the army.

A small valise packed, he left Williams to close up the house, and walked the five odd miles to the inn, his thoughts on his uncle. Much that he had discovered here unsettled him.

The sun set as he passed the church and entered the village, and he was more than ready for his dinner. He considered the village a pretty place, with black and white half-timbered cottages and roses spilling over the fences. In the distance, sheep and cows grazed in lush green fields.

Crossing the main street, Dominic touched his hat to a woman who looked askance at him, before bobbing a curtsy and hurrying on. Not exactly welcoming. How long, he mused, before his presence ceased to cause such a stir?

ON SATURDAY MORNING, Olivia woke filled with a sense of purpose. She dressed carefully in her best walking gown of apricot sarsnet, one she had worn in those halcyon days when, as the daughter of a respected man in the district, she was required to dress well. She pulled on a cream linen spencer because the breeze was cool.

Today, Lady Lowry was to visit friends for luncheon and spend the afternoon playing whist. She ordered Olivia to oversee the beating of the drawing room rugs while she was away, as the dust always gave her a cough.

If she hurried, there was time enough for Olivia to walk to Redcliffe Hall, put her proposal to the earl, and return before her mistress noticed. Once, after several glasses of sherry, Lady Lowry admitted to Olivia that she was the most competent housekeeper she'd had in her employ. It amused Olivia, for the woman was very hard to please at the best of times and paid poorly, dismissing staff on the slightest whim.

Olivia organized the rugs, and as soon as Lady Lowry was

driven away in the landau, she pulled on her cotton gloves and tied her bonnet strings. In her best walking boots, she set off for Redcliffe Hall. Would the earl agree to see her? Or did he intend to return to London? It hurt her chest to consider it, for too much hinged on the success of this venture. To clear her father's name, although his grave would remain far from her mother's and those resting in the church graveyard. If this gambit were successful, it would provide the means for her to rise above the dire straits she now found herself in.

Her only other choice, if she were to stay in this village she loved, would be to accept the farmer Ian Kershaw's proposal of marriage and become mother to his six unruly children. Although her chances of marriage had grown more remote with each year that passed, because of a sad lack of suitable men, she held onto the dream of holding a baby in her arms. Not Ian Kershaw's baby. She recoiled at his ignorance and unwashed odor.

How imposing Lord Redcliffe was, she mused, as she walked along. She'd tried, somewhat unsuccessfully, to forget their awkward encounter. The spark of intelligence and interest in his green eyes told her he was a man who rarely missed much. She feared she'd made a bad first impression, unsettled by the naked wheelwright. But she had not missed how attractive the earl was. With a rake's reputation, she reminded herself. Should he accept the proposal she intended to put to him, and she moved into the house, would she be out of her depth?

Olivia frowned. She could manage him, as she had other overly attentive men who acted with a lack of propriety on discovering she was alone and unprotected.

How long did he intend to stay? It all hinged on that, but she wasn't confident. A man such as he would soon tire of this quiet place. And he was sure to have engagements in London.

Redcliffe Hall gates stood open, and she passed through them. It was cool beneath the trees. Drawing her shawl around her shoulders as the breeze lifted her bonnet and stirred the hairs on the back of her neck, she hurried on.

The rambling mansion appeared through the trees. Nothing seemed changed, from here, it still looked deserted, with no servants bustling about. She stepped into the welcome summer sun and walked up the path to the front door. She breathed deeply to steady her nerves and took a firm hold of the knocker. A loud clang echoed, accentuating the empty spaces within. There would not yet be a butler or footman to answer the door.

Olivia stepped down onto the path and walked around to the kitchen and peered through the dirty windowpane. She didn't expect to find a bustling cook rolling dough and a scullery maid scrubbing pots, but were there no staff at all? Did this mean he intended to leave immediately? Sell the house? Disappointment lay heavy in her stomach as she retraced her steps.

Olivia rounded a corner of the house as Lord Redcliffe walked down the drive from the direction of the stables. She took another deep breath to steady her nerves while she waited for him to approach.

Olivia curtsied. "My lord."

He removed his hat and stood, feet planted, studying her. "We meet again. Miss Jenner, I believe?"

She considered his stance arrogant, but as it also showed off his fine physique to advantage, it sent another shaft of worry through her. "Yes, sir. I hoped I might have a word with you."

"I would invite you inside, but your gown will suffer from the dust." He glanced around and motioned to a garden seat beneath an elm tree. "Shall we sit?"

"Yes, thank you."

They sat at a discreet distance, his hat on the seat between them, and observed each other.

He folded his arms across a wide expanse of rust-colored waistcoat. "I am surprised to see you again, Miss Jenner. But it is a pleasant surprise. You wished to ask me something?"

He remembered her name. She wasn't sure why this bothered her, but it did. She studied his face. A slender, finely chiseled nose, his mouth full and wide and slightly sensual. There was that determined cast to his chin and jaw she'd noted before. How masculine he was. So strong, and self-confident. Why couldn't he have been spindly and shortsighted?

She forced herself to look into his penetrating green gaze. "I am here to offer my services as a housekeeper, should you wish for one."

He arched his dark brows. "Housekeeper? You're too young for such a post, Miss Jenner. Not above twenty-five at a guess."

"I'm quite capable of performing any duties required of me." Holding her age against her flummoxed her. She had intended to add a few years, but now found she couldn't lie. She huffed in a breath. "I hold the post of housekeeper at Lady Lowry's establishment, Spelling Park. She is satisfied with my work."

"Then why not stay there?"

"Because I wish to tackle something new."

"Audacious of you. And surprising."

"I don't believe so," she said, dismayed at where this conversation was leading.

His gaze roamed her face and then dropped unapologetically to her breasts. Her fingers twitched as she resisted placing her hands there. "What do you think the villagers would make of you living under my roof? I am unmarried and have, at this moment, very few employees." He spread his wide hands, palms up. "No household ones as yet."

So he planned to remain for the time being. "I assume you shall require servants, my lord?"

"My estate manager must go to Gateshead to find them." His warm, charming smile quite caught her off guard. "As much as I need competent staff, and I'm not doubting your abilities, Miss Jenner, I cannot hire you without causing a good deal of gossip I'd rather not have."

"But why? I am hardly in my first flush of youth."

He laughed. "Perhaps not. But neither are you in your dotage, and you're much too attractive for a housekeeper," he said bluntly.

"Lady Lowry expressed no such concerns."

"Why would she? It would only bother her if you were, er, distracting her male servants too much."

Her cheeks heated. "I can assure you nothing like that occurred, nor would it."

He nodded, waiting for her to continue.

"I am good at what I do. And few in the village would disapprove. They know I must work to earn my keep, ever since..." She stopped. She was making a muck of it.

"Since?" he prompted.

He was entirely too observant. "I shan't trouble you with my affairs, my lord, only to say I wish to work here. I believe I shall be an asset to you."

He stood and put on his hat. "I don't doubt it, Miss Jenner. And I regret having to refuse you. Now you must excuse me. I must visit the squire."

Olivia's heart sank. Deeply disappointed, she could only rise to her feet and curtsey. She watched him stride away to the door. He would return to London before long, but the need for staff told her he'd keep the house open. She'd never considered her failure to be engaged would be because of her age or attractiveness, though she knew in the back of her mind he had been correct about Society frowning on her living in the house without other female servants. What a double-edged sword! Her looks attracted the worst men and now ruined her chance of a position here. She straightened her bonnet and set off down the avenue. Gateshead indeed! He would have to go as far as Newcastle and send his agent to all the mop fairs to find a housekeeper. She would not give up yet.

CHAPTER THREE

A s Dominic drove the phaeton to the squire's at Northoaks, he recalled Miss Jenner's proud expression, and how her beautiful eyes clouded to hide her secrets. He found her bewitching. While he needed a housekeeper, he feared the temptation of having such a fascinating woman under his roof could be a problem. An inordinate time had passed since he'd bedded a woman. And Miss Jenner's full bottom lip invited a man to nibble on it.

In London, he'd rarely spoken to his housekeeper, and barely knew her, but here, there was so much to be done, and with no butler, he could see the need to confer with a housekeeper often on many matters. He had no intention of embellishing his soiled reputation, and that of his uncle, by stoking the ire of the villagers.

Pushing such musings away, he guided the phaeton through Northoaks gates. Passing the long, handsome, colonnaded house of red brick with a wide porch set amid well-kept gardens, he continued on to the stables.

As Dominic drove the pantheon into the stable courtyard, a magnificent black stallion jerked impatiently while a groom rubbed him down.

A groom rushed to take the reins. With another glance at the horse, Dominic confirmed his first opinion. The animal was a beauty, arched along the topline with a neat head. When he walked back to the house a florid-faced, balding man of some fifty years stood on the porch. He held out his hand.

"Lord Redcliffe, good to meet you. Your note set me thinking." He shook Dominic's hand, then gestured indoors. "Would you care for a drink?"

"Thank you."

Dominic sipped a glass of fine Scottish whisky in the well-appointed parlor while Jeremy Lancaster explained.

"Ordinarily, some months after spring foaling, I'd have no horse to offer you. But as it happens, I do have the stallion. But to be honest with you, Onyx is a fractious animal. He's not suitable for hunting, and I've had to keep him separate. He bothers my mares. I'm considering gelding him."

"The black stallion I saw in the yard?"

"Yes, handsome fellow, isn't he?"

Dominic nodded. "Why is he unsuitable for the hunt?"

"He has a mean streak. Likes to have his head. Tossed one of my grooms over a hedge."

Dominic smiled. Firefly had been of similar temperament in Portugal until they got to know each other. No one wanted the horse except Dominic, who was happy to take him on. Quite a challenge, but they'd become friends before he brought him to England. Still a moody beast, Firefly, but Dominic knew the signs and how to handle him.

He finished his whisky. "I'd like to meet Onyx."

Lancaster smiled and put down his glass. "Let's hope it's a good day for him."

In the paddock, Onyx danced agilely about, well-coordinated muscles rippling beneath sun-warmed, ebony skin. The horse turned his head to observe them as they approached and swished his tail.

Dominic walked up to him and placed a hand on the horse's glossy neck. Onyx's ears wriggled, and warning ripples raced across the coat beneath his fingers.

"It's all right, fellow." Dominic gave him a pat. He turned to Lancaster. "What's his history?"

"Sir Hubert Lowry owned him. After his death, they sold the horse to a brute of a man who didn't treat the animal well. I offered to buy him, and fortunately for the horse, he agreed."

Onyx lowered his head and forcefully nudged the sleeve of Dominic's riding coat, his teeth bared. Dominic chuckled. "I'd like to see if we will suit. May I ride him?"

"But of course. You must try before you buy." He smiled ironically. "Although you might change your mind if he's in an evil mood."

Dominic grinned. "I'll take my chances."

While a groom saddled the horse, Dominic leaned back with both elbows resting on a rail. "I'd like a word with your steward. He worked for my uncle some months before he died. I'm told he is now in your employ."

"Pike? He should be in the estate office. After your ride?"

Dominic nodded, watching the horse, now saddled, being led over to him. Entering through the gate, he stood for a moment while the horse observed him.

As he slowly approached, the horse pinned back his ears and his nostrils flared. Dominic spoke to him in a low, soothing tone, placed a foot in the stirrup, and swung himself into the saddle.

Onyx's head came down, and he took off at a gallop around the enclosure, swerving and changing direction to toss Dominic off.

Dominic kept a good tight hold on the reins but didn't force the horse to slow. "Steady boy. Steady."

They circled the paddock twice before he reined him in. "Open the gate, Lancaster," Dominic called.

"You're sure, milord?"

"If you will."

He guided Onyx through the gate and nudged his flanks. The horse needed little prompting. He careered across the grass, heading for the trees. When Onyx veered off before entering the path leading into the wood, Dominic let him have his head. He galloped to the top of a rise and along the crest and down a steep incline.

The sharp wind in his face carried the smells of dry grasses and earth. It had been too long since he'd galloped over the land, not since his father had passed away. He'd inherited the family estate in Surrey, but hadn't wished to live there. After his sister married Justin Trelawny and moved to Cornwall, Dominic saw no sense in hanging on to it. He'd sold the property within a year. It surprised him that apart from the deep sorrow he felt at losing his parents, he'd turned his back on the home he'd grown up in with no real anguish. Oddly, Redcliffe Hall already meant more to him, and he wasn't ready to hand the running of it over to Williams and return to London.

Twenty minutes later, the horse's coat glistening with sweat, Onyx obliged him by slowing at his command.

"Splendid fellow," Dominic said in a quiet voice. "Now, shall we return in a more elegant manner?"

They rode back toward the paddock where Lancaster waited. "You know horses, milord," Lancaster said with an approving lift of his eyebrows.

"Need to when you have to rely on them for your life." Dominic dismounted, giving Onyx a scratch behind his ears.

"Ah, of course. The war." Lancaster motioned to the groom to take Onyx back to his stall and curry him.

"I'll take him off your hands, Squire," Dominic said.

Lancaster nodded. "Before we settle the matter, shall I take you to my steward?"

They passed the hounds penned in a large enclosure. The dogs raced along the wire, barking. In a small building, Pike sat at his desk, account books set out before him. A short, dark-haired man with a narrow face and pale gray eyes, his purposeful actions as he put away his quill, blotted, and closed the ledger, gave the impression of a careful man. He stood as Lancaster introduced Dominic.

Dominic shook his hand. "Mr. Pike. You worked for my uncle?"

Pike nodded. "For several years, my lord."

"Can you tell me something about those last years? Did anything trouble him?"

"Not the last months, my lord. I wasn't there. Something disturbed the earl. But what it was, I have no notion. I'm told the accident changed him. During my tenure, I often found him irrational. I'd been delighted to get such a position, but it proved too troublesome to continue to work for him."

"Why?"

"He was suspicious of everyone. Accused the staff of robbing him and put them all off."

"And that business with Jenner," Lancaster prompted.

Pike nodded. "An argument over some bill, I heard."

"Jenner?" Dominic asked sharply. "What was it about?"

Pike slid a glance at Lancaster. "I don't know anything about it. I'd already left his employ."

"Where is Mr. Jenner now?"

"Dead. Shot himself when he ended up in financial trouble."

"A sad business," Dominic said, thinking he must be a relation of Miss Jenner's.

"As he didn't engage another steward, your uncle might not have paid his bills." Pike dropped his gaze. "I'm sorry to be the harbinger of such bad news."

"Thank you, Mr. Pike."

So this was why he was unwelcome here. Not his reputation, perhaps, but his uncle. Dominic nodded to Pike and stepped outside into the fresh breeze with Lancaster.

After arrangements were made for Onyx, he asked if Jenner had a daughter by the name of Olivia.

Lancaster nodded. "Sad business. Miss Jenner is now employed by Sir Hubert Lowy's widow as housekeeper."

Dominic left Northoaks, driving the phaeton back along the lanes. So, Jenner was Olivia Jenner's father. That explained her refined manner. She must be competent, to hold such a position. But why would she wish to leave it for a far more taxing one at Redcliffe Hall?

He had to admire her determination. It was hard enough to get ahead in this world, especially if you lived with the shame of your father's death at his own hand, in this small village.

He drew in the reins to round a sharp bend in the road. He doubted the villagers would warm to him whatever he chose to do. It was unfair, but to change their minds about him could take longer than his patience allowed.

As he drove on, he wondered about the cause of his uncle's death. Dominic's father passed away at sixty, which would make Alberic sixty-two. Some men were still robust at that age. It shamed Dominic to think he hadn't questioned it. He would speak to Alberic's doctor.

FOR THE NEXT few days, when not busy with the preparations for her mistress's garden party, Olivia's thoughts returned to Redcliffe Hall and the changes which took place there. Had the earl found a housekeeper? She remained confident that he hadn't.

Making the most of the unseasonably mild weather, chairs and tables had been arranged around the lawns, the garden beds resplendent with summer flowers. The cuisine was selected to Lady Lowry's satisfaction. Replies to the invitations Olivia had sent out arrived. Would Lord Redcliffe accept? Such men only attended when the mood took them, she thought darkly. The squire, Mr. Lancaster, wrote he would come. She held nothing against the man who lived at Northoaks but hoped not to meet him again, as she'd found their dealings in the past to be uncomfortable.

She did not expect she'd be needed once the guests had arrived and could retire to her room. With everything prepared down to the last tiny cucumber sandwich, Harold, their footman, and the maids would serve the guests.

At her desk in her office, Olivia read through the acceptances which arrived in the post today. One bore the earl's seal. She uneasily studied his reply written in an elegant, masculine hand. Would he give her away to Lady Lowry? The possibility horrified her. She would lose her position here and have nowhere to turn. It had been a gamble she'd considered worth taking when she'd approached him. Something about him made her doubt he would, but her nerves remained on edge. She'd be relieved when the party was over.

At breakfast, Lady Lowry ordered her to remain throughout the afternoon, to ensure the maids behaved appropriately. Olivia, unnerved, yet pleased for the chance to show his lordship her proficiency, took particular care with her appearance. It was not because she wished him to find her attractive, but rather to consider her a possible addition to his staff. She couldn't make herself believe that and made a moue of distaste in the mirror at her folly. Maisie, the upstairs maid who excelled in the arrangement of a ladies' hair, offered to arrange Olivia's "unmanageable black tresses," according to Maisie, in the current style. Olivia thought the elegant updo flattered her and promised the maid some satin ribbons to trim her bonnet.

The gown she'd sewn in her spare hours during the evenings was suitable for her position with its high lace collar. Blue ribbons trimmed the hem and bodice. It was not so girlish that Lady Lowry might object. Standing before the mirror doing up the gold locket her father had given her, Olivia wondered if after Lord Redcliffe viewed her in her role of housekeeper, he might then reconsider her.

A maid told them breathlessly over breakfast how handsome and imposing the earl was. He had crossed the road when she was on her way to fetch napkins from the haberdashery. "He raised his hat and smiled at me." She gazed around at them. "Like this," she said, aping him. She giggled. "Not at all uppity."

The maids gasped. "Fancy that," Harold said.

Olivia stood with Harold and Lady Lowry to welcome the guests as they came through the door.

His lordship had not yet arrived. Lady Lowry, rather put out at his tardiness, ordered Olivia to the kitchen to ensure everything was ready.

Olivia remained below to help Cook. But Lady Lowry soon summoned her. Olivia smoothed her hair and entered the drawing room. Harold offered the guests flutes of champagne, while the maids offered tea, sandwiches, and cakes. Seated on a sofa by the fireplace, her mistress was engaged in conversation with the earl. Something he said made her smile fade. She fiddled with her pearls and turned, then beckoned to Olivia. Olivia's pulse throbbed as she crossed the room. What had his lordship said about her?

Lord Redcliffe rose to his feet as she approached. "Good afternoon, Miss Jenner."

"My lord." Olivier bobbed.

An irritated crease formed between Lady Lowry's plucked brows. "His lordship tells me you met at the wheelwright's. You failed to mention it," she said testily.

Amusement warmed his lordship's eyes. "We met in passing, did we not, Miss Jenner? I wonder if I might ask a favor of you? Redcliffe Hall remains in need of servants. My estate manager has not had a great deal of success finding them. Might you have heard of anyone in need of work?"

Was this a hint that he'd changed his mind about hiring her? "No, but I will certainly make inquiries, my lord."

He smiled. "I would appreciate it."

"That is all, Olivia." Lady Lowry dismissed her. "The guests require your services in the garden."

His lordship raised his eyebrows slightly but said nothing.

Olivia bobbed another curtsy and left, conscious of his eyes on her. Stepping through the French doors, she allowed herself to hope. He hadn't given her away, but might he have changed his mind about employing her?

Clutching her cane, Mrs. Herrington stood helplessly at the foot of the steps, waiting for assistance. Olivia hurried to offer the elderly woman her arm. She led the old lady inside and settled her in a comfortable chair. Mrs. Herrington sat back with a relieved sigh. "Thank you, my dear." With a roguish wink, she glanced over at Lord Redcliffe, who was still with her employer. "Handsome devil. Lady Lowry obviously thinks so."

Oliva smiled but resisted a reply. The earl had again turned his head in this direction. Lady Lowry laid a hand on his sleeve to draw him back to her. But shortly after, he rose and took his leave.

After the last guests departed, Olivia sat in the kitchen with a cup of tea discussing with Cook the success of the dishes. When Harold came down to fetch her, Olivia found her mistress in the parlor, drinking a glass of sherry.

Pleased, Lady Lowry smiled. "The party went exceptionally well, did it not? Lord Redcliffe said he enjoyed himself. He met the best people today. I'm sure a host of invitations will follow. An unmarried man will need a good social life." She reached for the sweetmeats on the table at her elbow. "It proves to be a busy season. We must prepare for it."

"Yes, ma'am."

She frowned. "You failed to say you spoke to his lordship. Only that you saw him in the street. I hope you didn't push yourself forward, Olivia. It will reflect badly on me. You are a member of this household. I've sensed a defiant attitude in you, which you must correct. Your circumstances are not as they once were. You are a servant, and the sooner you accept it, the better it will be for you. And for me."

It was all Olivia could do to hold back a heated response. "Lord Redcliffe was at the wheelwright's. He needed a broken carriage wheel fixed. He introduced himself to me."

Lady Lowry narrowed her eyes. "Why would he approach you?"

"Out of politeness, I imagine. Our conversation was, as he explained, brief."

Lady Lowry's spiteful gaze flicked over her. "About what?"

"The weather, which differs from London," Olivia said, faintly astonished she could lie so convincingly. "The wheelwright was too busy to see me, and would deal with his lordship first, so I left."

"Very well." Lady Lowry waved an airy hand. "I suppose I shall have to take you at your word. But I must say I'm surprised his lordship remembered you."

Olivia stood her ground, anger tightening her stomach. "The servants have worked hard this last week, Lady Lowry. As you would be hard-pressed to fault them, I know they would appreciate a word of praise, if you should consider it appropriate." She didn't expect a gratuity, and neither did they.

Her mistress nodded slowly. "Yes...that might be prudent," she said after a moment. "Convey my thanks. I shall entertain more now the earl is here. A dinner party. I'll give it some thought." She put down her glass and idly picked up her fan, waving it before her face. "Redcliffe is a handsome fellow."

"I suppose he is."

She scoffed. "Of course he is. He stayed to talk to me over-long, I thought. I trust gossip doesn't spread." She laughed girlishly, then gestured with the fan. "You may go."

Olivia returned to the servants' hall, where the staff drank tea and ate the leftover cake and biscuits. Laughing, Vicky described how a lady had lost her pince-nez and it took her an age to find it in the grass.

Maisie giggled. "You looked ever so silly down on your knees."

"And I'll never remove these grass stains from me best gown," Vicky said, head bowed over her skirt.

Olivia passed on Lady Lowry's praise for their efforts and added hers. She left them and entered her office. How carefree they were, teasing each other. From her experience, money and status rarely improved a person's character.

Of course, nothing was intimated by word or gesture, but she remained hopeful Lord Redcliffe would change his mind about hiring her. And if he did? She hadn't missed how his gaze wandered over her at Redcliffe Hall. What was she to do if his interest in her wasn't entirely honorable?

What she always did, she supposed, although deterring an earl would not be so easy. She owed nothing to the Redcliffes, but rather, they owed a good deal to her father. If he took her on as his housekeeper, she would find what she sought, then put in her notice. She'd leave as soon as he found a replacement. Then her long-held dreams would become a reality.

CHAPTER FOUR

D OMINIC SAT IN the chilly breakfast room, on the north side of the house, where the sun never reached the windows. He stared into the steaming cup of coffee before taking a sip.

Yesterday, Williams returned from Gateshead with three servants in tow, but no housekeeper. Now settling in were Mr. Samuels, a cook with questionable references; a young house-maid, Polly, who had worked previously at an inn; a stableboy, Jim, too young to sprout a beard; as well as Jack, the cocky young footman Williams had promised.

A little rough around the edges, Samuels, with his sandy hair in a queue, would not be in great demand in London, but if the breakfast placed before Dominic was anything to go by, the new cook could produce good plain food and decent coffee.

Jack expressed pleasure his livery fitted but had little idea of what was required of him, while Polly, who at least made a bed competently, darted out of his sight whenever he came across her flicking her duster. According to Fellows, Jim, who expressed a love of horses, had become an asset in the stables.

Desperation finally forced Dominic to take Miss Jenner's offer seriously. At her employer's garden party, she looked demure in her gown but gazed at him as if she feared he would betray her. She obviously had a poor opinion of him.

Having heard of her father's troubles, he had some understanding of her predicament. Had her father suffered at the hands of his uncle? She might be of that opinion, whether or not it was true. Was that her reason to want to come to Redcliffe Hall? Or because she was unhappy in her present employment? Miss Jenner came from a respectable home and had fallen on hard times. But would it be wise to employ her? His reason not to had not changed. The pull of attraction he'd felt on meeting her rang in his head like a warning bell. Bemused by where his thoughts took him, he refused a second cup of coffee from Jack, who hovered with the coffee pot, then tossed his napkin aside and rose.

He approved of the library and intended to spend a good deal of his time there. It was a comfortable room with a wide cedar desk. An impressive number of tomes on bookshelves covered three walls. Above the stone fireplace hung a painting of a young family member. Dominic had first thought it to be Alberic. But as the hair color was wrong, he decided it was his father as a lad. Considering the family rift, he found it odd. But he knew so little about Alberic. Had he been a keen reader? The well-thumbed pages of the books Dominic flicked through made him think so.

Dominic sharpened the tip of his quill, took a sheet of bond from the drawer, and dipped the nib in the inkwell, intent on answering his sister's letter. He scratched out a greeting, then paused, gazing through the windows at the worrisome view where a wildly overgrown hedge bordered the front path. Alberic had let the gardeners go, too. Another matter to deal with. Even with the windows open, the room smelled deplorably stale, and the books were gray with dust.

He returned to his task, but the ability to write an entertaining missive to amuse Evelyn deserted him. How horrified she'd be to learn the state of things here. Might she be able to recommend a housekeeper? Thinking it over, he dismissed the idea. The miles lying between them made it impractical. Too much time wasted. And this house would not function without an experienced housekeeper to manage it.

Lady Lowry was a vain, silly woman. Working for her would be a trial. His understanding of Miss Jenner's plight made him consider her more seriously. Obviously, she was efficient, or the harridan would have sent Miss Jenner packing. And he'd watched her moving among the guests and approved of her easy manner.

There remained the question of the villagers' poor opinion of him. Some guests at Lady Lowry's garden party revealed little warmth toward him beneath their social manners. In London, it hadn't mattered a good deal. Here it did, and the unfairness of it rankled and made him feel lonelier than he'd been in the city after the scandal broke. But he reasoned he couldn't fall much further in their estimation if he took an attractive, young woman as housekeeper. And after all, he didn't intend to remain here long. He eased his tight shoulders. His uncle had certainly left behind a poor impression of the Redcliffes when he departed this world.

As his request for staff gave Miss Jenner a reason to visit him, which even her mistress could not object to, he expected her to call. Now he'd decided, he became impatient. Would she come? Or must he seek her out?

As the days passed, his wish to restore the mansion to something resembling its former glory strengthened. But he knew so little about running an estate of this size. In the steward's room, he flicked through the account books. After an hour, he found little to enlighten him. Apparently, the estate brought in a modest amount. But little appeared in the bank statements. His solicitor had remarked on it. Perhaps his uncle didn't trust banks.

Dominic found no mention of Jenner in the ledgers, which appeared to end with Pike's departure. Perhaps the parish constable had been called to investigate the dispute. He might inquire, but it was too long ago and, with Jenner and his uncle dead, impossible to get to the truth. Dominic discovered a discouraging pile of bills gathering dust in a drawer. He sighed. He would settle those immediately. It might go some way in developing trust among the shopkeepers and tradesmen. Williams had told him most had voiced their eagerness to continue doing business with the estate. But the coal supplier had made the comment, lords never settled their debts. And, regrettably, that happened. Dominic thumped the desk with his fist, stirring the dust. He was not his uncle, and he refused to be tarred with the same brush.

He quitted the room, wiping his hands with his handkerchief. This time, Polly failed to escape him in the corridor. "Dust and polish the library within an inch of its life," he ordered her. "And tell Jack I want him to take up the rugs."

The small, fair girl flushed crimson. "Yes, milord." She bobbed and hurried to carry out his order.

Dominic walked away, disliking how he'd scared her. This was not a task he was comfortable with. Miss Jenner. He must have her here. Hopefully, the townsfolk would come to accept it in time.

On his way to the stables, he admitted that coming north had proved challenging. He was not living the comfortable life afforded him as the earl, but he'd had years living without such comforts. It wouldn't kill him. And he admitted, that despite everything, he enjoyed being here.

Seated on a wall, young Jim polished a saddle. The lad jumped down and bowed as Dominic approached.

"No need for that." Dominic entered the shadowy, cool stables and found Fellows attending Onyx in his stall.

"He has good conformation," Fellows said of Onyx as he shut the stall gate. "But he's ornery."

Dominic stroked the horse's neck, pleased when the horse nudged him gently and blew through his nose. "He improves on acquaintance."

Fellows chuckled. "It's my experience that ornery women never improve on acquaintance, and I doubt horses do."

"Your love life needs improvement," Dominic said with a laugh, recalling an incident concerning Fellows and a fiery-natured woman when he was Dominic's batman in Portugal. She'd dumped a dish of stew over his head.

"I'm embarrassed to admit it," Fellows chuckled, "but I've found a friendly tavern wench here, so things could look up."

Dominic grinned as Fellows gathered up the tackle. "I wish you success."

"May I wish you the same, milord?"

"Does your wench have a friend?"

At Dominic's riposte, Fellows laughed and disappeared inside the tack room.

Yes, a woman's tender company would be agreeable, although he doubted he'd find one to suit him here in the north. It was quiet in the stables with the horses snuffling in their stalls. He leaned against the timber post and gazed with approval at his new acquisition. "We will become friends, you and I."

Onyx's big dark eyes fixed on him, his nose in his feedbag. The stallion pleased him because he railed against his lot and wouldn't submit to authority unless he saw the sense of it. That showed spirit and intelligence. Dominic folded his arms and breathed in the familiar smells of hay and a clean, well-run stable. He heard his coachman, Grimsby, whistling outside, sweeping the cobbles with the broom. With little to do, he cheerfully performed tasks not assigned to him.

Miss Jenner pushed her way into his mind again. At the garden party in her crisp dress, her hands held demurely at her waist, a slight frown in her blue eyes. Far too attractive and too often on his mind. Would she become a test of his character? It was an unusual occurrence for any woman he sought to refuse him. He carried no illusions as to the reason. It would be a mutual agreement, suited to both parties. But not Miss Jenner. No, most unwise! He shook his head, and straightening, walked out into the sunlight.

He'd discovered life in the country moved slowly, from sunup to sundown, the days unfolding with no undue interruption. The rhythm and cycle of nature, and the farming which worked with it. While he appreciated it after the fraught demands of London society, he would need to guard against becoming bored and restless. That could prove disastrous with Miss Jenner under his roof.

Should he invite Lady Anne? He rubbed his brow. Difficult, as they did not enjoy the familiarity of lovers. He'd left London before anything of that nature occurred between them. Lady Anne enjoyed her freedom after a disastrous marriage to a much older man, becoming a social butterfly. She would expect to find suitable accommodation and entertainment. That meant a house full of servants and guests. Every night, dinner parties and card parties, perhaps a ball. He chuckled at the sort of fare his cook would serve. Dominic could apply to an agency in London for a chef and experienced staff, but that would take time.

He imagined the hall polished and sparkling. A house party. He'd invite Shewsbury and Pennington and a few others. But an impossible amount needed to be done to make the house habitable. And he found that right now he lacked the enthusiasm for such an undertaking.

"We'll ride this afternoon, visit the gamekeeper and the farms," he said to Fellows, who had followed Dominic outside. "Onyx and I can get to know our new home."

"Right, milord."

The afternoon sun dropped to the west when, some hours later, after a tasty luncheon of fresh baked chicken pie, the crust as light as any French chef could make it, he and Fellows approached the gamekeeper's cottage. Clough had called to see Dominic, but he'd been away visiting the squire.

The gamekeeper, a tall, limbered man of some forty-odd years, emerged from the neat, thatched-roof cottage to greet them as Dominic dismounted. "Good to meet you, Clough."

"Milord." He turned to gesture at the doorway. "Will you come inside? Can I offer you both a tankard of cider?"

"You may indeed." Dominic was interested in trying the local cider. He bowed his head under the low lintel as he and Fellows entered the dim interior. The small room was orderly, which made Dominic confident about the state of his woods.

"Do we have a good supply of birds for a shoot in October?"

Clough turned from the sideboard, where he poured the cider into tankards. "We certainly do, milord. There's an oversupply."

Drawing up a chair, Dominic sat and drank the sweet cider. "Made here?"

"Indeed, it is, milord. From estate apples."

He studied the quiet, stocky fellow seated opposite him. "Did you enjoy working for my uncle?"

Clough widened his dark eyes. He tossed back the last drops of his cider, putting his tankard down. "He wasn't easy in the last few years, milord. Downright difficult if I'm honest."

"Bad as that?"

Clough nodded and rubbed his nose. "Knew he wasn't well, but he also suffered from what one might call demons. Drove him mad."

A half-hour later, Dominic emerged into the fading light, troubled by what he'd heard of his uncle's apparent descent into madness. Clough was rarely in his uncle's company, even so, his words set Dominic on a course to find out exactly what had taken place here. Were his uncle's claims someone planned to rob and kill him the ravings of a man who had lost his mind or was someone behind it?

Disturbed, he mounted Onyx, eager to be off. "Let's give these horses some exercise."

As they rode over the acres, the fresh breeze on his face dispelled some of his concerns. But not all.

THE NEXT MORNING, Lady Lowry lost her temper and dismissed Emily, the young housemaid. Olivia discovered the poor girl in tears in the servants' hall. She was one of ten children with a shiftless father, who spent most of his time in the tavern. There was no chance of her going home, and without a good reference, she was unlikely to find decent work. When she told Olivia of her intention to go to York, warning bells sounded. Olivia feared for the pretty girl with her creamy skin and dark curls. She foresaw her ending up on the streets just to survive, like other young country girls before her.

"Pack your things, Emily. While I'm not entirely sure, there's a chance I can find you a position at Redcliffe Hall."

Emily sniffed and wiped her wet cheeks with a finger, hope in her eyes. "Do you really think so, Miss Jenner?"

Olivia prayed she hadn't given the girl false hope. "Shall we go and see?" she said, aware Lady Lowry would disapprove.

When Emily emerged with her pitiful belongings tied up in brown paper, they left through the front door.

Before they'd gone down the path, Lady Lowry appeared and called to them in an outraged voice. "Where are you going, Olivia? What about your orders for this morning?"

"I shall complete them before I retire, my lady," Olivia said politely, turning to address the irascible woman she heartily disliked. "But Emily needs my help. She has no one to turn to."

Lady Lowry's face reddened. "That is not your affair. The girl is incompetent."

"Surely, it is not so terrible to spill a little tea in the saucer. Can you not give her another chance?"

"Certainly not! She has made a litany of mistakes since she entered my employ. The girl is clumsy. She will never make a good maid. Leave her and come inside."

"I will ensure everything is done to your satisfaction when I return, Lady Lowry." Furious that the woman would turn a young girl out onto the street, Olivia continued down the path with Emily's arm trembling beneath her hand.

"You may not have a position to return to, Miss Jenner," Lady Lowry called after her.

Her lips firmly closed, Olivia led Emily out to the street.

"I am clumsy. But Lady Lowry always makes me nervous." Emily gasped. "You will be in such trouble because of me, Miss

Jenner."

"Don't be silly. Given time, Lady Lowry gets over her bad humors." As there was no one in the village to replace her, Olivia expected her mistress to let the matter drop. After scolding her severely, of course.

"We're not going to Redcliffe Hall now?" Emily's voice was a nervous squeak.

"Yes. We'll see the estate manager. He is hiring staff."

Emily's brown eyes widened, and she stopped. "Oh, my goodness. D'you think he would take on the likes of me, with no character?"

"I can't promise anything. But come along. We won't know unless we ask."

Several inches shorter than Olivia, Emily hurried to keep up with her. "Me ma would be ever so pleased if I worked there," she said, hope lifting her voice. "Bert and I are the only ones workin'. We give Ma our wages." She smiled proudly. "Every month, sure as clockwork."

Olivia prayed the estate manager would take the girl on. Surely, they'd have need of her. The boy delivering groceries in the Lowry kitchen mentioned Redcliffe Hall was still short-staffed, and he doubted his lordship would stay long unless things improved. "Everyone hopes he will, Miss Jenner," Tom had said. "Ma says having Redcliffe Hall occupied makes the village prosper."

Olivia could only agree. The village had struggled for years, and it was true his lordship's presence would improve people's lots. Work had begun on the house. Tom told her the carpenter, Bill Green, was engaged to work there, replacing rotten timbers and broken windows. "Bill said there's enough work to keep him and his men busy 'til well past Christmas."

When she'd last visited the Sunday market, people expressed the view that working at the hall might not be as bad as they'd thought. One man planned to try his luck at the home farm and another, the dairy. Fred Aitkens wanted gardening work. The rumor of a ghost lurking about seemed forgotten.

While it pleased her for the villagers' sakes, she must keep in mind why she distrusted all the Redcliffes, and the reason she wanted to join the staff at Redcliffe Hall.

CHAPTER FIVE

T HE LATE MORNING sun warmed Dominic's shoulders and insects buzzed around the gardens as he strolled back to the house from the stables. As he approached the house, Miss Jenner emerged from the avenue of trees with a young woman beside her.

A new maid? He hoped so. He stood and waited as they approached, enjoying Miss Jenner's graceful yet purposeful stride.

She smiled, dipping into a bob. "Good morning, my lord."

"Miss Jenner." He removed his hat, pleased to see her, then turned to the girl beside her, who had dropped into a curtsy, deep enough for royalty. "And who is this?"

"My lord, I'd like you to meet Miss Emily Tomlinson." Miss Jenner grasped the younger girl's arm and hauled her to her feet. "We are here to see the estate manager. Emily is a housemaid and is looking for employment."

"Mr. Williams will be in the estate office. A footman will take Miss Tomlinson to him. I wish to speak to you, Miss Jenner. Will you come to the library?"

"Certainly."

After Jack escorted the girl to Williams, Miss Jenner joined him in the library, which Polly had cleaned, the air now scented with beeswax, and the rows of red and gold spines along the bookshelves gleaming.

"May I offer you tea or a cool libation, perhaps? It would have been warm walking from the village."

She removed her bonnet and put a hand to her dark locks. "No, thank you. I do hope Mr. Williams will hire Emily. She is grateful for the opportunity and keen to do well."

"I see no reason why not. Emily worked for Lady Lowry?"

"Yes." She frowned. "She was let go, most unfairly."

He nodded. Lady Lowry was probably a tyrant. If the girl weren't up to snuff, given time, she would improve. "I prefer to discuss the matter of your employment, Miss Jenner. As I remain in need of a housekeeper, I've decided to offer you the position." He paused. "Unlike the obviously smooth workings of Lady Lowry's establishment, I must warn you this position will prove difficult. At least until we have a full complement of staff."

Her blue eyes brightened, a smile hovering on her lips. "I enjoy a challenge."

"Well, yes...I suspected you might." He shifted his position on the chair opposite hers as he noted the stubborn lines of her sweetly rounded chin, then his gaze dropped to the smooth skin above her collar. Was he consigning himself to purgatory?

She waited for him to continue. He cleared his throat. "When you return, the housemaid, Polly, will show you the housekeeper's office and see to your bedchamber." He paused. He did not know where that was or what condition it was in, as bad as his had been? Worse, more likely. "Mr. Samuels is the cook. We have no butler. When might we expect you?" He hated the hopeful note in his voice, certain she had known from the outset he would need her.

"I'll come as soon as I can. I'm obliged to give Lady Lowry notice." Her expression darkened. "It might be as early as tomorrow."

She appeared upset—with her employer's treatment of Emily, plus a litany of things, he suspected. The lady might insist Miss Jenner remain in her employ until a replacement could be found. That might take weeks. "Very well." He must be content with that, although he doubted Miss Jenner would be. She seemed ready to gird her loins for a fight.

They rose together. "I'll wait for Emily in the foyer, my lord."

He strode to the door and opened it. Jack, slumping against the wall in the corridor outside, leaped up.

"Miss Jenner is to be our new housekeeper, Jack. Bring Miss Tomlinson to her in the foyer."

After Jack snapped to attention and hurried down the corridor, Dominic turned to her. "We shall expect you soon, Miss Jenner."

"Yes, thank you, my lord."

He closed the library door. Now perhaps he could concentrate on…

Returning to his desk, he sat and rearranged the papers strewn across it. Why did he feel as if something momentous had happened?

Dominic swiveled to stare out the window. The two women appeared in his view, chatting as they walked along the drive toward the park gates. Women were like flowers, he mused. They dressed up a place. Essential to a man's comfort.

He turned back to study the papers, an assortment of bills, invitations, and letters. Dash it all. He needed a secretary. He knew little about the running of an estate. He'd had nothing to do with his father's, and he'd sold the property almost immediately after his death. He admitted there was much to learn.

When Williams came in, Dominic waved him to a chair. "You hired the housemaid?"

"I thought it wise, milord."

Dominic nodded. "Miss Jenner is to be our housekeeper. Hopefully, she will begin soon. Perhaps as early as tomorrow."

"Good news. You still intend to visit the tenants and the home farm after luncheon?"

"Yes. Are you able to join me?"

"Certainly."

Dominic thought of the dull evening ahead. The local tavern

didn't appeal. When the house was ready, he would invite the squire and a few of the gentlemen he'd met at Lady Lowry's garden party to play faro. He indicated the pile of papers on his desk. "I must engage a secretary."

"Do you have anyone in mind?"

"One or two possibilities. My father was pleased with Collin Quin. Studied at Cambridge, quite an erudite fellow, but close to retirement age. I shall contact him and one or two others.

"Have you plans to visit London? That mended coach wheel needs replacing."

Dominic shook his head. "I've instructed my butler to take the knocker off the door in Mayfair." The city would be unbearable in the summer heat. And with little good company to be found, as the *ton* would have deserted it for the country. Nor would Lady Anne be in London. She stayed at her country house for the summer months.

When parliament reconvened, there would be much to organize; taking his place in the House of Lords, reopening his townhouse, the shoot in autumn here, and beyond that, the Christmas Season. His sister expected him to go to them. He would have to travel before some roads became impassable due to ice and snow. In the meantime, he'd work to make the estate lands more profitable and set Redcliffe Hall to rights.

Dominic glanced over at his uncle's portrait. He had a mystery to solve. And then, there was Miss Jenner. But she would soon whip the house into shape. He was already confident in her ability to cope with the enormous task before her.

"Probably won't see London for months," he said to Williams. "There is enough here to keep me busy. And more staff, Williams, dredge them up from somewhere."

"A few from the village are coming forward to apply for jobs."

"Then the rumor of a ghost has been put to rest?

"Not quite, but perhaps as time goes on."

Dominic shrugged with impatience. He must do something

himself to change people's opinion of what went on at Redcliffe Hall. Until then it was unlikely they'd have a full contingent of staff.

>>><<<

HAROLD, LADY LOWRY'S footman, opened the door to Olivia and Emily. He grimaced. "I've been told not to admit you, Emily. But her ladyship wishes to see you, Miss Jenner. She's in the parlor."

"I've come for me wages," Emily murmured tearfully.

Harold shook his head. "More than my job's worth to disobey my orders."

"Wait here, Emily," Olivia said. "I'll return in a moment."

She hastened to the parlor.

Lady Lowry raised her head from her embroidery. "There you are. I am surprised you have the temerity to return so late. You shall have to work into the night to complete those tasks I asked of you."

The tasks were menial and not meant for a housekeeper, but Olivia held her tongue.

"Was it a wasted trip to find that impossible girl a position?"

"No. Emily is to work at Redcliffe Hall."

Her ladyship narrowed her eyes. "I've heard they're having little success finding staff. It's rumored the house is haunted, so I expect they had no option but to take her, although they'll soon wish they hadn't."

"Emily hasn't been given her wages."

"The maid ruined a tablecloth, and I'm told she broke a plate. The costs were taken out of her pay."

Olivia frowned. "She has no one to care about her. Does that not concern you?"

Lady Lowry bristled. She stabbed at her embroidery with the needle and put it aside to glare up at Olivia. "You are impertinent. I don't know why I should put up with a housekeeper who talks so rudely to me. You force me to reprimand you."

"You won't need to, my lady."

Her ladyship stared at her. "What do you mean?"

"I am giving my notice. I've been hired as housekeeper at Redcliffe Hall."

Lady Lowry sat up straight. "You would leave me? Ungrateful girl! After I took you off the street without a reference."

Olivia swelled with indignation and anger for herself and for Emily. "Yes, you did take me in without references, Lady Lowry, and I am indebted to you for that. But a day hasn't passed when you failed to mention it. You forever reminded me that I have come down in the world. That my home is no longer my own and my family, disgraced. And although I have given you excellent service, you treated me like the lowliest servant."

Lady Lowry choked. "If you think you can get your hooks into Lord Redcliffe, you'll be disappointed. He holds no interest in a poor squire's daughter beyond his need for a housekeeper. He's an earl and will seek a well-bred lady." She gave Olivia a sly look. "Although he would be happy to bed you, should you offer yourself to him. And afterward, discard you without a second look."

Olivia wondered if Lady Lowry was jealous, or had hopes herself in that direction. She was certainly vain enough to believe it.

When Harold came, she pointed a trembling finger at Olivia. "Show Miss Jenner out. Send a housemaid to pack her bags. And don't admit her to this house ever again."

The footman gaped at Olivia.

"Did you hear what I said, Harold?"

He turned back hastily to his mistress. "Yes, milady."

Harold silently escorted Olivia to the front door and hastened to open it. He stood aside for her, his face crumped with distress. "I'm very sorry this has happened, Miss Jenner," he said in an undertone, after a quick glance back at the empty hall. "I doubt we'll get a fairer and more pleasant housekeeper than you in the future."

She forced a smile, her heart pounding, and her breath tight in her throat. "I pray you do, Harold. Give my best wishes to those belowstairs. I shall miss you all."

She doubted she'd get the wages due to her, either. Lady Lowry held her purse strings tight. She would look for any reason to withhold their money. On the porch, Emily waited, her parcel beside her. Olivia forced herself to smile reassuringly at the hopeful girl.

Her dreadful temper! After Olivia had no option but to work at Lady Lowry's establishment, the vicar warned her to consider her position and be humble. "Pride leads to disgrace, but with humility comes wisdom," he would sometimes remind her when she came to church in a desperate mood after something Lady Lowry said.

Well, she couldn't be humble! And she admitted to being gravely at fault.

She put an arm around Emily. "I'm afraid I failed to get our wages, Emily."

Emily smiled, her eyes filled with tears. "Oh, that's not your fault, Miss Jenner. You did your very best for me. And I'm that grateful."

After a wait, the front door finally opened. Harold, with a look of apology, placed Olivia's baggage on the porch, and after wishing them well in a hushed voice, retreated inside again.

Olivia ran to gather up her pelisse and spare bonnet, the carpet bag, and the portmanteau crammed with her underthings, stockings, and the gowns she had kept, the rest having been sold because she needed the money. She'd have no occasion to wear them, and they would only remind her of her past life.

How crushed her clothes would be and no competent laundry maid employed at Redcliffe Hall. "We have nowhere to stay tonight, and little money between us, Emily. We shall have to go straight to the hall.

Emily gasped. "But they aren't expecting us until tomorrow."

"We are a day early, but I'm sure they'll take us in."

She smiled, wishing Emily weren't so timid. A timid woman got nowhere in life. "It will be an adventure. I shan't miss working for Lady Lowry, will you?"

Emily gave a faint smile. "No, miss."

As they set out to walk to Redcliffe Hall again, Olivia wondered what Lord Redcliffe would make of it. But while her anger at the injustice of life ran hot in her veins, she hoped he wouldn't ask her.

CHAPTER SIX

DOMINIC ATE LUNCHEON in the dining room. On his way back to the library, the door knocker sounded.

At the entry, Jack admitted Miss Jenner and Miss Emily carrying their luggage.

Miss Jenner untied the ribbons of her bonnet with quick, determined fingers. "I must beg your good graces, Lord Redcliffe. I'm afraid Lady Lowry gave us no option but to leave her employ today, and we have nowhere to stay tonight."

He admired her display of confidence, although he caught sight of a flash of uncertainty in her eyes. She had grit and was protective of the young maid. "Today, tomorrow, it's of no consequence," he said, pleased to see her. He had feared it could be several weeks before she was free to start. "Have you had luncheon?"

"No, my lord," Miss Jenner said.

Emily, her eyes filled with tears, shook her head.

Dominic turned to Jack. "Organize the luggage and inform the cook to provide luncheon for two in the servants' hall." He turned to Miss Jenner. "After you've eaten, please join me in the library, Miss Jenner."

When she entered a half-hour later, he directed her to a brown leather armchair before the fireplace. "Would you care for a glass of madeira?"

"No, thank you." She perched on the edge of her chair, twisting the bonnet ribbons in her fingers while observing the state of the library with what he discerned to be a critical eye. "I am eager to take up my duties as soon as possible." Her gaze settled on his carved oak desk, dulled by years of neglect, which he'd banned from Polly's ministrations. He preferred not to put the estate books and his letters at risk from an upturned inkpot.

"You'll need to familiarize yourself with the house and meet the servants," he continued. "But there's no rush. Williams expects five more to arrive tomorrow. I can explain the situation more fully at dinner. You'll join us, of course."

She met his eyes with a troubled frown. "Do you think it's wise for us to dine together, my lord?"

"I understand your concern. But you've taken on quite a lot here, Miss Jenner, I thought it prudent to discuss it." What did she fear? Thought him a rake, did she? That he would engage in a persuasive seduction over the dinner table? All men were not crass beasts.

He tried to keep his gaze from her, but she drew the eye in the lemon-yellow dress trimmed with blue. How could such a modest gown appear so...suggestive? The pleated bodice clung, outlining her full breasts, and the thin fabric skimmed her hips, which made him contemplate how she would look undressed.

Aware of him, she tucked her long legs to one side and arranged her skirts.

"Would it matter if you shared my table?" The devil drove him to ask.

Her cheeks flushed as if he'd asked her to share his bed. "You initially expressed some concern about my presence here, fearing it might cause unwelcome gossip. Surely, it would be better if I deal directly with Mr. Williams?" She regained her composure and raised her eyebrows. "Unless, of course, you have any particular tasks you wish me to perform?"

He cleared his throat. "We shall discuss that later." He noted the determined set of her mouth. She hadn't been in the house above five minutes and already put him in his place. Irritated at being wrong-footed and deprived of a delightful dinner companion, he had to admit she made perfect sense. Gossipers had a way of catching one out. There seemed to be eyes watching everywhere. Even here at the hall.

Did she expect him to clarify how honorable his motives were? He had no intention of it. But he would never act like some men of his acquaintance. Some of the most repugnant peers believed it was their right to bed the female staff of the houses they visited.

"I shall confer with Williams. But please come and see me if any problems arise." He stood. "I won't detain you. Welcome to Redcliffe Hall."

"Thank you, my lord." She bobbed, her chin lowered in suitable deference, which made him regretful. He must have erred. He'd sought a rapport with her if nothing else. Was that impossible between a man and a woman? Especially one who was so dashed desirable?

Her eyes avoided his. "I'll see Mr. Williams now."

He walked with her to the door, conscious that she held herself at a wary distance from him. It had been a mistake. She didn't trust him. "Jack will show you where Williams's office is."

Dominic closed the door behind her. He feared her violet-blue eyes, ringed with long, black lashes, saw right through him, detecting his lustful thoughts, but how pleasurable it was to look at her. It would be so much simpler if she were fifty. But not nearly as fascinating.

Sighing, he sat at his desk and attempted to read over the letter he'd written earlier, but his mind wandered. Firmly pushing thoughts of Miss Jenner away, he considered inviting Williams to a game of chess after dinner. His estate manager disliked chess and was too easy to defeat, but it was better than reading week-old newspapers or the book he'd selected, which failed to hold his attention.

He sat back and questioned his reluctance to return to his

comfortable existence in London. He'd left under a cloud, but surely the scandal would have lost steam by now. The improvements to this house could continue without him. The prosperity of the estate placed in the hands of a good land steward. He fiddled with the pen, drawing it through his fingers. Something held him here, and he would stay until he'd discovered what that was.

Tomorrow, he would speak to the farm laborers, see what condition the home farm was in. That would take him away from the house for most of the day. Afterward, he hoped to return to a more orderly house, if not an attractive companion for dinner.

Dominic stroked his chin with thumb and forefinger. He suspected Miss Jenner's careful manners hid some resentment toward him. It made her intention to work here all the more surprising. Was it because of his uncle's dispute with her father? That was some time ago, and he was not his uncle. Nothing like him, in fact, as she would discover in time.

Miss Jenner had said she intended to remain with Lady Lowry until her replacement could be found. As disagreeable as the lady might be, he would like to know why she so ruthlessly turned Miss Jenner out onto the street without a reference. Was it because she assisted the young housemaid? Or was it something more serious? He hoped not the latter. He dismissed the thought of writing to request the reason from Lady Lowry. Give that woman an inch and she'd take a mile. He'd met her like before.

OLIVIA FEARED SHE'D made a mistake. Should she not have come here? Lord Redcliffe looked at her as if he were undressing her, and a pulse beat deep inside her, and she became flustered and warm. She expected working here would be difficult, but not...this. Could she keep her distance from such a potently sensual man? His green eyes held a promise of something wicked she didn't understand. It intrigued her. While he neither suggested anything she could take offense at nor made a move toward her, the air between them became charged, filled with expectation.

She'd dealt with men intent on bedding her, but it had been easy to bat them away because she remained coolly uninvolved. Apart from Lord Redcliffe's obvious good looks, what was it about him that made it so difficult to keep a cool head? The danger she sensed was not of violence but of promised pleasure and drew her like a moth to a candle flame. To dine and drink wine with him tempted her so much, she'd struggled to resist.

Chastising herself, she hurried downstairs to the kitchen to meet the cook, while Lady Lowry's nasty words rang in her head like a bell. *"If you think you can get your hooks into Lord Redcliffe, you'll be disappointed. He holds no interest in a squire's daughter, beyond his need of a housekeeper. As an earl he will seek a well-bred lady to be his wife, although he would be happy to bed you, should you offer yourself to him? And afterward, discard you without a second look."*

Although there was an element of truth in what her former employer said, for his lordship would certainly never marry her, it was pure spite designed to hurt her. Olivia would never contemplate such a scheme. But would Lady Lowry spread nasty gossip about her? The village would already be abuzz with conjecture. As long as she knew it to be lies, Olivia supposed she could endure.

But as Redcliffe Village had always been her home, and she intended to live there for the rest of her days, she must tread carefully. She would stay at the hall only long enough to find the answer she sought; the proof her father had not been paid the thousand pounds owed to him for the two horses he supplied the old earl. If proved she was the rightful recipient of that money, it would allow her to pay off Papa's debts and clear his name. She could execute her plan to live comfortably without being obliged to marry.

Entering the kitchen, the cook stood at the stove, stirring a pan, the preparations for the meal covering the table. Pots piled up in the sink in the scullery. There seemed to be no kitchen maids to assist him. But the flavors scenting the air were mouthwatering.

"How do you do, sir? I am the new housekeeper, Miss Jenner."

He turned to her. He wasn't old by any means, but the heavy grooves beside his mouth and on his forehead looked to have been born of years of hardship and suffering. "Samuels, Miss Jenner." He wiped his hands on the apron tied at his waist and took her proffered hand in a firm grip, while a cautious expression crept into his smoky gray eyes.

Samuels seemed an extraordinary choice for the earl's chef. His massive hand and scarred fingers rasped against her skin, and he wore his over-long, fair hair braided and tied back in an old-fashioned queue with a black ribbon. He seemed more suited to life a century ago. A highwayman perhaps, she thought, carefully hiding her surprise.

"Whatever you're cooking smells delicious. It makes me hungry."

His smile transformed his face, the deep lines softening. "I hope you will enjoy the meal."

"I am sure to." She gazed around. "You work under difficult conditions here."

He shrugged. "I have had worse."

A story she hoped he would someday tell her. "The new housemaid, Emily, can assist you. I'll send her to you, and we expect more servants tomorrow."

He nodded and turned to check on the roasting meat.

"We'll inspect the pantry and discuss the menus tomorrow." Olivia crossed to the door. "I'd best see what awaits me in the housekeeper's room."

"You've far worse to deal with than I," Samuels said over his shoulder.

"I believe we are both up to the task, Mr. Samuels," Olivia

said with a firmer conviction than at this precise moment she felt.

He chuckled. "I admire your spirit. You may call me Sam if you wish."

"Olivia, please, Sam."

She smiled as she left the room. This was proving to be a most unusual position. Her smile soon fell away when she discovered the state of the butler's pantry, which had been turned into a bedchamber with a mattress and bedding. In the housekeeper's office, mouse droppings tracked across the floor. Everything appeared undisturbed for years rather than months. Tattered yellowed ledgers filled the drawers. She could write her name on the desk's surface. Olivia sighed and mentally rolled up her sleeves. *Tomorrow.*

In her desk drawer, she found the housekeeper's keys and went in search of the maids. Encountering Emily talking to Polly in the servants' hall, she sent Emily to assist Samuels, then went upstairs with Polly to find the linen cupboard.

Olivia searched through the fine linen sheets monogrammed with the earl's crest and plain linens folded on the shelves. No evidence of moths or mice could be found, but they smelled musty. She would have some laundered and others sprinkled with dried lavender. The plant grew in abundance in the garden. But for now, they would have to make do. She removed some sheets, pillowcases, and toweling to ready the bedchambers.

In his office, Mr. Williams rose to greet her as the workmen hurried away to reach home before nightfall.

"It is good to have you here, Miss Jenner."

She immediately appreciated the man's calm manner and kind hazel eyes. "Thank you, Mr. Williams. I see there's a lot to do, and I'm eager to begin."

"We have a laundry maid, a Mrs. Hobbs, who is a widow and hails from the village. You might know of her."

"I don't believe so. I'll take the linens to her for laundering. Does his lordship have plans to entertain?" She might have asked Redcliffe, she thought darkly, if it had not been so...difficult. In fact, the less she saw of the earl, the easier it would be.

"His lordship mentioned a house party during the hunting season but nothing immediate."

She nodded, relieved such a large undertaking wasn't about to tax her limited resources. It gave them time to hire and train more staff. Over thirty servants worked for Lady Lowry, counting the gardeners and the stable staff, and the house was far smaller than Redcliffe Hall.

In search of her bedchamber, she left Williams and climbed the servants' stairs, which needed to be swept. She finally found it, three floors up under the roof and in a poor state, like the rest of the house.

Olivia assessed the small room, with its narrow iron bed, a candlestick on the table, an upright wooden chair, and a narrow wardrobe. Her room at Lady Lowry's was superior in comfort and size. But she wasn't sorry to be here. She would make it cozy. And she had a view through the dirty windowpane of the massive slate roof and chimneys and the two upper floors of the opposite wing, where the guest bedchambers were situated.

She opened the window and the warm summer breeze rushed in to banish the smell of the dusty rug and stale bedding. Then, turning with renewed energy, she stripped the covers off the mattress and made it with the fresh sheets. Then went to see how Emily fared cleaning her room. In the morning, Olivia would have the maids prepare the bedchambers for the new arrivals.

Olivia went down as the gong sounded. In the servants' hall, the staff ate their supper. Seated next to Jack, Emily giggled.

Weary, but pleased to see the maid less anxious and already feeling at home, Olivia sat down as Sam put a tasty meal before her.

CHAPTER SEVEN

T HE FOLLOWING AFTERNOON, Dominic rode with Williams to consult with the farmworkers who'd kept the home farm animals breeding and in good health, despite his uncle's neglect.

Jeremy Tate had worked for his uncle for over twenty years. He could not disguise his delight at Dominic's interest as he took them to view the animals, then into the fields to view the areas requiring new irrigation trenches. Tate squatted and dug his fingers into the earth. "Rich friable loam, milord, far superior to heavy clay, which makes plowing difficult."

When Dominic agreed to set the drainage work in motion, they walked on as Tate enthusiastically espoused the Norfolk four-course system, which meant they no longer required fields to lie fallow.

"I hope I haven't talked too much, milord," the big-boned country fellow said, his bristled cheeks reddening.

"Not at all. It's most interesting. Having never taken an interest in my father's estate, I have much to catch up on."

They passed fat dairy cows in a paddock. "They produce six gallons a day," Tate said. Farther on, a flock of sheep grazed on the last of the turnip tops, their lambs frolicking over the verdant grass.

Dominic's confidence in the estate grew. With increased production, it could become something his father would be proud of. His father spoke rarely of Redcliffe Hall. But when he did, his voice held a hint of melancholy, as if he'd left his heart here. Dominic could believe it. His father had expressed little affection for the home Dominic grew up in. He supposed that was why he didn't either.

As he and Williams trotted their horses down a lane bordered by daisy-strewn paddocks and freshly sown pastures, Dominic allowed himself to imagine Redcliffe Hall as the magnificent estate it must once have been.

They rode through the gates onto Willard Johnson's farm, where workmen wrestled with a huge log they'd dug out of a field, attempting to load it onto a dray.

Willard, a wiry fellow, came to greet them. He threw his hands up in defeat. "I'm about to bring the ax and chop it up here."

"Let's see if we can shift it." Dominic dismounted and tied the reins to the post. He climbed over the fence. The sun warmed his back when he stripped off his coat. Williams joined them, and working together, with muttering and curses, the four maneuvered the log onto the dray. A workman jumped aboard. He took up the reins of the solidly built draft horse and drove away.

Dominic eased his shoulders. He kept fit in London with bouts at Jackson's Boxing Academy, riding, driving his curricle, and swordplay, but manual labor tested other muscles which left him sore, but oddly satisfied.

"Good of you to help, milord." Johnson removed his hat and wiped his forehead with his forearm. "May I offer you both a glass of ale?"

"Thirsty work," Dominic said, reaching for his coat. "We would appreciate it."

They approached the farmhouse where Johnson's outbuildings and fences were in a sad state of repair.

"Lean times leave little money for such things, milord," Johnson explained when Dominic asked about it.

"I'll purchase some lumber. Let Williams know what you

need."

Johnson expressed his gratitude and introduced his wife, a small woman who had come out to greet them. They drank a tankard of ale while she cooked something delicious for her husband's supper and a shy child clung to her skirts.

"Johnson's supper smelled good," Dominic said after they'd mounted and ridden back the way they came. "I'm pleased with Samuels. He produces a tasty meal. Nothing fancy, but good English fare. How do you find the new servants?"

"I've had little to do with them. Miss Jenner is a remarkably efficient woman."

"Yes, I expected she would be." Dominic had met the housekeeper in the upper corridor earlier today. She and two of the housemaids had their arms full of linens. They'd bobbed, and he'd begged them not to drop them, producing giggles from the maids.

As she ushered the maids away, he was left with an annoying vision of Miss Jenner's hair hidden beneath a lawn cap. He liked to see a woman's hair. Admittedly, he would prefer hers down over her shoulders and mussed, preferably by him.

Remembering it made him groan in dismay at the direction of his thoughts.

"You spoke, milord?" Williams asked as their horses skirted a muddy patch.

"Nothing of import," Dominic said hastily. "Fancy a game of whist this evening?"

"That would be welcome."

Dominic chuckled. "You sound far more enthusiastic about cards than you do about chess."

"That I am, my lord," Williams said with a smile. "I might even best you."

Dominic grinned. "I wouldn't be too confident." He paused when an excellent idea struck him. "It's better with three people. Perhaps Miss Jenner will join us after dinner? I'll leave it for you to arrange, Williams."

"Certainly." If his suggestion surprised Williams, he gave no hint of it.

She could hardly refuse an order. His grin widening, Dominic nudged Onyx's flank and let the fractious horse gallop toward a fine copse of elms and a deep hedge in the distance, which marked the boundary of the gardens, the soaring roof of the house rising above them.

>>><<<

"ARE YOU PLEASED with the kitchen boy?"

Seated at the kitchen table, Olivia took a sip of tea, while Sam busied himself rolling out dough. Betty, the new scullery maid, bent her fair head over the pots, scrubbing furiously, while the two other kitchen maids cleaned the pantry.

Sam's rolled-up sleeves revealed a tattoo of a busty mermaid on his muscular forearm. "Henry's a keen lad, an orphan, and life hasn't been easy for him."

"No, so many have sad tales to tell," she said. "Were you in the navy, Sam?"

He nodded. "Joined up as a lad. That's where I learned to cook. When I left, I hoped to run my own eatery." Shook his head. "Didn't work out that way. Instead, I ended up in Newgate for three years."

"Newgate!" she cried, horrified. "What happened?"

"I got tricked is what. Landed with stolen goods. He used my business as a cover. I wanted to find the criminal and kill him when I got out, but he'd died before my term was up. It's left a sour taste in my mouth that has. Revenge is sweet, sayeth the Lord."

Olivia fell silent. She didn't want revenge, only justice and a chance at a better life.

Williams came to the kitchen door. "May I have a word, Miss Jenner?"

She rose. "Of course. Come into my office."

Williams glanced around appreciatively at her clean, well-organized room. "A great improvement." He eyed the vase of flowers on her desk. "And it smells a good deal better."

"It badly needed to." Olivia smiled. Next, she would tackle the steward's room. Which would give her the opportunity to search for anything pertaining to her father.

"I bear an invitation from his lordship," Williams said. "He has invited you to make a three for whist after dinner this evening."

Her heart thumped. She'd seen Redcliffe briefly this morning while she worked. He'd remained fixed in her mind. His perceptive green eyes and his tall, dark, good looks were a constant distraction. She shouldn't agree, but she would so enjoy an evening spent in their company. She'd played the card game often with her father and had become reasonably proficient at it. They would not be alone. Williams would be there.

"Please tell his lordship, I shall be delighted. I only hope I am up to matching wits with two skillful players."

Williams smiled. "As two gentlemen with only each other's company, I believe the pleasure will be all ours."

After Williams left, Olivia and the housemaid went to the steward's office, a small gloomy room near the laundry.

While Polly cleaned, Olivia searched through the record books. The estate steward, Mr. Pike, was the son of the former vicar, now deceased. Her father had asked him about the money owing to him, but Pike knew nothing to help. He had a cottage in the village. As steward, he'd collected the rents, attended to the leases, and supervised the tenantry. Lists of feed and seed purchases, plus other items, were neatly detailed at the end of each month. She ran her finger down each page. A tenant farmer wished to lease more land, and after Mr. Graves had passed away, his son took over the lease of their farm.

She found no evidence Pike had consulted the bailiff, which surprised her, as he alone dealt with the hiring and firing of workers. He'd settled two tenant disputes and oversaw the harvest and purchase of livestock. The records began several years ago when the earl must have been in better health and the estate well run. Pike's neat account keeping ended a few months before the earl died when he would have left the earl's employ.

After studying the books for over an hour, Olivia rested her head in her hands. Nothing she found supported her conviction that the earl had cheated her father. But she wasn't about to give up. There were several books of entries in Pike's crimped cursive to go through.

Polly gathered up her bucket, mop, and brushes. "I'm finished, Miss Jenner."

Olivia cast an eye around the room, smelling pleasantly of lemon and furniture polish. The floorboards washed, the fireplace swept, the woodwork gleaming, and the windows sparkling. The girl had been quick and thorough. "Good work, Polly. You are now the head maid and will assist me in organizing the other girls."

Polly grinned. "Thank you, Miss Jenner."

Olivia returned the ledgers she'd been examining to the shelf and left the room, wondering what among her few gowns she might wear to play whist. While she looked forward to the evening with pleasure, she cautioned herself to keep a professional distance from Lord Redcliffe. Once she found the proof of his uncle's trickery, she would restore her father's reputation and request the money owed him be paid to her. Then her position here would end.

She sighed. To see this beautiful old house restored appealed to her, and it would be hard to leave before its completion. But she would not change her mind. The sooner she escaped the temptation Lord Redcliffe might become, the better. But she disliked their association ending on bad terms, as it surely would.

Pushing such disturbing thoughts aside, she went to see if Michael, their new under footman, who'd gone on an errand for Sam some hours ago, had returned and wasn't dillydallying with a maid.

In the corridor, she caught sight of herself in the long, gilt-edged mirror. She smoothed her hair. The cap made her look the part of an efficient housekeeper, but she didn't much care for it. She wouldn't wear it again. In her bedchamber, she took her one evening gown, made at Lady Lowry's request, from the wardrobe. Olivia wore it at a weekend party where her employer insisted she attend to the guests. It showed far more of her breasts than she approved of, and she'd disliked how the male guests ogled her.

Should she wear it? The pretty gown suited her. She chewed her lip as the thrill of dressing to gain a man's approval made her remember her girlhood. But it was not Mr. Williams's approval she sought. Really, did the earl's opinion matter so much? Yes, it did. She wanted him to look at her as a man did a woman he found attractive. It was a risky way to think. She must remain alert should he attempt to lead her down a path that would end in disgrace.

In her shift, she washed herself using the bowl of hot water she'd brought up from the kitchen, which was now tepid. They left her soap and powder at Lady Lowry's. An oversight or her former mistress' vindictiveness? But she'd go without rather than ask for them. The soap she'd found in one of the guest bedchambers smelled luxuriously of roses. The scent made her feel feminine. After drying herself, she dressed. She'd taken a small, oval, gilt-edged one from the guest wing. She'd replace it when guests came to stay.

Leaning the mirror against the wall gave her a limited view of herself. The gown of printed muslin featured a blue border around the hem. Lace trimmed the scoop neck and the short sleeves. Her slippers matched. She wore the pearl earrings she would never part with, which had belonged to her mother. The gold, heart-shaped locket she wore around her neck was a present from Papa. He'd called her the belle of the ball on the night of her come-out party.

She'd danced the night away but had failed to fall in love with any of the men there. Nor in the ensuing years. She didn't have a London Season. Papa was happy to keep her home with him after Mama died, and as things went downhill, he needed someone to care for him. Olivia arranged the delicate link chain, glad her father would never know how difficult her life became after he died.

Her hands trembled as she pulled on the white cotton gloves. Her hands were not as pretty as they should be. She put her fingers to her cheek and nervously leaned closer to the mirror. The smattering of freckles across her nose were more visible, and she had no powder. She'd been out in the sun too much and must take care. She had an excellent recipe for Denmark lotion. If only she had the time and the ingredients to make it.

At the drawing room door, Jack's eyes widened as she approached him.

"Good evening, Jack." She sounded more composed than she felt as he rushed to open it.

Would she be the subject of gossip among the servants tomorrow? Another thing to worry about. She should have refused the invitation. Made up some excuse. But the chance to enter that world she had left, even for a few hours, was just too tempting.

The two gentlemen in evening dress rose from their chairs beside the fireplace. For the briefest moment, it brought back her life with her father when they'd entertained. She pushed away the sad memory, and with a smile, she crossed the floor to them.

"Ah, Miss Jenner, good evening." Lord Redcliffe averted his gaze from her low neckline and gestured to the sofa. "A glass of Madeira?"

"Thank you." He looked wonderful in a dark blue superfine coat and pale trousers. She swallowed nervously, in need of a glass of wine.

Williams sat on the sofa beside her. He smiled kindly. "A busy day, Miss Jenner?"

"Yes, indeed, sir. And still much more to do."

"I'm sure of it. A heroic effort is required, and I admire your fortitude."

Redcliffe handed her the crystal glass. "I notice you've tidied the steward's office. Mr. Pike now works for the squire. I have need of a new steward."

Her shoulders tensed. "I readied it for him. I expected you to engage one." A new steward would make it extremely difficult for her to continue her search.

"Thoughtful of you." Seating himself opposite her in the upholstered chair, he crossed his long legs. Raising his glass, he drank, his eyes thoughtful as they rested on her.

Did he suspect her? He had visited Northoaks. How much did Lancaster tell him about her father? Olivia took a hasty sip, allowing the flavorsome liquid to slip down her tight throat. She disliked being secretive, but it was necessary. "I've left the guest bedchambers to do because Mr. Williams tells me you have no immediate plans for house guests."

"Quite so." Some emotion darkened his green eyes. Was it mistrust? She would have sworn it was desire a moment ago—or had she been indulging in a fit of vanity?

Williams drew her into a discussion of the remarkable improvements the new gardeners made. "A pleasure to see the flower beds weeded and the lawns scythed."

She welcomed a change of topic. "Most particularly, the gardens around the fountain." She sat back as the wine soothed her. "Such a delightful vista. They will be quite lovely next spring."

Was she rambling? Olivia found nothing more to add to the conversation from her limited knowledge of gardening, and as neither Williams nor his lordship seemed inclined to continue, she finished the last drops of the Madeira and glanced down at her glass. She'd drunk it all.

The earl rose and took her glass. "Another?"

He must think her fond of drink. She couldn't look at him, but as it eased her nerves, she nodded.

He handed the glass to Jack. "A Madeira for Miss Jenner." He bent to offer her his arm. "Shall we begin our game?"

She rose and placed a hand on the fine material of his sleeve, breathing in his cologne, as they strolled the length of the room to the card table. A long evening ahead. How could she concentrate on whist? She feared she would play badly. If they invited her again, she would decline. Even the short time spent in this world unsettled her and made her yearn for something forever gone, which she'd thought she'd come to terms with.

CHAPTER EIGHT

THE MADEIRA HAD brought a flush to Miss Jenner's cheeks and made her eyes sparkle. She'd abandoned the slightly starchy manner she'd adopted since coming here, along with the mobcap. He fought a smile. She had Williams chuckling over something that occurred in the kitchen, which involved young Henry, the kitchen boy, and the plucking of poultry feathers. Dominic failed to follow the conversation. His attraction to her warred with his suspicions. Why had she gone out of her way to clean the steward's office? Her explanation didn't ring true. His initial thought that she had another reason for coming here resurfaced. But did it matter if she did her job well?

He put down a card.

Was she here to search for his uncle's suspected secret cache of money? Although he knew little about her, he struggled to believe she would act unscrupulously. But he wouldn't ask her about it. He was content to wait, hoping in time he would either discover her reason or she would confide in him. He preferred the latter.

The idea of valuables hidden somewhere seemed preposterous to him. He doubted the veracity of the story spread about by the community. People loved a mystery. And they loved to create one, he thought darkly, thinking of his recent past in London.

If he'd expected an evening spent in her company would cure

him of his interest in her, it hadn't. Watching Miss Jenner tonight only stirred a stronger interest in her and her past. She was obviously used to moving in social circles. Although shy at first, she was now at ease, amusing, and quite adept at whist. He'd made her banker, and having won the first of the three games, she detailed their scores in the book.

He'd played poorly and must give the next game his full attention, but again his gaze drifted back to her.

She would grace any ballroom in that gown. He enjoyed the intriguing glimpse of her breasts peeping above the lace, and how the simple lines of the skirts emphasized her tall, willowy figure. Just enough to make a man yearn to investigate the beguiling curves beneath, to touch and kiss.

He cleared his throat. He'd lost the thread of the last game. "You are an accomplished player, Miss Jenner."

She looked up from examining the seven cards he'd dealt her. "Thank you. Whist was a favorite of my father and me."

He stirred himself to discover more about her. "Squire Lancaster mentioned your father. He was the former squire of Northoaks?"

He regretted it immediately, for her eyes grew sad. "He was."

"A fine property."

"I haven't seen it for some time. It certainly was when I lived there." Her steady voice gave no clue to her feelings, but losing her father and her home obviously distressed her still.

Williams looked up from his hand. "Did you grow up at Northoaks, Miss Jenner?"

"Yes. I was born there. My mother came from Harrogate, my father's family owned Northoaks for generations. You may have heard of my grandfather, Judge Alistair Jenner."

She said his name proudly.

Dominic hid his surprise. "I heard the judge speak once in London. An orator of some note."

"Is he still alive?" Williams's voice was gentle as if he guessed the answer. Like Dominic, he had warmed to Miss Jenner and felt some sympathy for her.

"No. He died some years ago."

Dominic found himself caught up in a way he hadn't intended. "You have no living relatives?"

Her shoulders stiffened, the gesture barely discernable. "No."

She was alone in the world. Careful not to reveal the compassion she aroused in him, he asked, "Did you ride to hounds when at Northoaks?"

"Oh, yes. I loved to jump and had an excellent mount, but I was never there at the kill. I am too soft-hearted, I'm afraid."

"Not a bad thing for a lady to be," Williams observed.

Dominic left the table to fetch a bottle of champagne chilling on the sideboard, having sent Jack to the kitchen for coffee. He needed a moment to clear his disorderly thoughts, which were filled with her—the dimple in her cheek when she smiled, and how her blue eyes would cloud with some sad memory. He was coming to know her. Her gentle sense of humor. Her practical nature and her kindness. Spending this evening with her offered a further glimpse into her character. What drove him? Curiosity? Or the urge to get closer? He drew in a breath. He'd been mad to bring her here.

Filling her glass, a rousing but highly inappropriate thought forced its way into his mind. What if they were alone together? Of course, he wanted to make love to her. Had done since he first saw her. But he wanted more. He felt some sympathy for her. It was certainly no fault of hers that she found herself in this coil. But it wasn't sympathy that filled his thoughts when he thought of Miss Jenner.

He poured the champagne into the flutes, then sat to study the cards dealt him as the last game began. Williams having won the second. What a poor show he made of whist tonight. A smile tugged his lips. Dominic blamed Miss Jenner entirely.

He was in sore need of feminine company. That was the reason for it. He'd never gone this long without making love to a woman since the war, and even then there was a charming

Spanish lady. After casting an eye around Lady Lowry's garden party for someone ripe for a liaison, he'd quickly given away the idea. It would be unwise to conduct a discreet affair in such a small community, where he was the center of attention. And he had no wish to cement his reputation as a rake in people's minds. Country people were more prudish than the *ton*. And a romp with a tavern wench would never appeal to him.

As Jack brought in the coffee, Dominic returned to the possibility of inviting Lady Anne. He pictured them strolling the grounds and riding over the estate before breakfast. She might play the grand pianoforte that languished in the music room and sing for them. Her company in the evening would be far superior to old Williams, and should she join him in his bed, that, too, would be most agreeable.

Why should he not invite her and a few guests? The gardens looked splendid. The gardeners had made great inroads. And autumn was a few short weeks away. A beautiful time of year in Northumberland, he'd been told. The house looked and smelled considerably better, now with floral scents wafting from the vases of flowers Miss Jenner kept filled in the reception rooms.

He frowned. On reflection, he doubted Lady Anne would accept his invitation. Not unless a proposal was in the offing. And that was not his intention.

Miss Jenner, her coffee cooling beside her, studied her cards, dark lashes fanning her cheeks. He would lose again if he didn't pay attention. He discarded his hand and picked up the widow hand, dealt for the absent fourth player, which any player could exchange for his own. It was only marginally better than the one dealt him, but he could now play the queen of clubs.

Williams followed with a low club.

Miss Jenner a trump.

One thing Dominic was certain of, she would see to his guests' every need. Damn, but she played whist with skill. While he fought to concentrate and beat her in this last game, when his gaze rested on the soft skin of her throat, and down to the swell of her breasts above her bodice, his blood deserted his brain for another part of his body.

He took a deep swig of champagne.

Moments later, she looked up, merriment brightening her blue eyes as she put down her winning hand. "I believe I have your measure, my lord, and yours, Mr. Williams."

He tossed down his hand. Dash it all. It was mortifying.

"By Jove, so you have." Williams raised a questioning brow at Dominic's poor play. "Well done, Miss Jenner."

She laughed. "The luck of a beginner."

Dominic shook his head, amusement tugging at his lips. "You would be a sensation at White's Club in London."

"I fear I would," she said, raising her eyebrows. "Just by stepping through the door."

"We couldn't allow that. A gentleman's club is a man's last bastion."

"I confess such clubs are a mystery to me. Do they exist for members to escape from women, my lord?"

Williams chuckled. "Touché. I suspect Miss Jenner has you at point nonplus, milord." He drained his coffee cup and stood. "But rather than risk putting my point of view, I believe I shall retire. Good evening."

As the door closed behind Williams, Miss Jenner stood. "I, too. I have enjoyed this evening very much. Thank you for inviting me."

"You cannot retire on that note, Miss Jenner." Rising, he gestured for her to join him on the sofa. "Allow me to add something in a man's defense."

With an amused small shake of her head, she obeyed his request.

He joined her, sitting at a discreet distance. She had a refreshing view of life. She hadn't been brought up in that world where women expected their men to be away for long hours at their own pursuits. His arm resting along the back of the sofa, he leaned toward her and said, "Men, being of a simpler nature, enjoy each other's company without the complicated presence of women. We value our freedom, our clubs, our male pursuits: hunting; fishing, and boxing bouts, carriage races, which interests few ladies."

"I offer no objection to men seeking their own interests." She studied the gloves she held in her hand. "But sometimes they take men away too often from their families."

He could hardly disagree with her. Some men rarely went home after their sons were born. But some women could be merciless. Too many unhappy marriages in society, arranged or otherwise. He recalled a friend, Jeremy McConnell, who'd been discovered kissing a young woman with no chaperone present. The debutante and her mother plotted to trap him, and Jeremy, not much above twenty, faced with his father's threat of disinheritance, had little choice but to marry the girl. When in his cups, Jeremy miserably admitted to Dominic he did not love his wife, and worse, fervently disliked her.

"Not every man is capable of rakish behavior," he said, aware he had veered from the topic. Somehow, that she might think him a rake, mattered.

It was not long after young McConnell's experience that Dominic found himself unfairly branded a rake by society. The source of the rumor denied him, he had no recourse but to ignore it. He looked into her wide eyes, her smooth forehead puckered. Did she believe the gossip which had obviously reached the village all the way from London? Why did he feel the need to defend himself?

"Didn't Descartes say that perfect men are very rare?" she said with a hint of a smile curling her lips. "I take that to include women who can behave just as badly as men, while sometimes, good men are treated poorly."

"Descartes also said that you must never accept a thing as true unless you knew it without a single doubt," he said. "You've read Descartes?"

"Very little. A book of my father's."

He enjoyed talking with her. She was wise beyond her years, and her responses, were delightfully unpredictable. He couldn't remember having such a stimulating conversation with a woman before, politics certainly, poetry, even philosophy, but rarely discussed with a good deal of sense. It reminded him again of the life she must have enjoyed with her father, no longer hers.

Raindrops pattered against the windows, a warm, intimate sound. A pensive mood settled over them. As the silence lengthened, he sensed a sudden intimacy, tense with expectation. Their gazes collided. Her eyes widened. Her sweet, feminine scent drifted across to him. He battled against moving closer to seek her softness and her warmth.

Her tongue traced the soft spot on her upper lip he wanted to kiss. The unconscious gesture sent heat straight to his groin, and he almost groaned.

The grandfather clock in the hall outside chimed twelve o'clock with an annoying succession of loud bongs.

"I might get rid of that clock," he said with a husky laugh.

She gathered up her gloves. "I must go. It has grown late, and I have a great deal to do in the morning."

She sounded as unsettled as he was. The air seemed charged with unspoken emotion.

"Of course." He rose with her and took her slender, soft hand in his, tempted to raise it to his lips. He restrained himself.

She withdrew her hand.

He walked with her to the door and opened it, startling his drowsy footman. "Sleep well, Miss Jenner."

"And you, sir." She slipped out, leaving a trace of her perfume.

Dominic retreated into the room, stunned at what had just happened. He was hardly a green youth. And yet, he'd come within a hair's breadth of losing control. He was both relieved not to act in the rakish manner he'd just denounced, and conversely, regretful that he hadn't.

Miss Jenner hailed from the gentry. Her ancestors might well have been wealthy and important men, her grandfather undoubtedly was, but she did not live by the standards of the *ton*. And she gave him little reason to believe she'd behave as freely as some of the ladies of his acquaintance. With a heavy sigh, he poured himself a brandy. He hadn't been so unsure of himself since university. But thinking back to the first time they met, he'd somehow perceived that Miss Jenner, Olivia, would shake him to the core. He should have listened to the warning voice in his head. Several large swallows of brandy, and he accepted how glad he was she was here at the hall and part of his life, if only as his housekeeper.

OLIVIA SNUFFED OUT her candle and lay staring into the dark. She would never sleep. Her mind was filled with him. With little experience of men of Lord Redcliffe's ilk, she should never have placed herself in that position. But she'd so enjoyed their conversation. Being with him. Had he wished to kiss her, she wasn't sure she would have stopped him. And then, she could hardly accuse him of rakish behavior when she'd invited the kiss. He'd been adamant that accusing a man of such behavior was unfair to many. It made her wonder what might have happened to him to earn that title. She frowned. She mustn't make excuses for him. Or trust him when she barely knew him. And never put herself in that position again.

Perhaps he was motivated by sympathy for her straightened circumstances. She turned over in bed with a huff of annoyance. That was not something she wished. It weakened her and threatened her independence, to which she clung, drawing her fragile confidence around her like a warm shawl.

Olivia rolled over onto her back. Her father used to say there was no smoke without fire. Rakes would coerce a woman to get what they wanted. But this evening, his lordship's behavior was gentlemanly. She puffed out a breath. Just as well! What would she have done if he'd attempted to seduce her? Call for Jack's help? Push him away with old-maidish indignation? Pack her luggage and leave here? Or kiss him back? What nonsense. She must be a little drunk.

Growing increasingly annoyed with herself, she steered her thoughts to their card game. She beat Lord Redcliffe at cards! Admittedly, he seemed distracted through most of their play, but still...

Pulling the blanket up around her shoulders, she closed her eyes, but sleep seemed far away. She feared she would droop like a wilting lily in the morning.

Finally, she gave up on sleep, indulging in the memory of that moment, when alone in the drawing room with him, cocooned by the sound of the rain, their polite conversation had faltered. Always, in his presence, she was aware of this powerful, attractive man. But tonight, desire had sparked in his eyes, and she knew he wanted her. Her breath had caught.

Reliving it, Olivia curled her toes. To stir such a man's desire. Of course, she had no competition, she told herself sternly, fighting to bring herself back to earth. And anything more between them could never be. She must be careful. Her future depended on her remaining aloof from his charm. As Lady Lowry had been eager to tell her, such a man would only want her for a brief affair. And she wanted his respect and approval for what she could achieve here, not just to spark desire in him.

She wrestled her pillow into a more comfortable shape. To be alone with him after two glasses of Madeira and champagne was not only reckless, it could have been a grave mistake. She should have excused herself and left when Williams did. Why hadn't she?

She simply must never place herself in that position again.

The next morning, the arc of azure sky viewed from her office window held the promise of a sunny day. As Olivia worked on the menus and supplies for the following week, Jack knocked on her door.

"His lordship is at the Graves' farm, Miss Jenner. They are cutting and bailing hay. He wants you to bring him his luncheon."

Olivia stared at the youth. "Are you sure it wasn't you he wished to bring it?"

"No, said I'm to drive you in the trap. And you were to tell Cook his lordship wants a loaf of bread and butter, cold chicken, cheese, and pickles, two bottles of ale, and two pieces of the rhubarb pie served at dinner last evening."

Mystified as to why Lord Redcliffe should send for her, she left her desk. "I will see to it, Jack. Fetch the trap."

With a hamper loaded with plates, cutlery, glasses, napkins, and the requested food in the back of the trap, Jack drove Olivia along a lane for several miles to the small farm run by Ruben Graves. He took the rundown property over from his father after his death and struggled to keep the farm afloat.

The midday sun burned through her straw bonnet as Jack pulled the horse up at the pasture gate where his lordship's coat hung. Some distance away across the field, several men slashed at the hay with scythes, then loaded it onto a wagon. It was easy to pick out the earl; Graves and the other workers were shorter. Redcliffe stood and shaded his eyes with a hand, looking her way. Sighting the trap, he strode across through the row of hay bales, naked to the waist, a shirt trailing in his hands.

She gasped. He was magnificent. When he hailed them, he looked completely unabashed. A sheen of sweat burnished his lightly sunburned skin, and a trail of springy dark hair arrowed down from his molded chest to his narrow waist, disappearing into tight breeches. Olivia didn't know where to look as he pulled the white linen shirt over his head.

She busied herself placing a cloth on the grass and arranging the food.

He stood smiling down at her. "Good of you to come, Miss Jenner."

As if she had a choice. She tried not to look at him. His white shirt did little to hide the breadth of his chest and shoulders. He must enjoy physical work, she thought irrationally.

He bent to pick a yellow flower and held it out to her.

Olivia giggled. "That's a weed. Ragwort. It might give you a rash."

He raised his eyebrows with a half-grin and tossed it away. "It seems I have much to learn." He dusted his fingers and eyed the spread. "What have we here? A feast! Graves and I will enjoy it. The other men have brought their lunch with them. A man gets hungry when toiling in the fields."

How contented he was. When she'd first met him, he seemed quite different. She'd thought him arrogant, with a sardonic cast to his handsome mouth. An elegant lord tilling the soil side by side with a farmer? It came as a complete surprise to her. But she liked him for it. "There was something you wished to ask me, my lord?"

"Mrs. Graves is unwell. Graves tells me she is with child. As I have no wife to visit her, please call on her. Take anything you consider will be of help to her. You'll know what's best."

"I shall, of course."

He turned and hailed Graves, then threw himself down on the grass and grabbed a napkin, then picked up a chicken leg. "I'm considering a house party. When can the guest chambers be made ready?" He bit into the chicken and wiped the juices from his chin with the napkin.

Unsettled by his raw masculinity, not to mention his surprising announcement, Olivia stared at him. For a long moment, she struggled as to what to reply. The house was far from ready, and they had very few staff. But she didn't know why she should feel responsible for any inadequacies. "My lord, there is still much to be done," she finally gasped out.

He tossed the chicken bone onto a plate, wiped his hands, and leaned back on his elbows. With one booted foot crossed over the other, making her conscious of the length of his legs, his gaze caught and held hers. "I have confidence in you, Miss Jenner. I am sure you are well able to manage." How annoyingly casual he was. Used to getting everything he wanted, she thought uncharitably, whisking her gaze away from his before he might discern what she thought from her expression. "Shall we say…three weeks?"

Three weeks! This would be a test of her abilities. Could she do it? She must! He said he had confidence in her. Whether he'd intended his praise to inspire her or appeal to her vanity, she found she couldn't ignore it.

Graves came through the gate and his greeting gave her time to think. It was a huge undertaking, but they might manage at a pinch, and she refused to admit defeat. "How many guests, my lord?"

"Not a large party. A dozen or so. I shall furnish you with their names and other details later."

Her lungs expanded with her deep breath. "The house will be ready."

His gaze flickered over her breasts. Dark eyebrows rose. "Well done, Miss Jenner."

"Then if you permit, I shall leave you. Jack can fetch the basket later."

"Certainly." He smiled as if he knew what was in her head. It was just as well he didn't. Her thoughts were not charitable.

Jack assisted her into the trap. As he urged the horse to walk on, she turned for another glance at the earl as he and Graves filled their plates. Lord Redcliffe still watched her, but it was impossible from this distance to read the expression in his eyes. Surely it wasn't necessary to bring her all the way out here to convey his instructions? He might easily have conveyed them to her later in the day. How unpredictable he was. He constantly threw her off balance and did it on purpose, she suspected. Flustered, she forced her thoughts on to preparing the house for guests.

CHAPTER NINE

DOMINIC RODE HOME from the Graves' farm, thinking of his housekeeper. He smiled. He hadn't intended to rattle her but enjoyed the effect he had on her. Miss Jenner's prim demeanor didn't fool him. A telltale flush colored her cheeks, and she'd tried not to look at him. It brought a swift urge for him to be the one to stir her passions, to draw a heated response from her lips.

A man needed intimacy, a woman's softness. Women were a civilizing influence. He feared he might lose much of it with only Williams and Graves for company. When attending church on Sunday, he looked for a woman ripe for liaison. One or two stared at him as if he had two heads. Most were as prim as Miss Jenner attempted to be, but she outshone them in the beauty stakes. A widow coyly sent him a subtle message after the service, and while attractive, she failed to stir his interest. She would have, once.

It was definitely time to write to Lady Anne.

Dominic left Onyx to Fellow's care and walked to the house, planning to pen letters of invitation to several friends. He smiled. Miss Jenner, although at first shaken by his mention of a house party, rallied in that manner he so admired.

ON HER WAY to visit Mrs. Graves, Olivia had caught sight of Lord Redcliffe still toiling in the fields as she drove the trap along the lane. She tried not to look his way, as he'd stopped to watch her. He reminded her of a statue of Apollo she'd seen in a book, but warm and real, muscles shifting beneath satiny skin. She caught her bottom lip in her teeth. He was her employer. She must force herself to think of him in that fashion, and no other. But really, she thought crossly, Redcliffe—as she now thought of him—did not help. He seemed to invite situations that threw them together, and his manner toward her was a dreadful distraction.

Olivia's basket was packed with a tincture of chamomile, peppermint, and raspberry leaf, to ease the nauseating effects of pregnancy. She added one of Sam's meat pies from the larder for Mr. Graves, in case Mrs. Graves felt unable to cook his supper.

A mobcap over her chestnut hair, Mrs. Graves greeted her at the door, looking pale and tired. She expressed her delight at receiving a visitor. Her mother had passed away, she told Olivia, and the midwife was the only woman to visit her. Over a cup of tea, she spoke of how she and Graves had only been married a year and admitted to being quite wretched in the mornings.

"I hope the mixture makes you feel better."

Mrs. Graves unloaded the basket. "How very kind. It is so pleasant to have company. Will you please call me Mary?" She looked downcast. "With Graves out working, I find the days quite long." Her cheeks flushed. "I am most grateful for all we have. You must understand, but I miss reading. I so enjoy it."

"Please call me Olivia, Mary. What books do you like to read?"

"I was fortunate to be given a copy of *Sense and Sensibility*. It's by an unknown author. I should like to read more of theirs."

"I've read it and another novel by that author. A splendid writer," Olivia said, "I shall bring the other one with me next time."

"You will?" Mary enveloped her in a warm, lavender-scented hug. "It is something to look forward to. The books certainly but your company, especially."

Olivia smiled, pleased to have a friend when she'd lost so many after her father died. "I'm looking forward to our discussions." Someone to share books with was a delight. Most of the staff could do little more than sign their names, and few others had time to enjoy the pastime.

Olivia left, feeling sympathetic toward Mary. One of Lady Lowry's housemaids had hidden her pregnancy as long as she could but was quite ill before they found out and sent her home. The girl had said she would be unwelcome at home, and Olivia had worried about what might have happened to her.

Redcliffe had left Graves's field when Olivia drove along the lane. She arrived back at the house, determined to begin as the earl requested and prepare the rooms for his guests. She was never one to put off what she could do today and felt sure if she left all the six bedchambers for tomorrow, it would prey on her mind.

Olivia took Polly with her to the guest wing. She stopped on the first-floor landing. Here were the earl's and countess's suites. She had been in Redcliffe's, having supervised the cleaning and daily stripping of the sheets and towels, but never the countess's.

Halfway down the hall, Olivia opened a door and stepped inside.

Polly gasped in awe at the dainty, gilt-legged French chairs, the ornate fireplace, and the massive oil paintings. She tiptoed across the dense carpet to gaze up at the sky-blue velvet bed curtains spilling from a golden coronet just below the ceiling.

Olivia waited at the door. "Come, Polly. We have work awaiting us."

"Can we just have a peep into the dressing room, Miss Jenner?"

Olivia smiled. "It should be empty."

In the countess's boudoir, a full-length, gilt-edged mirror stood beside a pair of wardrobes. Olivia opened the doors. Expensive perfume wafted out from the countess's fine clothing.

Breathtaking silks, damasks, velvets, and furs folded or on hooks, some in cloth bags. Arranged on shelves was a vast array of dainty footwear: shoes, slippers, half-boots, and riding boots. All exquisitely made. Dozens of hatboxes occupied the shelves above. Polly opened a large hatbox with French writing on it. She removed a wide-brimmed hat of the finest straw decorated with curling ostrich feathers.

"This is so beautiful." Polly put it on her head and pulled the sheer veil over her face. She sneezed.

"Do put it back, Polly," Olivia scolded, tempted to try the hat on herself. Wondering if some of these materials might go toward making cushions and seat covers, she sorted through the gowns, examining a wide-skirted, gold silk damask gown in the style of the last century, which had yards of material, and another—a turquoise velvet evening gown, also voluminous and quite breathtaking. Corsets, silk stockings, and negligees still filled the drawers, and nightwear she could see her hand through, folded among lavender sachets.

How stylish Countess Redcliffe must have been. Olivia found it difficult to imagine her here with the old earl. She must have been far too elegant for the country. As she died many years before the earl, Olivia knew little about her, but she wanted to find her portrait in the long gallery, sure that she was beautiful.

"We might make these into something useful," she said to Polly. But she would need to discuss it first with Redcliffe. It was not a priority, for none of his guests would occupy this suite. At least, not until he married.

A door on the far wall opened onto a charmingly furnished sitting room, with another door that must lead to the earl's bedchamber.

They moved on to the guest chambers, Polly carrying her box of furniture polish and brushes. As they tackled the rooms, airing mattresses and rolling up rugs, Olivia wondered if the future Lady Redcliffe could be among the guests the earl planned to invite.

At the end of the long day, she sank onto her bed, long-unused muscles aching. She'd never had to perform a house-maid's tasks while at Lady Lowry's. How taxing the work was. But she and Polly had achieved a good deal today, which pleased her. She was confident she could fulfill Redcliffe's orders in time. Four of the guest bedchambers were ready, which only required fresh linens, towels, and the special touches of fresh flowers, biscuits, and perfumed soaps. Tomorrow, they would prepare two more.

She yawned and turned over on the narrow bed. Redcliffe, stripped to the waist, his smooth skin gleaming with sweat, entered her mind. Warmth spread through her. His future countess would be lucky indeed to welcome him into that sumptuous bedchamber.

Olivia rolled over again. She intended to leave Redcliffe's employ before he married, and so set some time aside in her busy day to continue her search through the steward's records. But the urgency which had driven her for so long seemed to have lessened.

Olivia groaned. Was it this old house, or the master, which fascinated her?

Of course, she knew the answer, and while it sent a thrill rushing through her, it gave her little pleasure to admit it. With a huff of exasperation at her folly, she closed her eyes and willed sleep.

Something woke her. A door or a window opening or clos-ing, she wasn't sure. Now wide awake, Olivia sat up in bed. She lit her candle and glanced at her watch. It was past two. Slipping from the bed, she pulled aside the curtains. A sliver of moon sent a silvery glow over the roof. Movement on the second floor of the guest wing caught her eye. Candlelight flashed in a window. As she watched, the glow vanished from sight. Who would be in the guest bedchambers in the middle of the night?

Whoever it was appeared to have gone.

She was about to return to bed when the light appeared again in another window.

Ignoring the urgings of her common sense to go back into bed, she shrugged on her dressing gown and donned her slippers. With her candle held high, she left the room. The corridor was black as pitch beyond the arc of candlelight. She made her cautious way toward the stairs, careful not to disturb the maids as she passed their rooms. Her first inclination was to wake Sam, but the men's sleeping quarters were at the far end of the corridor behind a locked door. While she possessed the keys to all the rooms, she could hardly venture into the area in her night attire. She would wake half the staff, and they might misconstrue her reasons for being there.

Olivia made her way to the main staircase and began down. A faint light shone below. She grasped the banister and peered into the dark. A man emerged, half in shadow. He crossed the floor below her, lighting his way with a candle. Might the restless soul be the earl? Whoever it was must have come from Redcliffe's suite, for only the earl's and the countess's were there.

He would have seen her candlelight. It must be Redcliffe. He might think she was up to no good. She shouldn't be wandering about in this part of the house, and certainly not in the middle of the night. Olivia preferred he didn't see her and moved away, intending to hurry back to her room.

But he had started up the stairs toward her.

"Lord Redcliffe?" she called, her voice echoing in the stairwell.

No answer.

He stopped.

It couldn't be Redcliffe. Then who was it? Finding no reasonable answer, Olivia's heart banged against her ribs. The man was only a dozen steps below her. He held his candle away from his face so she couldn't see who it was, but he was shorter, of smaller stature than the earl. Something flashed in his other hand.

She found her voice. "Who's there?" She backed up a step, clutching the rail poised to run. But to her horror, her knees weakened, and she feared if he came after her, he would catch her.

"*Redcliffe!*" Her panicked voice sounded husky and faint from her tight throat.

But it had the desired effect. The man swiveled and raced down, throwing the candle which snuffed out, plunging the stairs into darkness. Her relief was palpable, and she sank to her knees. Her candle wobbled in shaky hands, throwing a dizzying halo of light around her. She could hear the man's racing footsteps as he bolted down into the dark well of the hall below, and then his mad dash across the floor of the great hall, heading for the front door.

Her initial relief was short-lived when a cry echoed through the lofty space, then a thump, followed by a deep groan.

Jack! He was on duty tonight, stationed at the front door.

Fear felt like an icy hand on her neck as she sprinted down.

A lantern still burned on the table, casting shadows over the entry walls. Jack lay crumpled on the floor near the wide-open front door, broken glass scattered around him, catching the light.

"Jack!" Fear stilling her breath, she ran to him.

He was conscious and stared up at her. With a wince of pain, he gently touched his head. Blood dripped from his fingers. He struggled to stand up.

"No, Jack." She closed the door. "Stay there. I'll fetch help."

Redcliffe! She wasn't sure why she chose him over Williams as she ran for the stairs. Gaining the landing, she steadied her breath and rapped smartly on the door of his bedchamber. No sound came from within. Where else could he be? Did he remain to work in the library? She knew he often did. She hesitated, then deciding to make sure, she turned the latch. The room beyond greeted her with a wall of pitch black, the curtains drawn over the windows blotting out every skerrick of moonlight. She had been in this room while the housemaids cleaned, but it didn't help in the half-dark. Holding her candle high, she moved across the large chamber. It smelled of Redcliffe's tangy soap. But was he here?

Cautious steps led her across the floor until she came up against a padded chair in the small circle of light afforded her. The rough damask beneath her fingers, she fought the urge to turn and flee. She cleared her throat and whispered, "My lord?"

Nothing.

Two more cautious steps took her the carved oak bedpost. She edged around to the side of the bed. She could hear his breathing. A long body lay beneath the covers, his dark head on the pillow.

Shock at her sheer audacity diminished her bout of nerves, but her candle wobbled violently in her hand. She put it carefully down on the table and cleared her throat. "Lord Redcliffe?"

A soft snore.

She shuffled closer. Reaching out, her fingertips connected with warm flesh, muscle, and bone. His shoulder. She pulled her hand away as if burned. Did he sleep without nightclothes?

"What the devil? Who's there?" he asked, his voice thick with sleep. He sat up, his naked upper body illuminated in the pale glow of candlelight.

She swallowed, fighting the dryness in her throat. "It's Miss Jenner, sir."

"Miss Jenner? Is the house on fire?"

She quaked. "No sir, but…"

He reached up and before she knew it, she lay half atop him on the bed. "You had only to ask me earlier, Miss Jenner," he said, his amused, husky voice tickling the hair near her ear.

Incensed, she wriggled away from his grasp. "My lord! Someone broke into the house. They hurt Jack. They hit him on the head while at his post by the front door."

"Good God."

He rolled away and put his long legs over the side of the bed, clutching the sheet to his lap. Enough exposed bare skin confirmed her assumption. He slept without a nightshirt. She swiftly turned her back. "I apologize for waking you, my lord, but

I didn't know what else to do," she said breathlessly, scrambling over the other side of the bed. With no step, she jumped, landing awkwardly on the carpet.

"You were right to do so. Wait for me in the corridor."

Needing little encouragement, Olivia scuttled to the door without glancing back. She'd seen quite enough of his lordship's naked body for one day. His male smell and the memory of his hard body beneath her was enough! Any more of him would completely unnerve her.

He joined her in two long strides, shoes on his feet, his banyan flowing around the breeches he had quickly thrown on. "Right, come along."

She heard a pistol cock as he strode off down the hall.

A gun? She suppressed a shudder and hurried after him as he took the stairs two at a time.

When they reached the entry, Jack sat leaning against the wall, his hands on his head, obviously in pain.

Redcliffe put his pistol on the table and crouched beside him. "Are you badly hurt, Jack? Should I send for the doctor?"

"Not bad, milord. The fellow was a stripling." He gave a feeble chuckle. "I could have beaten him with one hand tied behind my back, but he took me by surprise. Hit me with that glass vase." He gestured to the flowers lying in a pool of water. "I must have closed my eyes for a minute, it being so quiet," he said sheepishly. "Or so I thought."

"Can you stand? I'll help you to the kitchen."

"No need, milord. My feet still work."

"If you're sure."

Redcliffe patted him on the shoulder and straightened. "Miss Jenner, will you tend to Jack's head wound? I'll look around outside, see if I can find where the man got in. Must be somewhere on the ground floor."

He snatched up his pistol, and holding the oil lamp high, went out into the dark, closing the front door behind him.

"That devil won't want to mess with his lordship if he's still lurking about," Jack said in a respectful tone.

"Let me help you to the kitchen, Jack. I'll see if that gash needs stitching and put a salve on it. There might be glass in the wound. I have feverfew for the pain."

Jack stood and tested his balance. "A bit of bump on the head won't bother me much."

"If you're woozy, you must lean on me."

"I'm fine, Miss Jenner." His gait was a little unsteady as he walked beside her. Keeping her eye on him while resisting taking hold of his arm and wounding his manly pride, they descended the servants' stairs to the kitchen.

When he sat down at the kitchen table, she went to fetch her box of salves and bandages kept in her office.

With the box in her hands, she hurried back to him. *Please God, let nothing happen to Redcliffe.*

The robber might have lashed out when cornered, but he was dangerous. That looked like a knife in his hand as he'd advanced silently up the stairs to where she stood. She tamped down a shudder. Did he think she was someone else? And then realizing his mistake meant to silence her? It was when she yelled out for Redcliffe that he'd raced downstairs. What would he have done had he reached her? Sensing evil, she shuddered as if someone had walked over her grave.

Jack slouched in the chair. He wiped blood from his hands with the cloth she gave him. "No need to be frightened, Miss Jenner. The devil won't come here again. His lordship and I will keep watch."

Olivia fought not to smile, touched by his concern. "I know you will, Jack." She carefully parted his hair to view the nasty gash. "I don't think it needs stitching," she said with some relief. "There is a small sliver of glass." When she plucked it out with tweezers, it bled more freely. "Press this clean cloth against it while I cut some tape."

After Olivia dressed his wound, she stoked the smoldering range and poured boiling water from the kettle into the teapot.

She brought out cups and saucers, sugar, and milk from the pantry, and joined him at the kitchen table.

They were drinking their second cup when Redcliffe walked in carrying a bottle of whiskey. He drew out a chair and sat down. "This might help, Jack."

Jack's eyes widened at the fine Scotch whisky. "Thank you, my lord."

She jumped up. "I'll get a glass."

He gestured for her to remain seated and poured the whisky into Jack's teacup.

"Would you care for tea, my lord?"

"First, you might tell me why you were wandering around the house in the middle of the night, Miss Jenner."

She stared at him. Was he accusing her? "Something woke me. I saw a light in a window of the guest wing and thought something might be wrong. The intruder started up the stairs toward me, but when I called out, he ran back down."

A frown snapped his dark brows together. "Did you get a look at him?"

"No, he threw his candle down."

"What about you, Jack?"

"No, milord. He wore a hat pulled low over his face. Not a big fellow, as I've said, and I'm sorry I didn't get a chance to take him on, but it happened so fast."

Olivia rose and poured hot water into the teapot from the kettle on the hob. She set another cup and saucer before Redcliffe with the jug of milk and the sugar bowl.

He thanked her with a nod and poured himself a cup.

"Did you find any sign of how he got in, milord?" Jack asked.

"None of the ground floor windows have been forced, all still locked." Redcliffe stirred sugar into his tea. "He won't hang around." He took a sip, his eyes meeting Olivia's. "In fact, I doubt he'll chance coming here again. But we'll take precautions."

Jack grimaced and rubbed his temples.

"I'll fetch you the feverfew, Jack," Olivia said. "You should rest tomorrow. I'm sure you agree, my lord."

"Yes. In fact, I insist on it." He raised his hand as Jack opened his mouth to object.

Clutching the feverfew, Jack left them, weaving slightly, though whether from the wound or the whiskey, Olivia couldn't tell.

"Stay with me a moment, Miss Jenner."

He held his cup of tea in long, lightly tanned fingers. Capable hands, she thought, distracted. "The fellow might not have been alone." His troubled eyes searched hers. "I found no sign of a break-in, and he appeared familiar with the layout of the house. That concerns me."

She stared at him. "Someone let him in?"

"It's possible," he said bluntly. "A pity we didn't catch them at it." He paused. "You saw no one else during your nightly excursion?"

"No." Hurt, she drew in a breath. He didn't trust her. But really, why should he? He knew little about her. "For a moment, I feared he would strike me down," she said in her defense. "He held something in his hand. It flashed silver in the candlelight. It could have been a knife. When I realized he wasn't you, I yelled your name, but I'm afraid it sounded like a raspy whisper." Her cheeks heated. What a poor thing he would think her now. "I felt his silent menace, and it frightened me," she explained. "I was relieved when he ran down the stairs. But then I found Jack."

"You believed he carried a knife? And yet you followed him down and went to Jack's aid."

Was that irony or suspicion, or heavens above, praise? "Jack needed help. It was all I could think of."

"And you came for me. Thank you, Miss Jenner."

His warm appreciation when she feared he distrusted her made her absurdly grateful. She ducked her head over her cup.

Braving Redcliffe in his bed hadn't been easy.

"I should tidy up and go to bed." She pushed back her chair.

"You should."

When he stood, he towered over her, causing her to hold her breath. It brought to mind the moment she'd lain against him in his bed, the sheets warm and smelling of his soap and innate maleness.

Redcliffe went to the door. He turned a hand on the door latch. "I appreciate your brave actions tonight."

"I merely did what anyone would do, my lord."

"But if it happens again, I will much prefer you remain in your bedchamber."

"I will, believe me."

He nodded with a slight smile. "I'll be in the library should you have need of me."

Olivia tidied away the tea things and attended to the stove. She didn't like his directive, but she supposed he was right. If it happened again, she had little desire to subject herself to further danger. And she would only get in Redcliffe's way. She rinsed the cups and wiped the table down, then went up to bed. Did he really suspect someone in the house had colluded with the intruder? She considered each servant for culpability. They all seemed such unlikely suspects. She couldn't believe it was one of them. But how the thief got into the house remained a mystery.

CHAPTER TEN

C LOSE TO DAWN, Dominic left the library, deeply troubled by the evening's events. Did one of his staff seek to undermine him?

Not Miss Jenner, who came to him for help when he failed to answer her call. He deeply regretted not being there for her. She'd come up against a violent man, and it could have ended badly. He rubbed the back of his neck, weary to his bones. Right now he needed a few hours' sleep, then he would work out how to best deal with this.

Some hours later, he rose from his bed, the sun high in the sky. He rang for Michael to bring his coffee and shaving water.

Once dressed in his riding clothes and his boots, which were a tiresome struggle without his valet, he was forced to admit, he left his chamber, intending to ride through the woods before breakfast.

He paused outside his door as a thought struck him. Miss Jenner said she saw the intruder emerge from this corridor. It was doubtful anyone had come into his bedchamber before her. He usually slept with one eye open, but admittedly, the demanding physical work at the farm and several brandies he'd imbibed while he mulled over a few demanding matters, caused him to sleep more deeply than usual. And then waking up to Miss Jenner's softly candlelit face hovering over him. At first, he thought he was in the middle of a very pleasant dream. He grinned. She obviously had some difficulty rousing him. Before he'd even come fully awake, he acted instinctively, taking her up on what he thought was an invitation.

He'd been mistaken. Pity. Her slender body would fit perfectly with his. Her eyes wide, she'd lain against him like an indignant fawn. A thick dark rope of braided hair rested on her shoulder. He wanted to unravel it, pull apart the strands, and lift her locks to his face. It would smell of her perfume, of her. And then discover the delights hidden beneath her modest dressing gown.

Annoyed with how easily he lost his train of thought, Dominic swiveled and went to his aunt's suite, which he'd only glanced at when he first arrived.

He stepped through the door and uttered a loud curse, eyeing the damage: the bed curtains ripped down; the countess's gold coronet lying on the floor; the cover pulled off the bed; and the mattress slashed, scattering feathers. In the dressing room, the desk drawers hung open. The thief had hauled his aunt's gowns from the wardrobes and upturned the hat and shoeboxes, the contents strewn about. Even the wallpaper suffered, shredded in some places.

Anger twisted his gut. For what did this devil search? His aunt's jewels were with Antonia, their widowed daughter-in-law, and the Redcliffe parure of diamonds still in a London bank because he saw no reason to take possession of them. What did the thief expect to find? Foolhardy to risk discovery by searching the house when occupied. In fact, it smacked of desperation.

Dominic feared for the safety of the women in his household, especially Miss Jenner, who was far too curious and bold.

He rang the bell. When Michael answered it, Dominic studied the under footman. While awaiting his instructions, Michael's mouth hung open as he gazed wordlessly around at the disorder.

Unlikely to be the accomplice, Dominic decided.

Clamping down his teeth, he tapped the riding crop against his thigh. "Fetch Miss Jenner."

He did not have to wait long before she hurried through the door, neat and fresh-faced, her smooth hair in place, with no sign of the ravages of a poor night's sleep.

"Heavens!" She stared around, aghast.

"Thorough, weren't they?" he said dryly.

"They thought they might find valuables here?"

"It appears so."

"I went through the countess's things yesterday," she admitted. "I intended to discuss with you what should be done with them. There are many good uses for such wonderful fabrics." With a deep sigh, she examined the slashed, jeweled bodice of a midnight blue silk gown, the paste jewels prized off and lying scattered over the rose-pink carpet.

"Williams must be informed," he said. "He'll need to speak to the staff."

"I'll gather them in the servants' hall after luncheon. The housemaids can tidy these things away. But it will take some time to repair the damage."

"Clear the room. Put everything in trunks in the attics."

She glanced at him.

Had he sounded heartless? "I never knew my aunt." Why he needed to explain left him momentarily baffled as they left the room.

She walked beside him. "I've never seen her. Does her portrait hang in the portrait gallery?"

"I believe so." He struggled to remember the family history told to him as a disinterested young lad. "My aunt left my uncle for a time and was very ill when she returned. She died soon afterward."

Miss Jenner's eyes asked a question she was too polite to voice.

"I believe she ran away to France with a lover."

"How sad for your uncle," she murmured. "He must have loved her, to take her back. And he kept her things and never remarried."

A romantic view. Dominic knew nothing of their relationship, but Uncle Alberic could have been a swine to live with. He felt he knew too little about his uncle to judge him, but his sorry life appeared to be unfolding before Dominic's eyes. "Nor did I know my uncle," he admitted. "I wonder if he were the sort of man who would hide his fortune from his heir. What is your opinion, Miss Jenner?"

She paused, giving his question consideration while he watched her. "If he suspected someone wished to rob him, he might. We seldom saw him in the village during his final years. His health seemed poor." Her brows met in a slight frown. "But if he secreted his fortune away in the house, you would expect him to leave some sign or message for his heir to find them."

"Yes, you would." His voice grated with sarcasm. "Both sons died before him. I'm not privy to what he thought about me as his heir. Still, that is an excellent point."

He continued down the stairs. "A man who refused to put his money safely in banks is not of sound mind, however. If my uncle left a map or a message, our visitor last night has not found it." He turned to her. "I'll speak to the parish constable. He might have heard of someone stealing from the big houses in the area. But we must make a thorough search of it from top to bottom."

"An arduous task in a building this size. But when news spreads that the house is being searched, it might deter the robber if he intends to return."

Dominic nodded, with little confidence that they would find anything. "I shall require your help, Miss Jenner."

She nodded. "Of course, the maids and I will…"

"I don't want the staff involved."

Miss Jenner raised her eyebrows. "But how…?"

"I will discuss it with you later when I have given it more thought."

She obviously disagreed but managed not to tell him so. "Very well."

He left Miss Jenner to her duties and went to consult with

Williams.

Leaving the house in search of his estate manager, he examined his reasons to invite Miss Jenner to aid him in his quest. While he did not wish her to uncover anything without him present to witness it, he also needed to keep watch while the house was under threat. But, if he were honest, he wanted her company, as she was an excellent sounding board. The last made him shrug at his folly.

When Dominic asked Williams to question the staff, his estate manager stroked his chin in thought. "The door between the female and male bedchambers is kept locked at night, but the staff are at liberty to leave their rooms. However, they know not to enter that part of the house with the footman on duty and you often working late in the library. Someone was bound to see them, as Miss Jenner did. But you might prefer to be there when I question them."

Dominic tightened his jaw. "I intend to."

Shortly after luncheon, he entered the noisy servants' hall. The staff had obviously been told of the break-in, although most would already have heard of it. Silence settled over the room as he nodded to Williams and Miss Jenner.

While Williams questioned them, Dominic, his arms folded, watched the proceedings. He wondered if there could be a traitor among them. Servants became close, like a family belowstairs. Anyone would find it hard to keep such an enterprise from them. He dismissed his footmen and the kitchen boy. And Emily and the younger housemaids, as they nervously twisted their hands in their aprons. Mary, an older housemaid, had recently joined the household but was hardly the type to involve herself in something like this.

Samuel stated calmly that he had not left his chamber. Dominic recalled the cook had a checkered past. But he didn't come from these parts, and Miss Jenner spoke well of him. He respected her judgment in this. Mrs. Hobbs, the laundry maid, a widow close to forty who hailed from the village, had been with them for only a short time. According to Williams, the reference from her last employer was excellent.

"If it happens again, I will send for a Bow Street Runner to investigate," Dominic said, once Williams had completed his inquiry. He doubted it would come to that and was extremely reluctant. He'd had a word with the parish constable earlier, who offered nothing useful, so he might have to act on it.

With a collective gasp, the servants gazed at each other. He'd expected the news would make them nervous when they were already upset by the break-in. The detectives from the Bow Street Magistrate's court in London rarely came to these parts, preferring the city and its environs. Some had unsavory reputations. Their presence here would cause suspicion in a small village.

The staff dismissed, Dominic asked Miss Jenner to join him in the library.

Moments later, she entered the room. From his desk, he watched her cross the swirl of patterned carpet. He gestured for her to sit. "Williams handled it well. Did you notice anything they said which might be suspicious?"

"No." She frowned. "I dislike how unsettled the servants are. I wouldn't want this to turn them against each other."

"That is unfortunate. But necessary."

"While I understand your concern, a house runs better with a happy household belowstairs."

"Then we must hope we have seen the last of the intruder. The fear of Bow Street Runners might give them second thoughts about trying it again."

"If a servant is involved. Are you still of that mind?"

"Until proven otherwise." He steepled his fingers, his elbows resting on the desk, watching the emotions flit across her expressive face as she considered his words.

"I'll look for anything your uncle might have left when the maids and I set the rooms in order."

"And report anything untoward immediately to me."

"Of course."

"The attics will be searched tomorrow. Shall we say two o'clock, Miss Jenner?"

Surprise widened her eyes. *"We,* my lord?"

"Yes. It is best to begin there."

"I can consign a footman and a maid… I'm in the midst of preparing the bedchambers for your guests, and there is much more that requires my attention."

"The staff are anxious. Let's keep this between ourselves. And it must take precedence."

She raised her eyebrows. "Have you reconsidered the house party?"

"I have." He noted the rebuke in her eyes. "Naturally, this has changed my plans. It must wait until I'm sure the danger is at an end. I trust an hour spent in the attics won't interfere with your work. The light will be poor. I'll bring a lantern."

She hesitated as if she expected him to throw something else at her. "Is that all, my lord?" she said finally.

"Yes, Miss Jenner. For now."

She left the library, her frustration evident in the stiff set of her shoulders. Had she wished to search the rooms on her own? Or was it dealing with him she found difficult? He rather thought it was the latter.

About to write to his solicitor to inquire if any correspondence his uncle sent him might prove illuminating, Dominic toyed with a quill, musing about his inclinations. He was no longer sure what drove him. Leaving London and coming here had changed his views on many things. When his sister objected to him selling their father's estate, he reasoned he deserved to live however he chose after he fought for his country against the French. But he'd enjoyed the satisfaction of achieving something here, and this happening made him angry. He was damned if some person or persons unknown was going to threaten him under his own roof. He thought he'd left that behind in London with the attack in Grosvenor Square.

He doubted their hunt through the various items stored in the attic would uncover anything to change his opinion that, apart from the estate, his uncle died a virtual pauper. But it suited him to have Miss Jenner search with him. He told himself it was not to spend time with her. Working side by side could tell him more about her. Why she wished to come here. The suspicion that she kept something from him still lingered. But he'd begun to trust her, and he hoped whatever it was she kept secret was not something to destroy his good opinion of her.

The next morning, Dominic went to the stables for his usual ride. He found Onyx in his stall, hanging his head.

"He's off his food again, milord," Fellows said as Dominic led the horse out into the quadrangle.

Dominic's concerned rub of the horse's neck failed to evoke a response. "Is he ill?"

"No. It's my guess he's lonely."

"Lonely? Ridiculous! He is not alone."

"That is true," Fellows said. "But he's taken a dislike to the carriage horses when they're together in the paddock. Tried to bite one yesterday."

"Puzzling." Dominic studied his dejected horse.

"Might I make a suggestion?"

"Anything."

"I was talking to the Lowry groom last night in the taproom."

Dominic turned from buckling the saddle. "What did he have to say?"

"Apparently, when Sir Hubert Lowry owned him, the horse had a companion."

"A mare?" Dominic smoothed his hair and jammed on his hat. It was not his plan to put the horse out to stud. Nor to geld him. Was all this sent to try him?

"A goat."

Dominic stared at him. "A goat? Are you mad?"

Fellows grinned. "Name of Peaches."

"Good lord! Why Peaches?"

"The goat often escaped into the orchard to eat the fruit, so they brought her into the stables to be with Onyx. Apparently, she and Onyx became inseparable."

Dominic scrubbed his hands over his face. "See if the goat still lives. If so, bring her here. I confess to being skeptical. The horse will probably kick Peaches out of the stall."

When Dominic entered the house after his ride, Jack stood in his place at the door. His usual upright stance had deserted him. He slumped against the wall.

"Not resting, Jack? I seem to remember giving you an order not to return to work for a few days."

"Yes, milord, but I…" He closed his eyes and swayed on his feet.

Dominic took his arm and drew him away. "Return to your bed. I'll send Michael for the doctor."

Dr. Manners promptly drove up in a trap to treat the patient. The brindle-haired man, a few years past sixty, reassured Dominic that with rest, Jack would fully recover. "He's a strong, young man, milord."

"A glass of wine or brandy?" Dominic asked Manners sometime later when he joined him in the library.

"Tea, thank you. Your lordship's brandy would be appreciated, but I have another call to make. I'd rather not arrive smelling of spirits. The doctor whose practice I took over was too fond of the bottle."

"Another time, perhaps." Dominic rang the bell.

Emily entered with the loaded tea tray and set it on a low table before them.

As they drank their tea, Dominic asked Manners if he'd ever treated his uncle.

"When he sought my opinion, milord. But he accepted his health was declining. He never fully recovered after the fall. Became most unlike himself. Reclusive."

"What killed him? Was it his heart or an apoplexy?"

The doctor raised brindle eyebrows. "Why, neither. His faculties might have been weak, but he was physically as strong as an ox."

"Then what…?"

"Took a tumble down the stairs and hit his head. Killed outright. Maisie, the old cook, found him and came for me. There was nothing I could do."

"I'm told my uncle had taken to sleeping in the butler's pantry."

"That is so. His living standards became chaotic. Said he feared for his life."

"Did he tell you why?"

"Suspected someone was after his money."

"Did you believe he had reason for such a claim?"

The doctor shrugged. "To be honest, I found it hard to take him seriously. He was addlepated at times."

"Could someone have struck him down?"

"Possible. But with such a head wound, it's hard to say. One would expect some bruises from such a fall, but there were none. A dead man doesn't bruise. But who would wish to kill him? The most likely scenario is that he lost his balance and fell headfirst down the stairs, killing himself instantly." Manners took another scone from the plate and bit into it with an appreciative sigh. "You have an excellent cook."

"Thank you. Where was my uncle found? On the grand staircase or the floor of the great hall?"

"No. The servants' stairs. He appeared to be on his way down from the top floor. Goodness knows what drew him there." He shrugged. "But as I say, he was not of sound mind at the end."

Disturbed by the doctor's words, Dominic walked into the garden after the doctor departed. He perched a foot on the stone rim of the recently cleaned fountain. Resting his arm on his knee, he watched the water spill onto waterlilies from a statue's upturned urn, vaguely aware of the twitter of birds and the thud of the gardener's spade. The breeze carried the smell of freshly turned soil.

He lifted his gaze to the servants' rooms and the attics above him. Why go up there? Could his uncle have hidden his valuables in the attic? Seemed a strange place to choose. Or was he rambling and half out of his mind?

Dominic brushed a leaf from his sleeve. Why hide them anywhere? If he was concerned about a thief, it was far easier to place any monies and valuables mentioned in his will with the trusted family solicitor.

He left the fountain and crossed the stone paving. As Alberic did not get on with Dominic's father, might he have hidden his money out of spite? But his father was already dead. Would his uncle's animosity extend to his son? Who knew what went on in a deranged mind?

Leaving the courtyard, he walked along the neat garden paths. Miss Jenner was right. There would be quite a show next spring. Would he be here to see it? Or would all this change his plans and drive him back to Town? He shook his head. He wouldn't leave until he had some answers.

What caused the rift between the two brothers? Whatever it was about, it lasted the rest of their lives. A sudden desire to know sent him striding to the house. He would write immediately to his sister, Evelyn.

Michael stood at the open door. With a nod, Dominic passed through into the great hall. He paused in the ancient lofty space. A rabbit warren of passages lay behind the walls of this old house, designed for servants to tend to their chores without intruding on the family. His father had mentioned hidden doors leading to secret rooms. Even a priest's hole was built during the reign of Elizabeth I when Catholics were persecuted. It hadn't interested him at the time, but now, with an intruder revealing some knowledge of the house, he needed to do some investigation of his own.

On entering the library, he walked along the walls of bookshelves, trailing a hand over the polished oak. No hidden doorway opened at his touch.

He dropped his hand and turned back into the room. He didn't have time for this. Miss Jenner would join him in a thorough search of the attics tomorrow. A start, but with a house this size, it could take him until Christmas to cover it all.

>>><<<

WHILE OLIVIA WENT about her chores, her mind remained fixed on the afternoon's meeting in the attic with Redcliffe. Why had he chosen her instead of a footman? Admittedly, Jack was not well enough, but Michael...she shook her head. Her pulse leaped at the thought and her breath quickened. Even while she struggled against his allure, her spirits rose at spending time with him alone.

She'd never felt like this. So up and down and unsure of herself. She considered herself to be a steady sort of person, not one to be in danger of succumbing to a rake's charm. If she had understood herself, her weaknesses, would she still have come here? Of course, she would have. She was being nonsensical. All thoughts of him must stop, she told herself with a mental shake.

"Polly, there's a coal smudge you've missed on the marble."

"Sorry, Miss Jenner."

She simply had to come to Redcliffe Hall. It was the only way open to her for a safe future, and she was perfectly able to withstand anything the earl threw at her.

Polly looked up from gathering her cleaning cloths. "Is the mantel clean, now, Miss Jenner?"

When Olivia failed to answer, the maid stared at her with surprise.

Olivia gathered her wits together. "Oh, yes, Polly. You've done well. We must move on. There's much to do before luncheon." She glanced around the guestroom she'd just searched. If she'd discovered the missing valuables or the old earl's letters, it would have put an end to all this. The mystery solved would stop the thieves. It would also stop the staff muttering darkly among themselves, as they had at breakfast. And there would have been no necessity to search the attics with Redcliffe tomorrow either. Now, why wouldn't that please her? Vexed with herself, she left the room.

CHAPTER ELEVEN

A LIGHTED LANTERN in his hand, Dominic climbed the short flight of steps that led from the top floor to the attics. He opened the door, holding the lantern aloft. The light revealed a cavernous room smelling of mice and dust, and crammed with aged rugs rolled up against the walls and furniture from a century ago, or older.

He made his way to a door at the far end that gave access to a section of the roof. Opening it, he allowed fresh air to flow in, though it did little more than stir the dust motes. He stepped out into the humid air. The slates glistened in the sun from an earlier shower of rain.

Could the intruder have entered the house this way? Three stories from the ground it seemed unlikely. Dominic walked to the edge and looked down over the low parapet. A rope-like creeper covered most of this wall and the west wing. Damn, he had not considered this possibility when he'd searched for the intruder's means of entry. A sure-footed man might climb up the creeper to the guest wing and enter through a window. Miss Jenner first saw a light in one of those bedchambers. He would have the locks checked on all the windows.

At the thought of her, Miss Jenner appeared in the doorway. Concern creased her smooth forehead.

"Ah, there you are." He had the absurd desire to say something amusing, to make her smile. She was so earnest, that she would think him mad.

The maid's apron she wore, tied snugly around her waist, offered a pleasing image of her womanly curves. He cleared his throat. "I have made an interesting discovery."

A keen light brightened her eyes. "What is it?"

He offered her his hand. "Come and I'll show you."

"Out there?"

"Yes. You won't fall. I'll hold onto you."

She stared at him uncertainly, hesitating before she put her hand in his and allowed him to help her out onto the narrow walkway.

He released her hand but took hold of her arm. It felt oddly right to be here beside her, to be touching her. Their eyes met, and for a moment, he thought she might pull away. "Look down. What do you see?"

She gazed over the edge, then took a quick step back, moving away from him. "Could he have climbed up the ivy?"

"It's possible. And gained entrance through a window in the guest wing."

"There are no broken panes."

"Could a window have been unlocked? Although Williams assured me they secured everything after the last break-in."

Her eyes widened. "Someone broke in before?"

"Before I arrived."

"We heard there were sightings of candlelight moving through the rooms after the earl died. It started the rumor of a ghostly presence."

He stood aside as she stepped back into the attic.

"Surely this must absolve the staff," she said as he ducked his head and entered after her through the low doorway.

How relieved she looked; and he wished he could tell her it did. "He'd have to be strong and agile to climb that creeper."

"We are not short of such men in these parts."

He cocked an eyebrow. "Mm. Well, where shall we begin?"

She pointed. "I will start this end, and perhaps you could begin at the other?"

"No. Best we work together. If you find anything even remotely interesting, show me."

"Very well. Some of this appears to have remained undisturbed for centuries."

"The chests bear searching for anything my uncle might have stashed there, be it documents or this cache of jewels everyone believes we will find. The chests, desk drawers, bureaus, wardrobes, and the bedchamber furniture." He pointed. "We'll begin with those."

She checked the locket watch she wore on a gold chain around her neck. "I'm needed downstairs at four o'clock."

"At which time we will stop."

He walked over to a large heavily carved oak desk, the legs gouged with deep cuts. He didn't like to speculate on what had gnawed it. While she opened a chest, he pulled out drawers.

"This is full of old curtains." She dragged one out and unrolled it. "A very fine damask in quite good condition, with only a few stains. What a waste."

He smiled, admiring her practical nature as he opened the bottom drawer of the desk. A stack of yellowed paper was inside. His pulse quickened as he brought them out and spread them over the desk. "What have we here?"

She hurried over to him. "Is it important?"

He held the papers up to the light, catching a hint of her perfume. "I'm not sure what they are. The writing is too faint to read." He shoved them back in the drawer. "Too old."

"Oh." With a sigh, she returned to the chest and pulled out another bundle of fabric. A metal box fell out of the roll and hit the floor with a bang.

Dominic moved to pick it up at the same time as Miss Jenner. They bumped into each other in their haste. Their eyes met and fingertips touched. Startled, they glanced at each other, then he chuckled. Her lips lifted in a smile.

"Allow me." With the lingering sensation of her soft, fragrant body having brushed against him, he levered off the lid.

She peered inside. "Reels of cotton, needles, buttons, hooks, and eyes." She put them to one side with the damask.

"What do you intend to do with those?"

"They will be useful. I'll give these to the laundry maid. The maids' dresses often require a needle and thread. The men's clothing, too."

They moved on, working silently, his gaze constantly drawn to her.

Dominic picked up an old china beer mug and examined it. "I wonder why this is here. Seems in perfect order."

She took it from him and turned it upside down in her slender capable fingers, and with the hint of a smile, showed him the crack in the bottom.

With a grin, he opened the doors of a French wardrobe. It was empty, and he moved on. He discovered more papers in a bureau drawer. Sitting on a satin chaise lounge, he examined them.

She came over to him. "What are they?"

"Sit down, and I'll show you." He patted the seat beside him, stirring dust.

She shook her head. "As I don't wish to change my dress, I'll remain standing."

He cocked an eyebrow. "It's only a little dust."

She ignored him. "Are they of interest?"

He shuffled the papers, glancing through them. "Letters, years old. I'll keep them to read later."

She turned back to the wardrobe where she'd pulled out a bundle of clothes and made a neat pile. No doubt with something in mind for them.

Did she fear he'd have her in his arms once she sat down? He smiled. Chaises had a well-earned reputation for assignations.

A half-hour later, they'd searched a third of the attic space. Olivia eased her shoulders, then consulted her watch. "It's four o'clock. I must go down."

Dominic wiped his hands with his handkerchief. "We'll continue at the same time tomorrow. Thank you for your assistance, Miss Jenner."

She shook out her skirts, then took his arm to descend the small rickety stairs to the next floor.

While she continued down the servants' stairs to the kitchen, he remained to examine the stair treads, searching for some sign of where his uncle fell. It didn't take him long to find the rusty blood stains splattered over a step and the banister. He went slowly up again, then down once more, checking to see if he'd missed something that might have caused his uncle to trip. Nothing. Had Uncle Alberic become distracted and lost his footing? Dominic accepted he might never know what happened.

He made his way to the gallery floor and down the grand staircase, crossing the great hall. A man stood in the entry.

Dominic hurried in.

"Your footman has gone to find you, Dom." George greeted him with his infectious grin. "So, you're still above ground? I grew worried when you failed to return to London. I expected you to grow tired of this place by now."

"What are you doing in these parts?" Dominic embraced him, surprised and pleased to see a familiar, friendly face. "Come into the library. I can offer you an excellent cognac."

They crossed the great hall. His dapper cousin brushed dust from his sleeve as he looked around. "Bit of an ancient relic, isn't it? I thought so on my last visit."

"I wasn't aware you'd been here."

George turned to look at him. "I'm sure I mentioned it. I'd hoped Uncle Alberic would remember me in his will."

"Yes, so you did." Dominic opened the door for him to enter the library. "But I assumed you'd written to him."

"He wouldn't have read a letter from me." George cast himself down in a leather armchair. "Had a few loose screws, Uncle Alberic."

Dominic turned from the drinks tray. "I'm interested to hear how you found him."

"Not much to tell. He didn't accept who I was at first. Then viewed me as one of his blood-sucking, distant relatives. Rude old fellow told me to get out. So, I did. Hell of a long way to come to be treated like an outcast."

Dominic handed him the cognac, surprised his uncle had acknowledged George at all. "From what I hear, that sounds about right for the old earl."

"But what are you still doing here, Dom? You can't enjoy it. No decent society and the accommodation is somewhat shoddy."

"It's improving." Dominic felt obliged to defend the old house. "The company is thin, I grant you. My fault. I've been caught up with the estate." He thought briefly about Miss Jenner. "And now you're here."

George chuckled. "Good shooting? Stables well stocked?"

"No on both counts. I haven't had time to take a gun out. And apart from my new acquisition, the two other horses aren't worthy of you, I'm afraid."

"No time? How do you spend your days?"

"I'm improving the estate, making it more productive. It is prime land, George, but there is much neglect to overcome."

George raised his eyebrows. "Is this my cousin speaking? The one who declared he would spend the rest of his life taking his pleasure where he found it? There are many ladies asking after you in London. Women seem not to forget you." He laughed. "Can't imagine why."

Dominic forced a smile, reminded of the rake's tag imposed on him. "I doubt it. No more of your insincere flattery, George." He swirled the flavorsome cognac around his mouth. It slipped down his throat, warming as it went. He'd spent only a short time here, and yet it seemed months since he'd left London.

"Not at all," George continued, unfazed. "Lady Anne seems rather put out by your absence."

"I had planned to hold a house party and invite her, but I've had to delay it. The house isn't ready for guests."

"I'll say it's not. Lady Anne here? Can't see it, myself." George laughed. "If you wish to secure her interest, you'd best hot-foot it back to London."

"Not for a while yet." Even the lovely Lady Anne Cranston failed to instill an urge to return to the city. He was glad he had not weakened and written to invite her. "How long can you stay, George?" he asked, changing the subject. "The news from the city can wait. Tell me what has happened to you in my absence."

George looked away. "This last Season wasn't lucky for me. As you know, I rely on my skill at dice. It takes a good deal of money to live the way I've grown accustomed. Clothes and rent, etcetera. But one must keep up appearances."

Dominic eyed George's apparel: the cut of his coat pointed to Schweitzer & Davison, his tighter styled boots designed by Hoby, his beaver from Lock & Co. When George finished his drink, Dominic stood. "Come to the stables. I want you to meet my new stallion."

"A stallion, eh? I'd like to see him. You must find me a mount, even a donkey. I intend to see the estate before I leave."

"No donkey, but I've yet to stock the stables. Hopefully, one of the carriage horses will give you a half-decent ride." George was a fine rider and a natural athlete, although he seldom did much to maintain it. Dominic thought of his carriage horses. Both objected to a rider on their backs, but he was confident George would handle it. "How did you come here?"

George finished his cognac and put down the glass. "Mail coach."

Dominic eyed him sympathetically. "That can't have been very agreeable."

"It wasn't."

They walked outside. For comfort-loving George to travel all the way from London on the mail coach, he must have a good reason. Dominic had his suspicions but would wait until George felt able to share. He would learn it soon enough.

WHILE THE VISITOR claimed Redcliffe's time, Olivia slipped into the steward's room to search it. She'd enjoyed spending the previous afternoon with him far too much. During the restless night, she admitted her attraction to him grew stronger each day. If a rake, he was a charming one, but weren't all rakes so? When he'd taken hold of her arm, a thrill skittered through her, and his green eyes told her he felt the same. Dear heaven, she was out of her depth. She feared something would happen between them if they spent too much time alone together.

Rakes, she'd heard, took what they wanted and damn the consequences. So far, at least, Redcliffe had not. But...should he step beyond the bounds of propriety, she would never stoop so low as to become his mistress. Not merely because of her sense of morality, such a life wouldn't suit her.

Those women became dependent on the whims of a gentleman, and some of the most notorious of them had starved in old age. Olivia doubted many would have married and had children. And she had not given up the hope of married life and a family, despite it becoming less likely with the passing years and too few eligible men to choose from.

If something scandalous occurred between her and Redcliffe, she would have to leave the village. Already, people questioned her life at Redcliffe Hall, and some who cared about her asked if the earl treated her well, while others gazed at her with suspicion. It wouldn't surprise her to hear Lady Lowry had spread scandalous lies about her. Especially as Redcliffe declined her former employer's recent dinner invitation.

Should Mr. Yardley persuade Redcliffe to go to London with him, it would give her some breathing space. But she doubted he'd leave now. Not with the possibility of another burglary. He seemed determined to search every room in the house. Must she accompany him while he pursued this unrealistic goal? The reckless, wanton part of her she'd fought to suppress urged her to, while the sensible part of her brain sounded a warning in her ear not to be alone with Redcliffe too often.

She took the steward's ledgers down from the shelves, sat at the desk, and opened the first one. Then her mind drifted. If she confessed to Redcliffe why she'd come here, and told him what she wished to find, would he be angry at her deception and dismiss her? Or would he understand and offer to help? She believed the latter, considering him a fair man. But he might fob her off while he dealt with his own concerns.

The days, weeks, and months would go on with no answer to the questions she sought. And before she knew it, Redcliffe would return to London, and she'd no longer have a position here. Another thought occurred to her. He might offer her the money without the proof her father never received payment for it. She would hate that even more.

Olivia leaned an elbow on the table and rested her chin on her hand. The writing on the page blurred. Her stomach tightened at the fear of being cut adrift again, as she had been when Papa died. She considered herself a practical woman and had always known that her time at Redcliffe Hall would end. Wiping a tear from her cheek with a finger, she sighed. "Enough of this." Moving a finger down the items listed, she focused on the task.

An hour later, she came away with the impression something wasn't right about the accounts, despite how ordered and precise they appeared. She didn't know the man and had no evidence of his dishonesty. Nor had she heard anyone accuse him of it. So it would be wrong to judge him. To date, she'd found nothing listed in the ledgers concerning the transaction. And as her father hadn't mentioned dealing with Pike, the steward might have left the earl's employ before the sale took place. She really needed to ask Pike, which she didn't like to do, behind Redcliffe's back. Olivia felt discouraged. She'd been so sure she'd find the evidence she sought.

On her way to oversee the housemaid's work and to continue her exploration of the guest wing bedchambers, she wandered the long gallery and paused before the large oil paintings of Redcliffe's ancestors, some of whom lived hundreds of years ago. She found Lady Elizabeth's portrait. Her name was on a plaque in gold lettering, but she would have known it was her by the fashions of the time. She was indeed a lovely woman, a feathery hat perched at a dashing angle on her piled-up fair hair.

A deep frill of lace dressed the neckline of her blue silk gown, a large bow beneath her full bosom. Even with an artist's license, her waist must have been tiny. Studying it, Olivia decided the countess looked unhappy. The artist had caught a suggestion of dissatisfaction around her mouth. It tallied with what Redcliffe had told her and made Olivia want to learn more about Elizabeth as she hurried away.

CHAPTER TWELVE

D OMINIC RETIRED TO the small salon after dinner with George and Williams for a game of faro. As he picked up his hand, George chuckled. "I take back everything I said about the accommodation, Dom. My every comfort was seen to, and that dinner was superb. My compliments to the chef. Where did you find him?"

"Williams was fortunate to nab him between positions." Dominic raised his eyebrows at his estate manager, who held his tongue.

George raised his glass for a refill from Jack, who looked a good deal better as he hovered with the wine decanter.

"And your housekeeper, Dom, you lucky fellow! What a lovely woman. Not sure how you keep your hands off her." George grinned at Dominic's obvious discomfiture. "But maybe you don't."

Williams ducked his head over his cards.

Dominic clenched his jaw. "Miss Jenner is an excellent house-keeper."

"I'm aware of it. She presented herself to me and inquired if there was anything I wished." George laughed. "It was all I could do not to tell her."

"I'm glad you restrained yourself," Dominic said stiffly.

"Don't worry, Dom. I shouldn't want to be the one to send

her packing." He put down a card. "Is your valet here?"

"No. I'll send for him soon."

"Poor old Cushing. Lounging about in London at your expense. Why don't you just let him go?"

"Cushing's a loyal servant. He's been with me for a long time. And invaluable when I'm in town." Dominic threw down a card.

George glanced at it. "Dash it all! I'd best concentrate. Pennyante stakes, but I can't afford to lose my touch."

When Dominic prepared for bed, he admitted to himself he'd found George's references to Miss Jenner distasteful. He feared he had lost his sense of humor.

What he'd begun to feel for Olivia unsettled him. In the past, friendship and respect seldom entered his decision to bed a woman—and never love. It was their mutual desire. While he valued Olivia's good opinion of him, it perplexed him that his body reacted with pure lust whenever she was near.

As George had expressed some eagerness at dinner to see the estate, they left the house after breakfast. The sweet summer scents floated on the breeze as they walked to the stables. A fine day by the look of it, with a scattering of white clouds dotted about the gray-blue sky. "Too far from London, but I have to agree it's a pretty place," George remarked. "Dashed if I do."

Onyx cavorted in the paddock, the small, gray-and-white goat following him sedately. When Fellows emerged from the stable interior, Dominic introduced George and asked for a horse to be saddled for him.

Fellows scratched his chin. "Which mount, my lord? Ransom? Tarian is a handful."

George tapped his crop in his hands. "Then I'll ride Tarian." He turned to view Onyx. "Why is there a goat in the paddock with your stallion?"

"The goat is the stallion's new companion," Fellows explained. "We thought the horse lonely and introduced the goat. Works like a charm."

George shook his head and laughed. "Well, now I've seen it

all. You're becoming quite the country gentleman."

Dominic called Onyx to him. The horse trotted over to the rail, and he patted his head. Onyx gently blew through his nostrils. "This is Onyx."

George reached over to pat Onyx's withers. "Athletic fellow, isn't he?"

Onyx snorted and backed away.

Dominic laughed. "He's sometimes standoffish."

They left the stables. Entering the bridle path, they rode through woods of oak, birch, and sycamore. He could find signs of the gamekeeper's care everywhere, with areas of bracken and rhododendron cleared and saplings planted.

After an inspection of the home farm and the dairy, they continued to Graves's farm. As Dominic expected of such an experienced rider, George handled Tarian firmly, letting the horse know who was master.

The Redcliffe Hall trap stood outside Graves's farmhouse, the carthorse pulling at the grass. Apparently, Miss Jenner had driven herself, for there was no sign of his footman.

"Please forgive me if I don't curtsy, my lord," Mrs. Graves smiled shyly at the door. "I believe I would topple over. Graves is in the big south field. But please come inside. Miss Jenner is here." Big with child and walking slowly, she led them into the small parlor, sweet biscuits fresh from the oven scenting the air.

Olivia smiled up at them. "Good morning, my lord, Mr. Yardley." She put the book she held down beside the tomes piled on a side table.

Mrs. Graves's best china, teapot, and a plate of the fresh biscuits occupied the larger table. It looked inviting, but Dominic resisted joining them. If George hadn't been with him, he might have.

"It wasn't necessary to drive yourself, Miss Jenner. You could have asked a footman."

Her welcome smile wavered, but she straightened her back. "I saw no sense in taking staff away from their duties, my lord."

He smiled. "Michael is a lazy fellow. Encourage him to earn his keep."

She returned his smile. "I shall find something to occupy him when I return."

"Good."

Mrs. Graves begged them to sit. "May I offer you gentlemen tea?"

"No, thank you, Mrs. Graves. Mr. Yardley and I will go in search of your husband. I'm keen to see how he has fared with the last of the hay baling."

As they mounted up, George said, "Why is your housekeeper visiting your tenant farmers? Surely that's not her role? You'd best watch yourself there, Dom."

Dominic scowled into the bright sunlight. "Because I asked her to."

"Even worse." George trotted his horse after Dominic's along the lane. In the distance, Graves worked among the bales. "Unwise to have such an attractive woman living under your roof."

One more word from George, and he would lose his temper. Grinding his teeth, Dominic urged Onyx into a canter.

Reaching their destination, they dismounted and crossed the field to where Graves stood waiting.

"My cousin, George Yardley," Dominic said.

"Good day, Mr. Yardley."

George wandered off when Dominic and Graves discussed the hay baling.

Dominic found himself thankful that George remained quiet and contemplative on the ride back to the stables.

George became more enlivened as they walked back to the house. "You're right about the estate, Dom. It's a fine one. With good men working for you, it could be made more productive. Money, of course," he said thoughtfully. "It requires a great deal of investment." He turned to Dominic. "But you have deep pockets, cous." He was silent for a moment. "I'd best go back to

London tomorrow."

Dominic found he wasn't entirely sorry. "Must you?"

"The creditors are banging on my door."

George had to be in desperate straits to have come all this way. "Can I help?"

"Yes, Dom, would you? I would be jolly grateful. To tell the truth, I'm deep in Dun territory," he admitted with a sheepish grin. "A run of bad luck like no other. You're a generous fellow, and after all, it might have been me who has all this." He waved his arm to encompass the now immaculate gardens and the handsome old mansion, windows sparkling in the sunlight.

"How much do you need to set things to rights?"

George rubbed an eye. "Twelve hundred should set me up."

"Come to the library. I'll write you a check."

"I knew you'd understand. You've always been a capital fellow." He followed Dominic along the corridor.

Seated at his desk, Dominic blotted the cheque for two thousand pounds. He handed it to George. "This has to be the last time, George. Pay your bills, for God's sake, or you'll sink deeper into debt and end your days in the debtor's prison."

George looked at the paper in his hand. His face flushed. "It is good of you, although it's easy to be generous when you have so much." He tucked the check into his waistcoat pocket. "I'll catch the stage tomorrow."

"No need. The coach will take you home in the morning. My coachman, Grimsby, has little to do here." He held up his hand before George could protest. "And it suits me. Grimsby can bring back Cushing and a few of the staff."

He'd been so pleased to see George, but he'd had enough. He'd never realized how little they had in common. George had introduced himself as his cousin at a race meeting just after Dominic sold out of the army. Not a close connection and they had never met before, but Dominic welcomed his friendship. It was different in London because they were always in the company of others. He rose and put a hand on the shorter man's shoulder. "You're on a dangerous path, George, and you should change it before it's too late. I say this because I care what happens to you."

"Kind of you," George muttered and banged out of the room.

OLIVIA AND MARY had been enjoying their talk about the novels they'd read when Redcliffe appeared with Mr. Yardley. Any hope of continuing their discussion of *Sense and Sensibility* became too difficult, because Redcliffe's presence, so earthy and real, blotted any book hero from her mind.

Soon after, she took her leave, promising Mary to return soon.

With luncheon over, Olivia collected the box of buttons and thread she'd brought down from the attic. The laundry maid was not at her work. The scullery maid, Betty, hadn't seen Mrs. Hobbs for some hours. "She is often away, Miss Jenner."

"Did she go to the haberdashery?"

"She visits someone in the village."

"A relative? I wasn't aware she had family here."

"She's never mentioned them. But she's not a chatty person."

In her office, Olivia opened the accounts book. She lifted her head, reflecting on Mrs. Hobbs. The laundress performed her duties well. Olivia could hardly disapprove if she cared for a sick relative. But she should have come to Olivia to explain and seek permission. She would talk to Mrs. Hobbs when she returned.

She looked up, quill in hand when Redcliffe appeared at the door.

"Good afternoon, Miss Jenner."

"My lord." *Why must her heart beat so fast when he appeared?*

He seldom came belowstairs, and she could hear the whispers in the kitchen. She bit her lip. Surely he could have sent for her? She rose from behind the desk as an uncomfortable thought entered her mind, but he motioned for her to remain seated. She sat back down and glanced up at him, wishing he wouldn't loom over her desk in that fashion. It made her catch her breath. "May I be of help, my lord?"

"Mr. Yardley leaves for London tomorrow morning. My valet and three servants, a young housemaid, and two men will return with the coach. Could you prepare their rooms?"

"Certainly."

His gaze swept over her face. "Did you find Mrs. Graves well?"

"She is very close to her time but remains in good health."

He smiled. "I confess to ignorance of such matters." He turned at the doorway. "You both share a love of literature?"

"Yes, my lord." An impish thought made her smile. "Not the sort you might read, however."

He raised his eyebrows in fake horror. "Not those awful Gothic romances?"

Olivia laughed. "No, but they are on our list."

His mouth quirked in a smile. "We'll continue our search of the attic tomorrow at the usual time."

A thrill shot through her, which she tried to suppress. It was reckless for them to be alone. She hesitated, determined to express her concern, but searching for the words. "Would it be prudent to take a footman or maid to assist us?"

His dark brows knitted. "And have all the staff agog?" He smiled.

"Little escapes the servants. They will gossip."

He shrugged his wide shoulders. "I expect that is so, but let's keep them guessing for now."

He was gone before Olivia could argue the point. In any event, she didn't feel up to the struggle.

Olivia returned to the laundry room. As she entered, the door leading to the garden opened and Mrs. Hobbs came in, removing her bonnet. She stopped, the bonnet in her hands, clearly startled to find Olivia there. "May I assist you with something, Miss

Jenner?"

"Where have you been, Mrs. Hobbs?"

The woman's thin face reddened. She emptied the package she carried onto the table. Haberdashery items scattered over the bench. "I required thread to match Emily's hem, which is coming down."

"Come into my office later, and I will reimburse you." Olivia gave her a wry look. "But you appear to need a lot of things, Mrs. Hobbs, for you go to the village often."

Mrs. Hobbs's eyes narrowed. "Has someone complained to you about me, Miss Jenner?"

"It's no secret, is it?" Olivia pointed to the box she'd brought. "Needles and thread and a few buttons which you might find useful."

"Oh." Mrs. Hobbs looked relieved. "They will be, thank you."

"I don't wish you to purchase items for Redcliffe Hall out of your own pocket, Mrs. Hobbs. Mr. Williams would have informed you of the rules when you came here. You may visit the village after church on Sundays and on your day off. But if you urgently need something, please advise me of it, and I'll send a footman." She paused. "Do we have an understanding?"

"Yes, of course, Miss Jenner." Mrs. Hobbs peered into the box, poking the items with a finger. She didn't look up. "I'm sorry. I didn't understand it was wrong."

Olivia left, puzzled by the woman's behavior and evasive attitude. All the staff knew they couldn't wander about the countryside willy-nilly.

Before supper, Olivia was called to Mr. Yardley's bedchamber. Wise to the ways of men, she took Jack with her.

Yardley glared at him. "I wished a housemaid to pack my luggage."

"Jack will do it, Mr. Yardley." Olivia gestured to Jack to pack the few clothes and items.

"Maids usually do such things. This is quite unorthodox." Yardley watched him. "Don't crease that coat."

"Was there anything else?"

Yardley smiled. "I wish to thank you for making my stay so pleasant."

"I am pleased you were comfortable, sir."

Yardley eyed Jack and then turned his back on him. "You are an excellent housekeeper, Miss Jenner. And an unusual one."

"Unusual?"

"Come now, you must agree. Where do you hail from?"

"From this county, Mr. Yardley," she said, fighting to hide her annoyance.

He nodded. Perhaps realizing his questions would bear no fruit. "You are preparing for house guests, Lord Redcliffe tells me. How many do you expect?"

"It is not my decision, Mr. Yardley. You must ask his lordship."

"Are all the reception rooms being opened up?"

"Again, I cannot say."

He scowled. "That is all. You may go. And you." He rounded on Jack. "You are making a complete mess of it. Leave it to me."

At cock's crow the next morning, while Olivia dressed, the coach clattered away along the drive. Mr. Yardley, departing for London. She couldn't say she was sorry to see him go. She'd disliked him questioning her and wondered what lay behind it.

Had she become too suspicious? Even doubting a cousin of Redcliffe's. Ever since the break-in, she looked askance at everyone. But Mr. Yardley had arrived at Redcliffe Hall days after the break-in. And he'd traveled there on the mail.

CHAPTER THIRTEEN

D OMINIC TURNED AWAY as the coach disappeared. It had been a cool goodbye before George mounted the steps. Earlier, he had thanked Dominic again for the money. "I shall prove you wrong, Dom." He patted his waistcoat pocket where he'd put the check. "I'll put this to good use. You'll see. It will do much to help me find my feet."

Dominic had clapped him on the back. "I wish you good fortune, George, and hope to see you here again soon."

He made his way to the stables. He hoped George would keep to his bargain but feared he would revert to his old ways. After all, they'd gone through this before, more than once.

Riding over the estate, he relished the misty, damp woodlands. The smell of mildew and wet leaves, birds twittering above. Onyx behaved like a lamb and was eager to join the goat, Peaches, when they arrived back at the stables.

Back in the library, he turned his mind to estate matters. Midmorning, Jack entered with coffee and the post. And Dominic sat back to read the crammed crossed pages in his sister's hand.

How surprised I was to find you still at Redcliffe Hall. And learn of your intention to stay awhile and improve the estate. Mama and Papa would be so proud of you, Dominic, as I am. I know a little about the history behind the family feud concerning Uncle Alberic. I was at an age when a young girl stuck in

*the schoolroom pounces on any intrigue. I listened at doors!
And later, I read correspondence not meant for my eyes! Will I
still go to heaven, do you think? Elizabeth came between Papa
and Alberic. I heard Mama discussing Elizabeth with a friend.
Mama accused Elizabeth of being immoral, but she might have
been a little envious of Elizabeth, who was wild and beautiful.
Mama was neither of those things, but oh so very good! She
firmly believed something scandalous occurred between Papa
and Elizabeth, after which Elizabeth promised to marry him.
But Alberic stepped in to claim her. And as he was the heir, she
accepted his proposal. Papa never forgave his brother, although
he admitted to Mama when he lay dying, that he had made the
correct choice of bride and had never been sorry for a moment.
Alberic might have regretted marrying Elizabeth when she ran
away with the Frenchman, but he took her back. And I don't
believe it was because of what people thought. He must have
loved her desperately. I suppose she was a woman who slayed
men's hearts!*

*It is possible that Alberic could have sent a letter addressed
to you to read in the event of his death, especially as you hadn't
sold out of the army and were difficult to contact. Although why
he wouldn't give it to the solicitor, I can't imagine. I'm afraid I
know nothing about it. But I will go through the correspondence
which came for Papa after he died. At least those his secretary
didn't take, which pertained to matters of business. Mama's
death followed so quickly after Papa's, and I was barely seven-
teen and shepherded off to stay with Aunt Abigail for my first
Season. When I returned, I could never face reading them. But I
have them here, somewhere, and shall let you know when I find
them.*

*I have no more room to add to this missive, Dominic, and
Trelawny will be cross at the cost of the postage. I wish you well
with your improvements and pray you will come to us at
Christmas. Our neighbor's daughter, Marianne, is still not
spoken for! All our love, Evelyn.*

He sipped his coffee, hot and strong the way he liked it, smiling at Evelyn's suggestion her husband would be cross with her. The besotted man was incapable of it. While her letter touched him, and he was pleased Evelyn and Justin enjoyed such a successful marriage, he was not in the market for a wife. He considered love to be the only reason for marriage, and he had not yet succumbed. A bachelor's life would suit him for a few years.

He pushed back his chair and wandered to the window. In the garden, a shapely figure stooped over the beds, a basket filled with flowers over her arm.

He left the library, strode to the front door, and flung it open. As he walked toward her, she turned to greet him with a smile.

"Good morning."

He pointed to a perfect blue flower. "That one."

"The delphinium?"

"Yes, the blue."

Olivia clipped off a stem. But before she could add it to the rest, he took it from her and held it close to her face. "I thought so."

She raised her eyebrows. "My lord?"

"It's the perfect match for your eyes."

The blush on her cheeks pleased him. He handed her the flower and motioned to the basket. "Why don't you send a housemaid to do this?"

Her slender wrist pushed back wisps of hair from her forehead. "I find it pleasant. A task I've enjoyed since a young girl." She touched her plush bottom lip with her tongue as if to end the thought.

His intake of breath took in the sweet scents of the garden. He raised his gaze from her mouth. "Picking flowers is a charming activity, which renders a man weak at the knees."

"Surely not."

He grinned. "Ah yes. We men still have one foot out of the cave, but women, they are God's supreme creation."

She smiled and shook her head at him. "You are in a poetical frame of mind today."

"I often am when inspired by such perfection."

She raised her eyebrows disapprovingly. As he knew she would. "I refer to the delphinium, of course."

"Then I'll make sure there's a vase of them placed in the library every day," she said crisply. "While they are in flower."

"Thank you." He smiled. He shouldn't tease her, but he loved how she bit back at him.

"Did you have a pleasant ride?" She turned back to the flower bed with a change of subject.

"I did. Now that Onyx behaves himself."

She moved along the garden and selected another flower with pink petals. "He has been troublesome?"

He explained about his and Fellows's concern for the horse and the success with Peaches.

"How delightful!" She laughed.

He wished she'd laugh more often. "I assume you ride, Miss Jenner?"

As if a cloud passed over the sun, the smile faded from her eyes. "Yes. Papa put me on a horse as soon as I could walk."

He regretted upsetting her, and yet he had to know more. "You must miss the exercise."

She bent to pick a daisy with a bright yellow center. When she straightened to add it to her basket, she said, "I rarely think about it."

He didn't believe her. Riding was obviously very much a part of her life at Northoaks. An invitation for her to ride with him hovered on his tongue. He firmly closed his lips. It would stir unwelcome gossip and she would refuse, sensible woman that she was. He wished she weren't quite so sensible. That he might take her in his arms. Bend her to his will? He hated the thought, but it didn't quash the desire.

She added another daisy to the basket. "Mr. Yardley enjoyed his stay?"

"I believe so."

"He seemed quite interested in the house."

"George approves of the changes." He raised his brow. "Why, did he tell you so?"

She bent and picked a leaf off her gown. "Yes, when he asked me to come to his bedchamber. He wished his portmanteau to be packed."

"I see." He eyed the slight flush on her cheeks. Did George proposition her? He expressed a desire to. Dominic scowled. He wished he'd known about it.

"If you'll excuse me, I must put these in water."

She picked up the secateurs from the ground, offering him a glimpse of her nicely rounded derriere. Dominic repressed a sigh. "Then I shall see you later this afternoon, Miss Jenner."

He swiveled and returned to the house. At the corner, he turned to watch her make her way to the servants' entrance through the kitchen gardens. When the time was right, he wished to learn about her life at Northoaks and what happened afterward.

Dominic stepped up onto the front porch, admitting he was infatuated, even to the extent of being jealous of a harmless fellow like George. He cursed softly, raked his hair back off his forehead with his fingers, and entered the house.

Michael stood at the door. His eyes widened at Dominic's perplexed scowl. "Is anything amiss, milord?"

"Nothing that cannot be fixed, Michael," he muttered, wishing it were true.

Dominic strode to the library, relieved to have engaged a secretary. He'd written yesterday to confirm it. Joseph Grant was Oxford educated, his father the owner of a successful Spitalfields import business. Joseph explained he had no desire to work for his father in his business. He hoped one day to write academic treatises. Liking the sound of him, Dominic was prepared to wait the few weeks until Joseph could take up the position. In the meantime, he must deal with all this himself. It bored him; he'd much rather be out in the air riding or working on the land. He laughed. Laboring like a born farmer. What would his friends make of him? Charles, such a correct duke, would good-naturedly chide him, and Nicholas, who found great pleasure in running his estate, would secretly approve while ribbing him unmercifully. He sighed. He missed them since leaving London.

He returned to his work. A good steward had proved difficult to find, although equally important as a secretary. Williams took care of some of those duties, as did Miss Jenner, who did more than a housekeeper should.

Olivia Jenner. He knew from the first moment he saw her he would find it challenging to have her under his roof. His days seemed to revolve around her, leaving him wishing his nights did, too. She was in his blood. Her smile, her laugh, even her thoughtful frown. Her sense of what was right. And he did not know what to do about it. Was this love? He fought for a cool response to the alarming question and changed the nib of his quill while considering the possibility. It sent a rush of fear through him—and a vulnerability he'd never experienced. An attraction strengthened by their proximity, he decided, and quickly banished the notion. He took a piece of bond from the drawer, dipped his quill in the inkwell, and forced his mind into more mundane and less emotive thoughts.

THE FLOWERS ARRANGED, Olivia ordered Polly to put them on tables in the entry and around the reception rooms. As she stood back to admire those in the drawing room, she thought of Redcliffe and their earlier conversation. She'd been far too pleased by his flirty suggestion her eyes were the color of delphiniums. Attempting to dismiss his comment as a rake's flattery failed to diminish her delight. Dominic didn't treat her the way other men did. Not in the lustful manner of the wheelwright or the farmer, Ian Kershaw, who didn't love her, yet saw her as a mother to his children. Mr. Yardley, too, had behaved in the insolent fashion some men had. As if she were someone they could dominate for their own pleasure and then forget. Redcliffe listened to her and respected her opinion, even though he might not always agree.

At three o'clock, she nervously climbed the rickety attic stairs.

Entering, she found him searching through a cupboard, the lantern placed on a table nearby. He turned as she came in with a smile of greeting. "If there's something here, we should discover it today."

Anticipation curled through her, tightening her stomach. She tied the strings of the apron around her waist. "What if there's nothing here?"

"We'll continue in another part of the house."

She wished her heart didn't leap at the prospect. "That will arouse the servants' suspicions."

He rested his hip on the corner of a desk and swung a long leg, drawing her gaze there. How well proportioned, and how graceful his movements. "I've considered that. We'll look for secret passages. The staff are unlikely to find us then."

It sounded like a liaison. "Are you sure there are any here?" she asked faintly, imagining them crushed together in a tiny space.

Dominic nodded. "My uncle would have been familiar with them. My father talked about how they played in them as children. I wish I'd been more attentive." He slid off the desk. "We should begin before the light fades."

Olivia examined the chest she'd intended to search yesterday. Inside was a roll of royal blue fringe and a bolt of India muslin. She shook them out and laid them to one side.

"My Scottish nanny was thrifty," Redcliffe said, observing her.

She smiled. "I remind you of your nanny?"

He captured her gaze. "Not even remotely."

The room filled with expectation.

He laughed. "She was stout and had gray whiskers."

"Were you fond of her?"

"I was. When I broke my arm falling from my pony, she seldom left my side."

She smiled at the picture of him as a small boy, then turned away to examine a cabinet. When she opened a drawer, her skirt caught on a sharp piece of wood. She bent to free it.

"Allow me." Redcliffe came over to her. "You won't want to tear it."

She certainly wouldn't. She had few suitable gowns to wear and had been putting money aside for the local dressmaker to make her another.

Her balance unsteady, she resisted holding onto his shoulder while he squatted down to examine her skirt. As he worked to release the sharp piece of wood embedded in the fabric, his hand, strong and warm, swept over her leg. She stilled, watching his bent head, and closed her eyes, resisting the temptation to touch his thick brown hair.

"That's got it." He tugged down her skirt. "There's a small tear. Shame."

She opened her eyes to find his face level with hers. So close, there were intriguing deep blue depths around the iris of his arresting green eyes. For what seemed a long moment, their heated expression held her captive. Warmth threaded through her, a tug of desire, down low in her belly. She swallowed and looked away with the pretense of consulting her watch. "It is almost four o'clock. Shall we leave it for today?" Her tight throat made her voice sound strained.

"I suppose we must," he sounded regretful. When her reluctant gaze rose to his, he looked as if he'd made an important discovery. "Allow me to assist you down those wobbly steps."

His calm assurance made Olivia suddenly suspicious. Did he have this effect on every woman? Despite her determination to remain indifferent to him, he could render her nonplussed with a mere glance.

She wanted to refuse his offer. She was hardly in need of it, being sure-footed, but if she refused him, he would know the reason. Such a perceptive man. Quite maddening!

His warm hand on her arm sent further sensations skittering through her. He knew how he affected her! His smoldering gaze told her so.

When they reached the landing, she could respond to him calmly.

He thanked her. "We've searched all the obvious hiding places. There's still some we might return to later. Tomorrow, the library for that secret passage. I suspect it's behind the bookshelves."

The prospect of entering a secret passage with him shocked and tantalized her. "But if we find the passage? What then?" She'd hoped to sound unaffected, but doubted she'd managed it.

The corner of his lips quirked. "We'll embark on an adventure, Miss Jenner."

Good heavens! The man was incorrigible! Olivia left him, her knees still unsure as she went downstairs.

She sat in her office, staring into space. She didn't trust Redcliffe's motives. Why did she ever think she could manage such a man? And why had she been so sure she could resist him?

She must!

With a sigh, she opened her record book to list items needed for the following week. Was it wrong to want love and a happy life for herself? Not wrong, merely foolish. She refused to cry over the past when her life as she knew had come to an abrupt end.

CHAPTER FOURTEEN

I T WAS STILL early when Dominic rode Onyx along the lanes to the Graves' farm. His mind stubbornly returned to the previous day with Olivia in the attic. When he untangled her skirt, he'd accidentally touched her ankle. He might have drawn a hand up her leg for the effect it had on both of them. She gasped, and his body tightened. The cavernous attic space quieted, the only sound, their breathing. When he stood, he fought the impulse to put a hand on her lower back and settle her against him, for her to acknowledge his desire. He now knew, without a doubt, she struggled with their attraction, too. Knowing that was like a gift. He wanted her. She wanted him. What could be more natural than to proceed accordingly? And when the time came for them to part....

He cursed. The pleasurable thoughts vanished, replaced with cold, hard logic. He could not seduce Olivia and then abandon her to her fate. So independent, he was sure she wouldn't allow him to help her financially. If she welcomed his advances, he feared he would never want to leave her. And where would that leave them?

Resist her, he must, but it was becoming damnably difficult. He should stop searching the house and see her only when necessary. Even as he thought it, he doubted he would call a halt to their delightful time together, even though it no longer seemed urgent since the intruder hadn't made another attempt. It might, in fact, never happen again. And what did he care if Uncle Alberic left a hoard of money? He shook his head. Another sticking point. He cared. Not about the money, which would go to those who needed it, but he looked for further insight into his uncle's motives, which might point to what happened to him.

Who was this man who unforgivably cheated Dominic's father by snatching away the woman he loved? Was he a thoroughly despicable human being? Or did overwhelming passion destroy his life? Dominic was becoming more sympathetic.

"There I go, romanticizing like one of Olivia's novels." He considered himself as rational as the next man. He'd proved it to himself by remaining cool under fire during the war. But now? Perplexed by the change in him, he shook his head.

He rode through the gate and up to the farmhouse. Graves met him at the door, his eyes wide and dark with anxiety. "It's my wife's time. She's been this way for over two days. I fear her strength is failing."

"Is the midwife with her?"

"Yes. She says it's a difficult breech birth."

Dominic wasn't sure what that entailed, but it obviously wasn't good. "Have you sent for Dr. Manners?"

Graves rubbed his eyes. "Hours ago, but he hasn't come."

"I'll send my footman to urge him to hurry."

"Thank you. I wonder if you could do a further favor for me, Lord Redcliffe?"

"Of course."

"Mary asked for Miss Jenner. Could you spare her for a few hours?"

"I'll bring her to you."

Graves visibly sagged, exhausted. "We would be most grateful. Miss Jenner is a calming influence."

Dominic nodded. "I'll return as soon as I can."

Olivia calmed everyone except him, Dominic thought, as he

galloped home.

At the stables, he ordered his curricle brought around. On reaching the house, he sent Jack to the doctor and went in search of Olivia. He found her in her office. His sudden appearance obviously startled her.

He smiled. "Did I alarm you?"

"Certainly not." Her cheeks grew pink. She closed the ledger and put away her quill. Then she gazed up at him. "Is there something you require?"

Her flat denial charmed him, but Graves's plight remained foremost on his mind. He quickly explained.

"Sam can prepare a basket of food from the larder so that Mary can rest and recover." Olivia was up from behind her desk and reaching for her keys as she spoke. "I'll fetch towels and linens and meet the footman in front of the house."

She called him Sam. Dominic wondered how close she and the cook had become. "I'll drive you."

She nodded, then hurried away.

A remarkably short time later, she joined him in the curricle, resting a basket on her knees, a bag of linens stored behind. "The midwife is there?"

"Yes. There's mention of breech birth. Is that serious?"

"Yes, it can be. Oh, poor Mary. The baby needs to be turned. Can't the midwife manage?"

"Some complication. Doctor Manners has been called."

He drove along the country lane in silence, mulling over something. "You call the cook, Sam?"

"Yes." She frowned at him. "Do you disapprove?"

"No. I wondered how it came about." He steered the horses around a sharp bend.

"Sam has told me a little about himself. He's had a difficult time."

"In what way?"

"I cannot betray his confidence."

"For goodness' sake, Miss Jenner. I am his employer."

She turned to look at him, her lovely eyes questioning. "Would you or Williams not have asked those questions when he applied for the position?"

"We direly needed a cook. And to his credit, he's proved a more than capable one."

She crossed her arms over the basket. "Then surely, there is no more to be said."

Recognizing the obstinate set of her chin, Dominic turned his attention to guiding the horses through the gate. "You are an infuriating woman," he observed, bringing the curricle to a stop before the house.

She merely arched her brows.

Hmm. Innocent, he thought darkly. But loyal, he had to admit, as he jumped down and went to assist her. He took the basket and bag from her, Graves anxiously waiting on the small porch.

"Miss Jenner, thank you for coming." Graves led them inside. "Mary will be so pleased to see you." He shrugged. "A man feels so helpless in these matters."

"Try not to worry, Mr. Graves." She disappeared into the bedchamber with Graves, where his wife moaned in pain.

The distressing sound sent a chill through Dominic. Women died in childbirth, even those from the wealthiest families. Even Princess Charlotte, the Prince of Wales's daughter.

"The doctor will be on his way," he reassured Graves when he came out again.

Dominic left the house and grabbed a bottle of whiskey from the curricle. He held it up for Graves's approval. "A shot will give you much needed energy."

"Kind of you, milord. I'll get some glasses."

Graves returned and held them out with a shaky hand. Dominic poured three fingers full and handed it to him. The farmer tossed it down and coughed.

The jingle of the trap heralded the doctor's arrival. Doctor Manners strode in with his bag.

"I want to make it clear, Doctor. Mary must survive if it comes to a choice," Graves said in an anguished voice.

Manners put a hand on his arm. "I'll do my best to save them both." He disappeared into the bedchamber and shut the door.

Graves continued pacing.

The murmuring voices and Mary's sharp cries continued as the sun moved high in the sky.

The midwife, Mrs. Crandle, emerged, her face creased with worry. "I did my best, Mr. Graves. I can do no more."

Graves halted in his restless stride. He dug some coins out of a jar and handed them to her. "I know you did. Mary and I are grateful."

Surprised to see the woman go, Dominic wondered if Manners preferred Olivia to assist him. An hour passed; Dominic suggested leaving, but Graves begged him to stay. Graves gave up pacing and threw himself into a chair. When Mary's cries grew more frantic, he hid his face in his hands.

It didn't surprise Dominic Graves loved his wife or that she meant everything to him. It had been that way with his parents. But sometimes, in the world he came from, with an heir being of such importance, a baby's life took precedence over the mother's. It shamed him to think of it. Rattled, he wished he could do more.

A baby's cry brought Graves to his feet.

He stared at Dominic, not really seeing him, joy mixed with anxiety in his watery blue eyes.

Several tense minutes passed until the door opened. Olivia carried a bundle Dominic thought at first was linen until it howled. "Mary needs you, Mr. Graves. But first, you must see your son."

Graves gasped as he pulled back the swaddling blanket to view what Dominic considered a tiny wizened face like a red turnip. Judging by his lusty cry, the babe seemed none the worse for his prolonged birth.

Graves was unashamedly sobbing as he hurried into the bedchamber.

Manners emerged. "It was a difficult birth." He washed the blood from his hands and forearms in the bowl Graves had provided for him, then wearily reached for the towel. "But a good result."

Dominic gestured to the bottle. "A shot of whiskey, Manners?"

"Thank you, my lord." He gave a grateful smile. "I won't say no this time."

When Dominic handed him a tumbler, the doctor raised it to Olivia. "You make an excellent nurse, Miss Jenner. If you ever wish for a change, contact me." He winked at Dominic, downed the drink, and said, "I'll be off. Another patient to see. This time I'm not worried about whiskey on my breath, my lord. My patient is Smithson's sow, which is ailing."

Dominic laughed.

After Dominic offered to provide any assistance Graves should need and Olivia promised to call again tomorrow, they settled in the curricle.

He took up the reins. "I found this profoundly moving. Mother and baby appear in good health."

"Yes, thank the Lord."

"Pity their son doesn't favor either of them."

She turned to him. "You don't think so?"

"Horribly wrinkled little fellow, but I'm sure quite endearing for all that."

She laughed. "Many babies look like that when first born. Perhaps even you, my lord."

He shook his head. "I believe I was quite handsome."

"Your mother would have told you so."

He glanced at her with a smile. "You are entirely too heartless."

She chuckled, more with relief than humor.

He wondered if she wanted babies. It was mostly every women's wish, was it not? If her father had prospered and lived, she would be married with children by now. He felt a wave of compassion for her, but knowing how proud and independent she was, he fought to hide it. "And you, Miss Jenner. I am sure you were a beautiful baby."

"I don't know, but I shan't argue with you."

He laughed. "You don't wish to take the doctor up on his offer?"

She raised her eyebrows, a smile lurking in her eyes. "No. Unless you want to be rid of me."

"Definitely not." He smiled as he hurried the horses along through the lanes, the smell of warm grass in the air. "I'm relieved."

"Why?"

The question brought him up short. He glanced sideways at her amused profile, tempted to tell her the real reason that he wanted, must have her in his life. But that would open Pandora's box and heaven only knew how it would end. And while he was sorely tempted to throw caution to the winds, he resisted. "Because you are an excellent housekeeper."

"Thank you," she said briskly.

He grinned. "Was it not praise enough? Should I embellish?"

She giggled. "No, please don't."

They traveled on while he considered how much he enjoyed her laughter.

"I'll take some more provisions tomorrow if that's all right," she said. "And a twist of tea. It's so expensive. Mrs. Graves drinks a watery brew."

"Add a couple of bottles of claret from the cellar. Graves will appreciate it."

"You are a kindhearted man, if I may be permitted to say so."

"You may." He felt inordinately pleased. Any crumb. What a sad fellow he'd become. He spurred the horses along. What happened to the man accused of rakish behavior in London? He almost preferred him to the man he now was.

"You are scowling," she observed. "Has something upset

you?"

"A man can have many sides to him."

"Indeed. I admire kindness in a man."

Before long he'd be holding her skeins of wool while she rolled them up, he thought darkly, aware of how unreasonable he was. Fighting an almost overwhelming urge to stop the horses and pull her into his arms, he fell silent as the curricle took them home.

WILLIAMS WAITED FOR Redcliffe in the entry. "There's been word of a fire in the barn at Willard Johnson's farm, milord."

"I must go at once." He turned to Olivia. "Leave the library until tomorrow, Miss Jenner."

"As you wish, my lord."

Olivia was relieved. She was getting behind in her work and feared she became forgetful. Discussing the menus and provisions with Sam this morning, he had to prompt her twice. And when she apologized, the wily man gave her a second glance. He must suspect something but made no comment. Sam never would. Live and let live was his motto. He'd told her more about himself over a cup of tea. She understood. Events beyond their control had blighted their lives. It made them unusual friends.

Seated in her office, Polly came to ask her a question, and she put thoughts of the heartwarming experience with Sam aside.

She did not see Redcliffe again that day. She visited Mary, who was brighter and in good spirits, holding the dear baby in her arms.

"Did you hear about the master's goat?" Jack had asked while driving her back to Redcliffe Hall. "He brought it here to keep his stallion company because he thought Onyx was lonely."

Another thing to admire about Redcliffe. He was kind to animals. Heaven help her. Was there anything to dislike about him to enable her to arm herself against him?

Her night was restless, filled with yearning to experience the love the Graveses had for each other and their baby. Redcliffe appeared in her dreams. It was hazy, but she was sure he'd kissed her. Pushing the startling dream away, she bathed and dressed while applying her mind to the tasks which awaited her.

Redcliffe was gone before breakfast. She learned from Williams that he rode over to Johnson's farm to organize the building of a new barn to replace the one razed by fire. He was still absent when Jack drove Olivia to the Graves' farm with the provisions. They returned immediately, leaving the tired but happy family to their rest.

The earl was in for luncheon, Emily informed her, having taken him a tray in the library. And at three o'clock, Olivia, before brushing down her skirts and tidying her hair, knocked on the library door.

"Enter."

At his desk, Redcliffe's cravat lay undone, baring the strong column of his throat. She swallowed, her gaze caught by the tuft of dark hair in the vee formed by his shirt. He rose and came around to lean against the desk, folding his arms across his chest while he studied her.

She wished her heart would cease thumping. Her chest rose and fell, drawing his attention there. "I trust you're well?"

"Perfectly well, thank you," she said crisply, annoyed. He missed little. Was there no way to escape his penetrating gaze? "Did Mr. Johnson lose much stock in the fire?"

"Yes, all the hay stock and the beets. We will replace the stock losses when the barn's finished. The carpenter and every spare man lent a hand, and the frame is already up."

"I know the Johnsons from church. Such nice people."

"Most people here are."

"Is it your intention to search the library today? Because if not, I will...."

"It is." He straightened and crossed to a wall lined with bookcases. "Shall we begin?"

Olivia glanced up at the row of bronze busts high above them set in an alcove crowned by the coat of arms. "Very well."

She joined him, and they moved along the shelves of gold and red spined tomes, prodding each section. Over an hour had passed when they finished. No book or shelf gave an inch. Redcliffe sighed and stepped away. "Disappointing. I was confident we'd find a secret door here somewhere."

She walked over to the fireplace. "I seem to remember reading something about a hidden panel in a book."

He came over to her, watching as she investigated around the sides of the marble mantel. "One of your gothic novels, Miss Jenner?" he asked, amused.

She ignored him and bent down to feel under the lip of the mantel. Her pulse galloped. "There is something here."

He came closer, his shoulder brushing hers. "Let me see. Some kind of lever," he said after a moment. He wrestled with it. "It's stiff."

She held her breath.

"Ah, yes, that's got it." He pulled it all the way down. Noiselessly, a door opened, taking a dozen rows of bookshelves with it.

He turned to her, his eyes alight with the anticipation she felt. "I should have paid more attention to my father."

Olivia stared into the small room at the dust-laden table and chair. The smell of the ages drifted out with the powerful odor of vermin, which she tried to ignore. A passage led off, which looked decidedly uninviting.

"I'll see where it goes." He lighted a candle in the silver candlestick on the mantel. One foot in the doorway, he turned back to her. "I don't expect you to join me if you'd rather not."

"I shall, my lord." With a shiver of excitement, she stepped in after him. She wasn't about to stand back and wait for his return.

"Stay behind me."

They crossed the small room.

"Who would have spent time in such an unpleasant place?"

she asked, her voice sounding hollow.

"Those with a need to hide." When he entered the passage, she glanced behind her. Would the door close and shut them in? She shivered and hurried to catch up with him.

Cobwebs hung from the low ceiling like a wispy curtain. Redcliffe had to stoop slightly, the ceiling an inch above his head. Fearing it would be airless, she took a deep breath of dry, dusty air.

They trod carefully in the half-dark, the candle held aloft in Redcliffe's hand as they moved deeper into the recesses of the house.

She batted away a cobweb. "Where do you think this leads?"

"Somewhere near the kitchen, perhaps." He paused and turned to her. His face, illuminated by the candlelight, revealed his approving grin. "Shall we find out? Or do you want to go back?"

She rubbed her arms. "We've come this far. We may as well go on."

With a soft laugh, he continued along the dark, narrow passage.

What would they find? Had she been too hasty in wanting to come? She swallowed the dust in her mouth. Growing a little desperate, she resisted hanging onto his coat.

"All right there?" he asked, aware of her discomfort.

She firmed her lips on a complaint. "Of course."

His chuckle made her frown. He enjoyed this too much.

A set of steps came into view through the gloom. They led upward, not down to the lower floor, as he'd suggested.

"Not intended for the servants' use." He put a foot on the step. "I trust these wooden treads aren't rotten."

The steps creaked under his weight. She followed, her skirt stirring a cloud of dirt and dust. They safely reached the top. The passage led in a northerly direction.

Olivia sneezed and pulled out her handkerchief to blow her nose. She couldn't stop as he didn't, and she didn't want to lose sight of him.

"All right there?" he asked, looking over his shoulder. "Not frightened?"

"No, my lord." Olivia didn't have the breath to be outraged at his assumption she was too delicate to cope. Right now, she'd agree with him. She gasped, longing for fresh air. "How horrid if one was trapped in here alone."

"Mm. Never fear, there is a reassuring absence of skeletons."

She bit her lip, tempted to poke him in the back.

They came to a dead end.

"This can't be right." Olivia's voice lowered in disappointment and dread at having to go back the way they'd come. "It *must* lead somewhere."

"The door could be boarded up on the other side."

"Oh no," she murmured. Must they go back?

He held the candlestick high.

"Is that a handle?" Olivia pointed to a brass object bright in the candlelight's glow.

"I believe it is."

He reached for it and gave a hearty tug.

A panel snapped back. Weak-kneed with relief, she stumbled out after him and filled her lungs with fresh air. Sunlight streamed through the window, alighting on the bed and expensive furnishings. They stood in Redcliffe's bedchamber, having exited from the oak-paneled wall.

She eyed him with suspicion. "Did you know where this led, my lord?"

He widened his eyes. All innocence. "A cruel thrust. This surprises me as much as you, Miss Jenner. My ancestors were royalists. This would have been a way to escape the Roundheads. One of many such tunnels, I expect." He blew out the candle and put the candlestick on a bureau. "Shall we investigate the others?"

His gaze teased her.

"Please come and tell me about it. I will be very interested to hear what you find."

He grinned. "You weren't afraid?"

"I don't scare so easily, my lord," she lied.

His green eyes filled with laughter and something else, far more unsettling. "No?"

Stepping close to her, he reached up and gently removed a cobweb from her hair. "You have an admirable, adventurous spirit, Olivia."

At his use of her first name and the longing in the husky tone of his voice, her breath became trapped in her lungs. She was alone with him in his bedchamber. It was entirely improper. Well, this entire situation was, and she had only herself to blame. Why had she allowed him to lead her astray? Her reason deserted her around Redcliffe.

"You are an amazing woman," he said softly. "Capable of so much more than your life permits."

"No...I'm not." Her skin warmed, and she raised her gaze boldly to his. The air around them filled with anticipation. She yearned to stay and discover what she was capable of. To be with him. *Go, go now.*

"Indeed, you are."

He reached out and clasped her arm as she turned to the door. The warmth of his fingers through her muslin sleeve held her back.

"I must go down."

His hand slid down and tugged her wrist, bidding her stay, and put an end to her flight. "Wait." His voice was a low plea. Eyes the deep green of the sea sought hers, then settled on her mouth while his thumb stroked her galloping pulse.

She stilled, guilt and apprehension warring with insatiable desire.

He leaned down and kissed her. A tender touch of lips, a sharp intake of breath, and his mouth lingered on hers.

His lips were firm, demanding. Her hand sought his shoulder, her fingers gripping his coat as desire and need threatened to overcome her. His kiss tempted her into a sensual world she knew nothing about, beguiling and dangerous.

When he moved away, the heat in his green eyes caused a pulse to beat low in her stomach. She touched her lips with a finger, as warmth spread across her chest and up her throat. Did she blush? It would show her inexperience and no doubt amuse him. Had she, by her behavior, invited such impropriety? She came to her senses with a shock and stepped away from him. "You mustn't."

"Mustn't I?" His voice was low, husky, inviting.

The warning voice in her head stabbed through her wavering desire. *Oh, he was so persuasive. What woman could resist him? He was a charming rake.*

She took several quick breaths and bent to dust her skirts with shaky hands. "I am an ordinary woman, unworthy of such praise. As interesting as this hidden passageway was, my lord, it has proved a waste of time."

She settled her shoulders, relieved to bat away what had just occurred between them. But had she? She could neither forget the touch of his lips and the warmth and desire it evoked nor ignore the still rapid beating of her heart.

A corner of his mouth lifted in a smile. "Not an entire waste of time, surely."

She consulted her watch with trembling fingers. "It is well after four. The servants will have need of me."

Regret in his eyes, he sighed. "If you must."

Her stomach fluttered, caught by his sad capitulation. He was unpredictable, and she was out of her depth.

"Are we friends, then?" he asked.

Her heart, which had been beating furiously, slowed down as cold reason took hold. Where would their friendship lead them? She feared herself as much as him. She shook her head slowly. They were not friends and never could be. Before she reached a point where she could no longer resist him, she rushed to the door and left the bedchamber without looking back.

Olivia hesitated on the staircase, fighting the voice in her head urging her to go back into his arms and the promise they held. Oh, he would be a superb lover, of that she was sure. But she still had a shred of common sense left. She hurried downstairs. To end up in his bed would mean the end of her life here. And she wasn't ready to leave. But was it only her need to discover the truth which compelled her to remain under his roof? Or was it Redcliffe himself?

Chapter Fifteen

"*Dash it all!*" Dominic's gruff voice penetrated the quiet as he paced the library. He was blue deviled by the need to explain himself. But nothing he thought of to say sounded right, and would only be a lie. He wouldn't blame her if she didn't trust him. He wanted to make love to her, and the fear that she could be gone from his life within days saddened him.

He glanced around what had become his retreat. The solitude he'd once enjoyed now made him restless and lonely.

To rid himself of these thoughts, he left the library in search of Williams, planning to ride out to see the gamekeeper before it grew dark.

After learning from the gamekeeper about the overstocked grouse, which meant less food for the birds and resulted in disease, Dominic decided he and Williams would take the guns out tomorrow to shoot a brace for the table.

Back at his desk, he set a firm plan in place for a shooting party in the autumn. With extra servants, Olivia would make the house ready for guests. If she were still here to organize it. He frowned. When had his life become so dependent on her being in it?

A quiet evening followed, a game of chess after dinner and a discussion about the machinations of the Napoleonic wars. Williams, a keen student of history, prodded Dominic to relate his experiences. He reluctantly obliged him after imbibing several glasses of brandy. The alcohol numbed the worst of those memories and eased his restlessness, which he suspected was due more to what occurred between him and Olivia in his bedchamber.

He must apologize. Tell her he wished the kiss had never happened, which was an outright lie. Assure her it wouldn't happen again and hope to keep to his word.

Planning his usual morning ride, he dressed in his riding clothes and left the house, pulling on his gloves. Before he'd reached the stables, the Redcliffe coach lumbered up the drive carrying the servants from London.

Dominic instructed Grimsby to let them down at the front door instead of around the back at the servants' entrance. He wished to see them, and more particularly, Olivia, who would be called upon to deal with them.

Michael ushered them into the great hall to be greeted by Williams. His valet, Cushing, cast an aggrieved eye at Dominic's carelessly tied neckcloth. "We'll have your cravats put to rights in a jiffy, milord. I brought my special flat iron."

"Thank you, Cushing. Your expertise has been missed."

With remarkable restraint, Cushing did not ask why Dominic hadn't sent for him earlier, but his glance said it all. Dominic sighed. Right now, he didn't give a hoot about his damn linens. "Find Miss Jenner," he ordered Michael.

A few moments later, she came into the hall dressed in the gown the color of which reminded him of ripe apricots.

"Sorry, my lord." Her voice brisk, she looked past him at the servants. "Mr. Samuels is making jam and bottling the summer fruits."

She greeted the recent additions to the household. A quiet word with her would be impossible today. Frustrated, he strode to the stables, planning to visit the Johnson farm to check on the new barn.

Preferring to ride alone with his jumbled thoughts, he took

his usual route along the bridle path through the woods, which joined the lane farther on. Rain during the night had softened the ground, the trees dripping, ruts in the path filled with muddy water. As he guided Onyx around a deep pothole, the soil caved in and the horse stumbled, throwing Dominic forward in the saddle.

A shot ricocheted through the trees. It slammed, white-hot, into his shoulder.

Spooked, Onyx reared and took off at a gallop. Dominic fought to rein him in, struggling to keep his seat. When Onyx finally slowed, they'd traveled some distance.

Dominic stroked the horse's foam-flecked neck, his low voice calming the animal. He fought the urge to return and accost the gunman, but he had no gun, and blood dripped from his arm onto his riding glove, making his grasp on the reins slip. He transferred them to his right hand. If the devil had hung around, he could pick him off, and finish the job. And if the fellow knew him, he would expect it. Fighting mad at his helplessness, Dominic studied the wound in his shoulder and made a promise to find him as soon as he'd had it tended to.

He took a shorter route along a rough, heavily wooded path, emerging from the woods onto the gravel road. Who would want him dead? That was no stray shot from the gamekeeper's gun. Clough worked miles away in another section of the woods.

His shoulder was numb. The sleeve of his green riding coat had turned the color of claret, the wound bleeding profusely. He became damnably dizzy and swayed in the saddle. "Take me home, Onyx," he murmured, hunched over the horse's neck.

His eyelids grew heavy and despite his fighting it, they closed. He struggled to stay in the saddle, barely aware of the horse's rhythmic gait.

"Milord! What happened?"

"Shot." Dominic opened his eyes and looked groggily at Fellows. Onyx had done as he asked. Damn fine horse, he thought vaguely.

"Let me help you down."

Fellows dragged Dominic off the horse and called for the stable boy and Grimsby to assist him.

"Well done, Onyx," Dominic mumbled. "I'll be all right, Fellows. Just get me to bed."

His knees gave way and blackness descended.

⟶⟩⟩⟩⟨⟨⟨⟵

IN THE SERVANTS' hall, Olivia instructed the new arrivals, then sent them to their chambers to freshen up. She needed a walk to order her still rampaging emotions. Rather than send a footman on an errand, she entered the village, intent on purchasing a few items at the haberdashers. Friends halted her progress along the main street. Mrs. Buckhurst spoke in glowing terms of her daughter Reanna's engagement to Jack Dowd. Miss Franklin expressed her joy about the Graves' newborn, praising the Lord that mother and baby survived. The christening would be this Sunday.

When their curious questions turned to inquiries about Redcliffe, Olivia made her excuses and entered the haberdashery, where a customer talked about the rebuilding of the Johnson's barn. "Unlike his uncle, the earl is a very generous man," she gushed. She patted her bonnet and left the shop.

Mr. Mockford turned his attention to Olivia. "Good to see you, Miss Jenner."

"How are you, Mr. Mockford?"

"Looking forward to spending my days in the garden."

"You don't yet have a buyer for the haberdashery?"

"Not yet. But I'm confident someone will."

"I'm sure of it. It is a tidy business."

She kept her plans to herself as she gave him her order.

He wrapped her parcels in brown paper. "You look a trifle peaky. I have an excellent tonic I can recommend."

"I'm merely a little tired, but thank you." She smiled and gathered up her parcels. "I shall rally presently."

"I'm pleased you have a good position. Lady Lowry has dismissed your replacement, Mrs. Turner," he said, halting Olivia at the door. "Her ladyship has gone to Newcastle in search of another."

Olivia suffered a swift pang of sympathy. Meg Turner had been a dear friend once and had been Lord Willowbrook's housekeeper until he died. What could have happened? "Poor Mrs. Turner. She is extremely competent. I'm sure it was unjustified. What about the rest of the staff?"

"Still there." He leaned on the counter.

He loved a chat, and while Olivia wished to learn more about his retirement plans, other matters needed her attention. The most prominent: what to do about Redcliffe. But she was relieved to learn Lady Lowry's servants kept their positions. Work was scarce. Gaining confidence, Emily had proved to be an excellent housemaid, and Olivia wouldn't hesitate to hire any other staff member Lady Lowry might take it into her mind to let go. She'd found them all very capable.

After waiting for a wagon to pass, she crossed the street, intending to take the short way home, across the meadow to Redcliffe Hall. Her journey into town failed to help her sort out her problem, and she wasn't confident the few miles back would, either. How did one stop their heart from loving the wrong person? If she disapproved of him or knew him to be a scoundrel, it would be easier. But apart from wanting her, he'd done nothing to make her dislike him. And much for her to admire.

Her walk took her down a different street from the usual way. As she turned a corner, she caught sight of Mrs. Hobbs entering through a cottage gate. It was not the laundress's day off. Prepared to give Mrs. Hobbs the benefit of the doubt, Olivia still wasn't happy about the woman's tendency to be secretive.

She went a few steps farther, then stopped. Wasn't that Mr. Pike's cottage? The one with the green gate and well-tended hedge. She remembered her father pointing it out to her once. She turned back for another look to make sure. It was. Olivia continued on. Apparently, Pike and Mrs. Hobbs knew each other. Were they related?

As she expected, thoughts of Redcliffe returned to plague, yet perplexingly thrill her. Still indecisive, she passed through the Redcliffe Hall gates. If she were sensible, she would hand in her notice. She was sure he would supply her with a good reference. But to her dismay, she discovered she wasn't the sensible woman she'd thought herself. Although she knew it was inevitable, leaving Redcliffe Hall and its owner seemed too painful to contemplate.

A team of busy servants filled the kitchen with the preparations for the next meal covering the big, scoured oak table, along with a bowl of eggs, a basket of fruit, and vegetables. The kitchen maids greeted her as they chopped herbs, while Henry peeled potatoes.

Sam turned as he stirred gravy in a pan for a beef and kidney pie, the pastry for the pie already prepared. The smell wafting about the kitchen was delicious.

"They need you upstairs, Olivia."

"Why? What has happened?"

"Someone shot his lordship."

Her heart leaped, and icy fear rushed along her veins. "Shot? Will he be all right?"

"They've called the doctor. He's in his bedchamber."

She tore off her bonnet and threw it down on a chair, then snatched up an apron hanging on a hook. Racing up the servants' stairs, she tied the apron around her waist.

When she entered the earl's bedchamber, Doctor Manners was tending to Redcliffe. "Ah, Miss Jenner, just the woman I wished to see." He eyed her apron. "And you've come prepared."

"Anything I can do, Doctor." Olivia approached the bedside. How still Redcliffe was, when he always seemed so vitally alive; his face, usually a light tan, so pale, it scared her. But his bare chest rose and fell with each deep breath, his shoulder and arm covered in blood. She almost gasped aloud. *He must live!*

"Will he..." she swallowed, not wishing him to tell her if it was bad news. "Will he be all right?"

"I believe so. He's a vigorous man. But he's lost a lot of blood. The ball needs to come out. You can help me. You're not squeamish at the sight of blood, are you?"

She shook her head. "I'll have whiskey, hot water, and towels brought."

"No need. Jack has gone to fetch them."

A moment later, Jack, his arms full, hurried in.

Doctor Manners opened his bag and withdrew a long pair of tweezers. Holding them over a basin, he doused them with whiskey. He did the same with a small knife before arranging them on a rolled-out cloth.

Redcliffe stirred and opened his eyes. "I need to remove the shot, my lord," Manners said.

"Go ahead."

"I trust you know how it's done?"

"Had one dug out of my arm during the war."

"A little whiskey first."

Redcliffe took the bottle from Jack and drank. He sank back on the pillows. When liquid sloshed down his chin, Olivia dabbed it with the towel.

"Miss Jenner," he murmured. "You make a splendid nurse."

"More," Manners commanded.

While Jack held the bottle, Redcliffe swallowed an alarming amount.

His eyes unfocused, he peered up at her. "You still here, Miss Jenner?"

"Yes, my lord." She was relieved he didn't call her Olivia.

"I'm glad." He closed his eyes.

"We shall begin," Manners said, knife poised. "Hold the patient still, both of you."

With Jack on one side and she on the other, she held Redcliffe's arm as the doctor first enlarged the wound with the knife, then pushed the tweezers into the cut. It must have been dreadfully painful. Redcliffe jerked and groaned.

A few minutes later, the shot pinged into the bowl.

"Good." Satisfied, Manners washed and dried his hands at the washbasin. "I'll clean the wound. Then can I leave you to bandage the area, Miss Jenner?"

Olivia raised her anxious gaze from Redcliffe's face. He'd lapsed into a faint during the procedure. "Yes, of course."

The doctor put his instruments back in his bag while Olivia picked up the bandage he'd brought. "Put a pad on the shoulder and bandage him like this," Manners said, showing her. "To support the arm."

She nodded.

"I'll call again tomorrow."

"Jack, see the doctor to the door." Olivia cut off a large piece of bandage and fashioned a pad with it.

The door closed. She worked silently, carefully wrapping it as he'd shown her. A hand resting lightly on his broad chest, her fingers brushed over smooth skin and crisp, dark hair.

"Have you trussed me up like a chicken?"

He slurred his words, but his heavy-lidded eyes watched her.

"I have never trussed a chicken." She kept her voice calm as she cut the end of the bandage. "But I suspect it would be easier than this."

"Why?"

"You are a good deal larger than a chicken, my lord."

"That's true."

"You must feel bad. You aren't arguing the point with me."

"I never argue."

"Yes. You do. And I suspect you like to keep on until you win." She would settle a few matters between them while he was in his cups.

"But I haven't won yet," he said, his voice husky.

She tied the knot, her fingers trembling. "Incorrigible."

"You feel confident you can scold me, Olivia," he said, surprising her, "because I cannot retaliate."

She shook her head. "You don't frighten me, even when you act like a thwarted lion."

"Fighting words." His lips quirked in an endearing grin. "I shan't forget them."

She expected he would. Certainly hoped he would. "Who shot you?"

"Devil if I know."

She frowned. Then the man was still out there somewhere. "The parish constable has been called. He will want to speak to you tomorrow. If you are well enough."

"I am well enough now. The gunman's trail will grow cold if it rains tonight." He tried to raise himself up and grimaced.

She pushed him gently down and smoothed his blankets. "You must sleep. Or you won't be fit to speak to him tomorrow."

He closed his eyes. "Will you lie down beside me? Keep me company?"

"I most certainly will not. Why must men behave like children when they are ill?" She remembered the fuss her father made over a badly bruised toe when, like Redcliffe, he was fearless in tackling more serious matters. "All that whiskey. You are cup shot."

"Where did you learn that expression?"

"I heard my father's stable staff use it."

He glowered at her. "Well, you're wrong. Come over here, and I'll prove it to you." He sounded alert and not the least bit drunk.

Her heart fluttered. "I see you are going to be a difficult patient."

He groaned. "I'm sorry, Olivia. I'm not angry at you. Being bedridden and useless is the worst thing to happen to a fellow. Especially now when I need to find the man who shot me."

"I know. But perhaps the constable will."

"He won't. He doesn't know the woods like I do."

"Then you must be patient."

Watching the pain which he fought to hide marring his ruggedly handsome face, she decided not to put in her notice. Helpless, he was even more appealing, if that were possible. And he needed her. How could she contemplate leaving now?

She gathered up the roll of bandages, scissors, and the bottle of whiskey. "I'll look in later. Perhaps a little meat broth at dinner."

"Delicious," he muttered through his teeth, but he was asleep before she left the room.

CHAPTER SIXTEEN

A COOL HAND rested feather-light on Dominic's forehead. He breathed in a flowery scent he recognized, and reached up to grasp the hand, but it had moved out of reach. He opened his eyes. Olivia stood beside the bed in a gown the color of apricots, far too attractive for a nurse. Sunshine flowed through the window, alighting on her glossy black locks. No cap. He smiled approvingly. "Olivia. Is it morning?"

"It's midday. You've had a good sleep. There's no evidence of fever."

Jack came in with a tray.

Olivia stood aside. "Here is your luncheon, my lord."

"I fancy a big slab of beef and a glass of burgundy. Good for the blood."

"Chicken broth." She bent over him and arranged the pillows behind his back as the footman placed the tray on his lap.

He wanted her to stay close to him, but of course, she didn't. "Thank you, Jack."

"You're welcome, milord." Jack looked cheerful as he left the room. Dominic took that as a sign he was rallying. A good meal would get him on his feet.

He stirred the pallid stuff with his spoon. "This looks like gruel."

"Oh, would you prefer gruel?" Her innocent expression didn't fool him. "I'll ask Sam to make you some."

He narrowed his eyes at her and took a sip, wincing as a sharp pain pierced his shoulder. The broth was tasty. "Not bad."

"Sam is an excellent cook."

"He is. Will you sit awhile and talk to me?"

"Until you finish your broth." She sat on the chair by the bed. "I plan to visit Mary and the baby this afternoon."

"Come and tell me later how they fare. It's dull lying here. I will get up this afternoon."

"Doctor Manners will call in a little while. You can ask him about moving around, but I doubt he'll approve."

He frowned. "It's only a slight wound."

"No gunshot is slight. Fortunately, there's no damage to bones and arteries. But Doctor Manners says to treat such a wound with care."

His eyes roamed her face. "Were you worried about me?"

"I was concerned, but you look much better. You might get up and sit in a chair tomorrow."

He tightened his lips on a curse. "We shall see."

"I trust you'll be sensible, my lord."

He put down the spoon. "I'll leave common sense to you, Olivia. You have enough for both of us."

"You've had enough broth?" She rose and removed the tray, placing it on the table. "Perhaps you might sleep a little."

He laid his head back on the pillow, discovering he was still damnably tired.

"A dashed good shot," he mumbled, his tongue thick.

She tucked the covers around him. "Who is a good shot?"

"If Onyx hadn't stumbled, he would have shot me in the head." He heard her gasp as he fell asleep.

When Dominic woke again, the doctor stood beside the bed with Olivia. Both appeared relieved. Judging by the level of the sun creeping over the carpet, it was afternoon.

"You've been out for twenty-four hours," Manners informed him, feeling his pulse. "We feared you might turn up your toes, milord."

Dominic raised a questioning eyebrow.

"You had a high fever and were rambling." Olivia looked at him, concern in her eyes. It made him wonder what he might have said. An erotic dream? She would certainly feature in it. "But you've come through it." She glanced at Manners. "Isn't that right, Doctor?"

"On the mend. Fever's broke."

"I'm tougher than that." Dominic struggled to sit up. Vague memories of lost hours returned. Olivia spooning nasty medicine down his throat, her soft breast resting against his arm as she sponged his brow with blessedly cool water.

His shoulder throbbed, and he gave up the struggle, falling back, weak as water. He gritted his teeth with annoyance. He'd be damned if he'd admit it. "When can I leave this bed?"

"Tomorrow, for a few hours," Manners said in that infuriatingly calm way of his. "If you continue to improve." He snapped his bag shut and walked to the door. "I'll call in the morning."

"Thank you, Manners. I owe you a good deal."

"Thank your devoted nurse," Manners said as he went out the door.

There were shadows beneath Olivia's eyes. How long had she remained beside his bed last night, forgoing sleep?

She leaned over to adjust the sling on his arm. "You must rest if you wish to get up tomorrow."

Impossible to remain in bed for even one more day. He needed to be his usual strong self now, more than ever. Find that gunman if he still lurked on the estate. And he wanted to throw back the covers, snatch Olivia up and twirl her around, make her laugh, and banish the fatigue around her eyes. With a faint grin, he promised himself he would soon.

"I'm not sure what you find amusing, my lord." Eyeing him, she poured more of that awful stuff the doctor prescribed and held out the spoon. "I distrust it. I'm sure it was wicked."

"Unfair, Olivia. I'm helpless as a babe," he murmured, then

swallowed the spoonful with a grimace. "No more of that tomorrow."

She tidied things away. "Wait to see what the doctor says."

He patted the bed invitingly. "I must talk to you."

Ignoring his offer, she chose the chair.

"Has anything come to light while I've been abed? What does Williams say?"

"Williams and Phillips, the parish constable, have made inquiries. No one reported anything unusual."

"Bah. Inquiries will get us nowhere. I need to speak to Williams. Send Jack up with a meal. I'm ravenous."

She smiled. "That's an encouraging sign. Sam will prepare you a hearty luncheon."

He arched an eyebrow, a smile twitching his lips. "No chicken broth."

She laughed. "No broth."

"Beef. With all the trimmings. And a glass of claret."

She rose. "That might prove unwise."

"I'll settle for nothing less."

"Very well." She walked to the door. "I'll come back later with Polly. You can bathe, and we'll change the bed linens."

"Polly isn't to lay a hand on me, Olivia," he barked.

She left the room giggling.

Once he was on his feet and could ride again, he would examine the area in the woods where he'd been shot. The gunman would turn up again, but this time, Dominic would be armed and ready for him. Couldn't have the man wandering loose on the estate. It placed everyone in danger.

He groaned with helpless frustration. Who would want to harm him? A question he kept asking himself while finding no answer. The one person who would benefit from his death was George. Even if Dominic could contemplate such a distressing occurrence, George was in London.

And the intruder? Were they the same man? His head throbbed. This wouldn't resolve itself while he was stuck here.

He would get up tomorrow, come hell or high water. Or any objections from Olivia. Olivia. A far more pleasant subject, although an even more frustrating one.

At the end of the fifth long and tedious day, brightened only by Olivia's welcome attentions, Dominic, frustrated beyond endurance, was determined this would be his last spent in bed.

When he awoke the next morning, he felt more himself. He picked up his pocket watch on the bedside table. Nine o'clock. He left the bed, and ignoring a slight weakness, rang for Cushing while testing his shoulder. It hurt, but satisfied it was manageable, he pulled the bell for hot water. Going to the window, he drew back the curtains. Rain threatened, dark clouds hovering low.

His valet hurried in minutes later. "Oh, your lordship, it is splendid to see you out of bed. We have all been dreadfully concerned."

"Thank you, Cushing. I'm afraid I don't deserve it. My riding clothes if you will."

Cushing's eyes widened. "But the weather, milord. It's about to teem with rain."

Dominic raised his eyebrows. "Not an unusual occurrence, is it? Hurry please, I will breakfast downstairs."

Cushing, who never tarried when given an order, disappeared into the dressing room.

"I'll dress myself, but you can help with my boots," Dominic said when the valet returned.

"But your sling, milord?"

Dominic slipped it off. "Unnecessary."

"Shall I choose your waistcoat?"

"No waistcoat, Cushing."

His boots on, he dismissed Cushing, disliking how he fussed around him as if he were on his last legs. His shoulder nagged at him as he pulled on his riding coat, leaving it unbuttoned over his shirt. He checked to ensure he hadn't caused the wound to bleed, then ignored it. He conceded he needed a neckcloth and was battling with it when someone knocked on the door.

"Enter."

Olivia raised her eyebrows. "You're up, my lord? They did not inform me the doctor had come."

He smiled. "You know full well he hasn't. Tie this for me? I've sent Cushing to have his breakfast."

"Where is your sling?"

"Unnecessary."

She frowned. "Shouldn't you wait for Doctor Manners before venturing out?"

"If he arrives before I leave for my ride, direct him to me in the breakfast room."

"You're planning to ride?" She gestured to the sky beyond the window. "Surely you won't go out in this. And what could you possibly find after a week?"

"Some hint of who the fellow is." He arched an eyebrow. "Or would you prefer I wait until he takes me by surprise again?"

"He won't have to if you die of pneumonia."

"Spare me all the sensible reasons I shouldn't go, Olivia. I am not listening."

"Men are so stubborn," she murmured, tackling his cravat.

He gazed down at her with a grin. "Are we indeed?"

Dominic enjoyed her closeness, her womanly scent, and speculated on how well she would fit against him. He rested a hand on her slender waist. "Still a little unsteady," he said with an apologetic smile.

Satisfied with her simple arrangement, she stepped away. "If you are as unsteady as you say, I suggest you return to bed. It is most unwise to ride. You might fall."

"I haven't fallen off a horse since I was eight. Although, there was that time when..." He paused as she waited, her delectable lips parted. He fought the powerful urge to kiss her. "But I suppose it's best I don't go into details." Not a romantic tale. He'd gotten thoroughly soused after a nasty encounter with French troops, and Firefly, affronted, had tossed him over his head.

She glowered at him. "Is there nothing I can say to change

your mind?"

"No. But thank you for trying."

She followed him from the room. "What shall I tell Doctor Manners if he comes after you've left?"

"Convey my sincere gratitude. I'm sure he saved my life. I shan't require his services again. Make sure Williams reimburses him, oh, and gives him a couple of bottles of the French cognac from the cellar."

"Very well, my lord." With a heavy sigh, she turned and left him.

Dominic went downstairs, hoping one day to hear his given name on her lips.

OLIVIA'S THOUGHTS WERE on Redcliffe as she supervised the housemaid, polishing the silverware. He was definitely better. She'd observed his grimace when he'd moved his arm, but he was much stronger. He no longer had need of her. She must return to her duties, where she belonged.

Olivia faced the truth of her feelings. She ached to have him touch her in all those places that longed for a man's touch. For her to touch him, his smooth skin, his hair, his body, which held fascination for her. To be held in his strong arms. Safe from a world that wasn't kind to women. But she was alone and would remain so. And must leave Redcliffe Hall soon. She could see no other way. Falling in love with Redcliffe would only bring her heartache and eventual disgrace.

She would carry in her heart her time with him here, his wicked humor, his heated glances, and his desire for her, which thrilled her. She'd come to know him: his impatience, restlessness, kindness, and his grace. A man she would never forget, for she would not meet his like again. She came here with a poor opinion of peers, resolved to find the means to defend her father's memory. And while still determined on that course, she was no longer impelled to seek judgment against the old earl.

At the window, she watched Redcliffe ride away through the rain in his oilskins, relieved to be alone in her office when sobs escaped her lips. She blew her nose and rose, intending to search the steward's records again while he was away. If only she could find evidence to point to the truth, which she must have before she gave her notice. Had she missed something in the steward's neat, flawless accounting? There was nothing listed about the horses purchased from her father. Pike left at about that time. She did not know him, so she could not judge him. But Mrs. Hobbs did.

Olivia went to the laundry room. She'd been meaning to ask the laundress why she visited Pike, but when Redcliffe was shot, she'd forgotten everything while tending to him.

The laundress was busy at her work with the housemaid, Jenny, who now assisted her. There was a neat stack of laundered and ironed linens on the table, and several of his lordship's white linen shirts. The woman was efficient.

Olivia smiled at Jenny, the maid who had arrived in the coach from London. Quite an adventure for a young woman of twenty, but she appeared to be adjusting well. "Would you leave us for a moment, Jenny?"

"Yes, miss." Jenny ducked her fair head and hurried out the door.

Mrs. Hobbs put aside the flat iron. "May I help you, Miss Jenner?"

"When returning from the village the other day, I saw you enter Mr. Pike's cottage. You were not to leave Redcliffe Hall without permission. I thought I'd made myself very clear, Mrs. Hobbs."

"I looked for you, Miss Jenner. But you were not in the house, and Pike had urgent need of my help."

"Is he a relative?"

"My cousin. He's been ailing. But he sent word he's much

better. He'll be out of bed in a few days. I shan't need to visit him again."

"Who delivered the message to you?"

"A friend of Pike's."

"No one mentioned a caller. Did he come to the kitchen door?"

A slight flush painted her sallow cheekbones. "No, this one." She motioned to the door. The laundry was at the northern end of the building and set apart from the kitchen, with a few steps leading down. There was a screened area to dry the washing. It was possible no one saw him.

Olivia met the woman's hard, defensive gaze. She doubted her, but Olivia gave up questioning her further. The woman's thin lips had tightened. She would learn no more from Mrs. Hobbs today, but it sparked her interest to find her so defensive.

The new housemaid talked to Polly as she cleaned the servants' hall.

"Jenny, did anyone come to the laundry door to see Mrs. Hobbs while you were there?"

The maid shook her head. "No, Miss Jenner."

The gardeners would have noticed if a stranger wandered across the lawns. "Thank you, Jenny. Go back to your work. Come with me, Polly. While his lordship is away, we'll attend to the library."

"Yes, miss."

While Polly dusted the library bookshelves, Olivia tidied the papers on the desk. Redcliffe had been gone for hours. He could have taken a groom with him, she thought with annoyance. But he wouldn't want to place anyone in danger.

She retrieved a letter fluttering in the breeze from the open window and caught the last few lines "... and pray you will come to us at Christmas. Our neighbor's daughter, Marianne, has not yet been spoken for! Signed, Evelyn, Lady Trelawny."

Redcliffe's sister had found a suitable bride for him. Olivia had always known Redcliffe would choose a wife from his own class.

Heavy-hearted, she moved away from the desk. This should not hurt so much. She had always known it. Redcliffe wanted her, but as his mistress, not his wife. Earls did not marry their housekeepers.

"Finish up here, Polly. You'll find me in the steward's room."

She left Polly to her work. Could Pike's ledgers contain the vital piece of information she sought? Had she overlooked it?

Her head bowed over the ledger, a finger on the list of entries. She was so engrossed, she didn't immediately look up when the door opened.

"What are you searching for, Olivia?"

She released a long, shuddering breath. Redcliffe home safe. His wet hair slicked back, dark eyebrows raised.

He strode across the room and planted his hands on the desk, leaning toward her.

Her throat dried as she met his cool green gaze, dismayed to have him find her examining Pike's old ledgers. "Did you discover anything in the woods, my lord?" She glanced at his shoulder. "How is your wound? I hope it isn't bleeding again. Would you like me to look at it? The doctor has come and gone. I gave him the Cognac." She was rambling, her heart skittering with distress, her gaze darting away from his.

He reached across and placed a hand beneath her chin, raising her gaze to his. She found disappointment in his eyes. "Answer my question."

She edged back out of his reach. "I will, but you might wish to dry your hair and change your damp clothes first."

"Damn it all," he demanded. "You'll tell me now."

"Very well." She swallowed to ease her dry throat. "Your uncle insisted he'd paid for two horses my father sold him. Papa swore he had not." She didn't mention her father's resulting despair and tragic end, although she desperately wanted to.

Redcliffe folded his arms. "So, you sought a post here to expose what you believe is a fraud perpetuated by my uncle?"

She'd never seen him so angry. "I want justice. To clear my

father's name."

"And the thousand pounds."

"Yes!" She raised her chin. "Why not? Father would want me to have the money. It would help me set up my house and buy a business."

His eyes shadowed, he searched hers. "That remains your intention?"

She swallowed and licked her bottom lip. "Yes, it does."

A tick appeared in his jaw. He waved a hand over the books. "You've found no such evidence?"

She shook her head miserably.

"It could be impossible to prove. I'll give you the money, Olivia. You had only to ask me."

She sighed. "That is why I didn't come to you. I knew you would want me to have it. I won't take it unless I know I have a right to it."

"How will you find out? Pike doesn't appear to know."

"Oh, yes. Pike." She told him about the laundress's secret trips to Pike's house and the man who came unannounced to Redcliffe Hall to see her.

"There might be something amiss. I'll look into it." He walked to the door. "And if your father was right, and I pay you? You will leave us."

It wasn't a question. She wanted to cry out, to tell him she hated to go. Avoiding his troubled eyes, she said, "When you have found a suitable replacement."

With a nod, he left the room, closing the door quietly behind him.

She put a fist to her mouth to stop herself from calling out, fighting the urge to run after him, to have him hold her, and be supported by his strength. As angry as he was, she knew he wouldn't turn her away.

He wouldn't miss her once the house ran smoothly. Williams could find a housekeeper in York or one of the big towns. It shouldn't be too difficult. At Christmas, Redcliffe would meet the lady his sister wished him to marry and forget ever having known her. The thwarted desire of a rake would mean little as the years passed. She frowned. That was mean and unworthy of her. Nor could she believe it of him. Was what they shared more than mere desire? It was for her. While she would never be privy to his true feelings, she sensed it was for him, too.

She returned to the ledgers in the hope of finding proof that would make matters right between her and Redcliffe. Life had to go on, and it would distract her from her anguish.

CHAPTER SEVENTEEN

A T HIS DESK in the library, Dominic inspected the ball Manners dug out of his shoulder. He recognized the type. Made for a flintlock rifle and sold by Manton's in London. He didn't know if they were available here. Certainly, no poacher would have such an expensive rifle. But he didn't expect the shooter to be a poacher.

Earlier, while searching the woods, he'd scooped up the gold disk half-buried in the mud on the bridle path. He'd ridden back to the house, deeply disturbed, and sought Olivia to discuss it with her. When he found her in the steward's office searching through Pike's books, he'd come away without revealing it.

He felt oddly cut adrift. He could discuss most things with Williams, but not this. It was Olivia, more and more he'd turned to, knowing she would listen and offer sound advice. Had he been a fool to trust her? But was it fair of him to expect her to be honest with him from the beginning? He had to earn her trust, too. And he'd failed when he kissed her.

Dominic rubbed his aching shoulder. He'd expected to wear her down, to make her see the sense of an affair. Then once the affair ended, as it inevitably would, he'd insist on securing her future, to ensure she would never have to work again. But his anticipation of a delightful liaison was a pipe dream when he knew what a determined, moral woman she was. What a blind fool he'd been to believe it, while, every day, his feelings for her deepened. And when they parted? But they would never be lovers. The thought left him strangely hollow.

He pushed his fingers through his hair. In London, periods of solitude and introspection followed the war, his brief affairs a distraction. But he realized he wanted more, a companion who shared his doubts, dreams, and his love.

His sister, Evelyn, knew better than he what he needed. To marry and put down roots, she'd told him, after he sold their father's estate without a backward glance. He had been dismissive and thought her a romantic. Now, he saw clearly how right she'd been. Had the war changed him so much? Turned him into a cynical loner? He didn't want to be that man.

Olivia sparked a hungry need in him, and to his shame, he'd turned their attraction into a reckless pursuit of selfish pleasure. While she, with far better instincts than he, saw what he refused to acknowledge. He had drawn her close to the edge of dangerous ground, which she would not cross.

He groaned as he considered how badly he'd handled things.

What he wanted to show her, this disturbing discovery left him deeply concerned. He shoved aside his dark thoughts, telling himself it could not be. But whoever shot him had known of his habit of choosing that path, when very few would. No one had stalked him. He'd developed an acute sense of danger during the war. It was possible he might have spied that shooter, too, if he hadn't been concentrating on guiding Onyx over a tricky patch of ground.

Beyond the window, the rain clouds had drifted away, the sky washed a clear blue. Putting the rifle ball in a desk drawer, Dominic left the house. He walked to the stables, where his coachman must answer a question, one he'd hoped to avoid.

A gray cat atop a wall stopped cleaning its fur to observe him as he entered the stable quadrangle. Grimsby looked up from washing the coach, surprised to see him back again, as Dominic approached. "Milord?"

"Did you put Mr. Yardley down in London, Grimsby?"

"Not London, milord. He asked to be taken to his aunt's home."

Dominic's throat closed. "Where?"

"Oxford."

Disturbed, Dominic went to stroke Onyx's black head thrust over the stall gate, Peaches resting contently on the straw beside him. George might intend to stay away from the London gambling dens for a while. To do as he promised and set his life in order. Dominic hoped profoundly this was so because it was possible for George to be back here within a couple of days. Pushing the nagging worry aside, he strode back to the house.

As he walked along the gravel drive, his fingers closed over the small object in his pocket he'd found on the bridle path near where he was shot. He took it out. The handsome button matched those on the riding coat George had worn when last here. Dominic remembered them because he'd remarked on the unusual cupid at a fountain etched into the gold. He and George had taken that route, and if a button were missing when they'd returned to the house together, he hadn't noticed it. George hadn't mentioned its loss either after he'd changed his clothes. He prided himself on being a dandy and was most particular about his appearance.

Dominic tucked the button into his coat pocket again and made his way around to the kitchen gardens and staff entrance.

The burly young undergardener vigorously applied a garden tool to the weeds taking over the kitchen garden.

"Barlow, isn't it?"

He lowered his hoe and straightened up. "Aye, milord."

"You've been working on these beds during the last few days?"

"Oh, aye."

"Seen anyone come to the house you didn't know?"

He turned and gestured to an unruly, tall hedge in need of pruning. "Mister Pike came. He met the laundry mistress there, behind the hawthorn. Very friendly like, they were."

Dominic tensed. "Pike?"

"Aye, milord. Wore his hat pulled low and his collar up, but I'd recognize him anywhere, skinny fellow that he his." He flushed. "Pardon, milord. Perhaps I shouldna have said it."

"You don't like Pike?"

He shook his head. "Seen him in the taproom. He's there every night 'til late. It's a bully he is, treated the barmaid bad last time I was there. I'll teach him a lesson if he does it again."

Dominic eyed the set of the gardener's shoulders. "I prefer my staff not resort to such means to settle an argument, Barlow." The sturdy young Scot dropped his gaze to the hoe he held in his powerful hands. "It would be an unfair fight."

Barlow glanced up, a twinkle in his brown eyes. "Aye, milord. I ken that."

With a nod, Dominic walked on to the house.

He entered through the kitchen door.

Samuels turned from stirring the bubbling pots on the stove, filling the room with fragrant steam. "Milord?"

When on the way to Graves's farm, Olivia refused to tell him what she knew about Samuels. He had asked Williams. Dominic knew the cook served in the navy, but it surprised him to learn he'd spent time in Newgate for a fraud.

"When the fellow, whose evidence put him behind bars died," Williams had explained over breakfast, "he left a letter clearing Samuels of any wrongdoing. Wasn't much use as he'd almost completed his sentence. I thought he deserved another chance."

Dominic watched Samuels wipe his hands on a dishtowel, assessing his character. Olivia approved of him. "I wish to talk to you. Come to the library at three o'clock."

The cook raised his shaggy eyebrows but didn't question it. "Yes, milord."

Back at his desk, Dominic opened his mail. A letter from Evelyn. He scanned it quickly, passing impatiently over details of parties and dinners and the vicar's sermon, which had so annoyed Justin. He found what he looked for in the last two paragraphs written on the side of the page in small print.

I found an old letter from Uncle Alberic addressed to Mama. She was most dreadfully ill and passed away within two weeks of Papa, so it was overlooked. I have sent it to you under separate post. Dearest Dominic, I am so sorry I missed it. But it isn't too late. You will still gain much from it. I shall say no more until you have read it.

Dominic searched fruitlessly through the rest of the mail, then sat back with a muttered curse. The letter wasn't there.

Frustrated, he tugged at his neckcloth, one Cushing called *l'Orientale,* which in his opinion resembled a noose. Why the devil he needed such a fancy arrangement in the wilds of the country eluded him. He tied it in a comfortable knot, which would have his valet in hysterics, and went to the window to stare bleakly out. He did not like to be on bad terms with Olivia. It bothered him far more than he thought possible. Once he'd cooled down, he admitted what a difficult position she was in, and his deep sympathy for her reasserted itself, along with the determination to solve the mystery surrounding her father.

For a startling moment, he thought he'd conjured Olivia up when she walked into sight along the path leading down to the lake. He'd allowed himself to envision them in the summerhouse together, away from prying eyes. A few cushions, some wine, kissing every inch of her.

An odd time for her to go for a stroll, when luncheon would soon be served, but there she was in her straw bonnet, hurrying as if she had some purpose in mind. Was it to meet someone? He took himself to task for his unreasonable jealousy as he went after her.

OLIVIA PASSED THROUGH a green archway on a path leading away from the house. Alone, she could face what had occurred. Her world had turned upside down. Redcliffe thought poorly of her. It was of little comfort to know he now knew the truth. After wiping her cheeks and blowing her nose, she'd forced herself to continue her hunt through Pike's ledgers for evidence of her father's innocence.

She'd had no luck to date. But it was difficult to be sure if the accounting during Pike's time at Redcliffe Hall had been recorded accurately, or designed to hide his criminal activities.

Another wasted hour, but she had persisted, because to give up left her with nothing and nowhere to turn. She'd scrutinized the last few pages again. Several items stood out. Six months before the earl purchased her father's horses, Pike had ordered a large amount of feed for the stables. She found it curious when the earl had few horses. Bags of flour and items for the kitchen pantry seemed excessive, too, with the house almost empty of servants. There was a large order for a load of lumber from the sawmill. Pike had noted it was for the renovation of the summer-house. But where were the bills? She'd searched everywhere. Odd that Pike, who seemed so orderly, would not have kept them.

She'd wanted to show this to Redcliffe, but as things stood between them, decided against it. Instead, she left the house and walked down to the small lake.

It had turned into a perfect summer's day. She couldn't help admiring the beautiful scene as she went down the slope. Sun sparkled on the rippling waters where a pair of elegant swans glided over the surface. Waterfowl squabbled among the reeds.

The timber structure stood majestically on a crest of verdant grass above the bank, the posts entwined with wild rose, almost bare of its pink petals, the last of them dropping to add to the fragrant carpet over the ground, the perfumed air intoxicating.

Olivia climbed the steps to search for any evidence of recent repairs to the woodwork. It all seemed untouched, the aged beams of the ceiling solidly in place. She leaned on the rail to watch the busy birds, while the perfumed breeze blew across her face, stirring her hair. It wrenched her sore heart to think she would soon have to leave here. But to leave Redcliffe hurt her far more. He meant too much to her, and that was a good reason to go.

She took herself to task and wandered around the octagonal building, checking the rail and the timber posts for signs of rot that would need replacing. Or new timber already in place. But to her unpracticed eye, it all appeared to be the original timber and in good condition.

"What are you doing here, Olivia?"

At his low, melodic voice, which was almost a caress, her pulse raced. He had come up the steps behind her.

Turning to face him, she gazed into his smiling green eyes and sighed with relief. He was no longer angry with her.

The wall she'd built to protect herself from further hurt threatened to crumble and lay bare her need for him. She clutched the banister, barely aware of the roughened wood beneath her hands, and steeled herself to answer truthfully. After all, she had nothing to lose. "I came to check on something I found in Pike's accounts ledger. He ordered a large amount of timber to repair the damage here." She waved her hand to encompass the space, annoyed by the tremble in her voice. "But I can't find any sign of repairs. Can you?"

He studied the roof and moved around the building. "No work's been done. Why would it be? Repairs to the house would surely take precedence."

He came to stand beside her. Not trusting herself, she watched the charming scene on the lake, barely taking it in. "And there are other questionable entries, too. Feed for the stables when it was almost empty. If you wish, I can show you."

She turned to go.

"Yes. Later." His hand brushed her arm. "Stay awhile."

She took a step back and pressed herself against the rail. "The staff will wonder where I am," she murmured, her voice horribly weak.

He took her hands, holding them lightly in his long-fingered clasp. "I came to apologize, Olivia. I had no right to be angry."

Conscious of his touch, she said, "You have every right, so don't apologize. I should have come to you. Explained, but I was afraid you wouldn't understand." She smiled slightly. "And you would dismiss me before I could investigate further."

He tilted his head. "You think so badly of me?"

"No...no. I don't."

He smiled. "Not now?"

Must he drag a confession from her? "Now that I know you better," she said evasively.

"I would like you to know me better still."

Redcliffe's endearing grin drew her gaze to his mouth. She noted the deeper grooves there, and the fine lines radiating from the corners of his eyes. Signs of his recent suffering had not been evident before. Her fingers curled with longing to touch them.

She swallowed. "I really must go back."

"Why rush away?" He searched her face, his eyes settling on the pulse beating too fast in her throat. "I planned to bring you here."

"You did?"

He slowly nodded, passion darkening his eyes.

She yearned to move closer, the desire so strong, she shut her eyes to hide it.

"*Olivia.*"

Her heart beat madly at Redcliffe's soft entreaty. She was suddenly in his arms, held against his taut body, his cheek against her hair. "I miss you when you're not with me."

She trembled and buried her face in his coat.

He raised her chin with a finger and brought his mouth down on hers, a hard, demanding kiss, his breath quickening to match hers. Her hand went to his nape, her fingers sliding into his soft, thick hair.

When his tongue pushed at the seam of her mouth, she

opened for him and moaned. Her knees buckled, and she would have fallen had his arms not held her. Her body pulsed with a desperate need to be with him. Wholly and completely. Overwhelmed, she pushed away from him. She shook her head. "No, Redcliffe."

Not like this. They could be close to discovering the truth. She owed it to her father. Then she must leave. She turned away from him to the top of the steps, her heart still thudding, unsure of her footing.

He came to hold her arm, which only unsettled her more as he assisted her down. "We're not finished with this, Olivia. Don't think we are."

"Redcliffe...don't, please." She swallowed and pulled away from him.

He let her go as they crossed the lawn. "I intend to look into Pike's activities. You were right to question the man."

He took hold of her elbow, stirring her senses, as they climbed the slight incline. She could manage, but she didn't dissuade him. She was greedy for his touch.

"I was going to search the stables and the storage sheds for anything Pike might have ordered." She glanced up at him, trying to steady her voice. "What if he falsified the records and pocketed the money?"

"Hard to prove after such a long time. But I agree, Pike grows more interesting by the minute. And Mrs. Hobbs, who was seen with him in the garden."

"I don't trust her. Shall I replace her?"

"Not yet. She may prove useful."

He stopped. Turning toward her, he reached up and gently tucked an errant wisp of hair behind her ear. Her breath stilled. "Olivia, when all this business is at an end, we must talk. I want you in my life."

She shook her head. "We have to stop this."

She broke free of him and hurried along the path.

They startled a groundsman, who removed his hat and

bowed.

Whatever course Redcliffe was so determined to take, it could not have a happy outcome, because none was possible. If they found the truth of what had happened here, and she grew more hopeful now that they would, she must leave before they had that talk. Because her future lay beyond the gates of Redcliffe Hall, and she no longer had the strength to refuse anything he asked of her.

CHAPTER EIGHTEEN

I N THE LIBRARY, Dominic stood before the painting of his father as a lad, hanging on the far wall. He saw something of himself in his father's stubborn stance and the impatient way he held the reins of his pony. As if to say, *I'd rather ride than endure this nonsense.* It made him marvel at his own self-control when he was with Olivia in the summerhouse. Her soft lips when she moaned against his mouth, he almost lost control. And would have if she hadn't drawn back.

Impatient to make her his, he would first have to deal with what worried her most. With Samuels's help, he might do it.

The cook entered wearing a clean shirt, having discarded his apron. He still looked tough and disreputable. It might be his long hair held back in the queue, but Dominic imagined it went deeper, to the very core of the man. He had a right to be angry about the injustice he'd suffered, but it hadn't weakened him or made him fall by the wayside.

Dominic abandoned his desk for the sofa. "Sit down, Samuels."

Seated on an armchair, the cook waited for him to speak. Dominic estimated Samuels to be about forty, but his eyes looked a good deal older than his years.

"I'm told you've been in prison." Dominic held up a hand as Samuels, startled, seized the arms of the chair. "Mr. Williams dug into your past. My discovering it earlier would not have changed my mind about hiring you. You are an excellent cook, Samuels. Untrained, but with a natural talent."

Relieved, Samuels relaxed back against the squab. "I'm very fortunate to work here, milord. I'm extending my range with some fancy dishes."

Dominic nodded, impatient to get to the point. "When I entertain, you'll have a sous-chef to assist you." He ran a hand along his jaw, choosing his words carefully. "In the meantime, I require help from someone of your experience." He smiled. "And skills, hopefully."

Samuels's eyebrows rose. "I'm not sure what you refer to, milord. There's not much more to me than what you see."

"You survived in Newgate for some years, surrounded by murderers and robbers. No mean feat."

Samuels slowly nodded.

"It can't have been easy."

The cook folded his arms. "It wasn't."

"Did you learn anything helpful from the thieves who shared your cell? How to pick a lock, for instance?"

Samuels's eyes brightened. He leaned forward, hands loosely clasped between his thighs. "I can. Spent a year with one of the best in the business. Drove me out of my wits, gabbing on about his lucrative robberies." He grinned. "Never mentioned the one that got him tossed into Newgate."

"What I'm about to ask might prove dangerous for someone with your record, should it go wrong, Samuels. It won't go badly for you if you refuse."

"I'm listening, milord."

"I intend to search Mr. Pike's cottage. I won't give you the reason. Let's just say I'm looking for evidence to support a theory."

"Couldn't you put the parish constable onto him? He would haul Pike in for questioning."

"And have Pike destroy or remove the evidence I seek? He

considers himself safe, and I prefer to keep him thinking he is."

Samuels nodded. "That's smart, milord. Wouldn't have thought of it. I suppose that's because I'm the cook and you're the earl."

Dominic smiled. "A few noblemen would do well with your smarts and your toughness, Samuels. We'll search Pike's cottage while he is at the tavern. I'm told he drinks there every evening."

Samuels nodded, his eyes keen. "Just say when, milord."

"Tonight. We'll make use of the full moon. Meet me at the park gates as soon as it's dark." He thought for a moment. He could take the phaeton, but he preferred to ride. "Ride a horse, Samuels?"

"Grew up on a farm, milord."

Dominic nodded. "I'll bring you one."

The cook rose to his feet. "Lookin' forward to it."

When Samuels left the library, Dominic pulled the bell cord to summon Jack. He was confident the cook would be a handy partner in crime. And there was no one else. Williams had departed for London that morning on the mail coach and would be gone for a week. But he wouldn't have involved him in this.

WHEN DOMINIC ARRIVED at the hall gates riding Onyx and leading Tarian by the rein, Samuels loomed out of the shadows, his dark clothing rendering him almost invisible.

Dominic handed him the reins, and the cook leaped into the saddle.

"You brought an implement to open the door?"

Curiously, Dominic found he was enjoying himself. It felt good to hit back at whoever sought to hurt him and those he cared about.

"A tool to jimmy the lock, milord. And a knife to save my skin, should it be necessary."

"It won't come to that. I'd prefer not to have a death on my conscience. Either yours or Pike's. Can you open it but leave no evidence?"

"I'll be as gentle as a dove, milord."

A prickle of excitement ran down Dominic's spine as the horses cantered down the road. He refused to be the prey of some assailant. He much preferred to turn the tables and hunt the fellow down.

The moon, like a glowing silver coin, lighted their way. A night bird called, the wind soughing through the tree branches. A hedgehog scuffled about in the undergrowth bordering the road.

Walking their horses gave Dominic time to think.

Unwise to tell Olivia. She'd have some fool notion that he did this for her, or she'd try to talk him out of it. She deserved the truth as much for her father's sake, but he also owed something to his uncle's memory. And he couldn't allow the danger and uncertainty to continue.

He must consider the safety of his staff. But was he right about Pike? His instincts told him so. But should the man prove innocent, Dominic's actions tonight were disreputable. He was willing to take that chance. If Pike stole from Jenner and his uncle, he'd have to watch how he spent it.

A steward's pay wouldn't be much. He couldn't throw money around in the village. It would bring unwelcome attention. Nor leave his position with Lancaster to spend it elsewhere. Nor cash a banknote if Alberic had issued one to pay Jenner. Dominic's solicitor would have mentioned such a sum. What puzzled him was why Pike hadn't moved away. Set up somewhere where he would be free to spend his ill-gotten gains? What kept him here? Was it his partner in crime, Mrs. Hobbs?

Had Alberic accused Pike of cheating him and threatened to call in the magistrate? Pike would need to act quickly to silence him. Not such a fanciful theory for a man who carried a knife and savagely attacked his footman.

Pity that the letter Evelyn sent him hadn't arrived. Something in it might allude to Pike, despite it being written sometime before his uncle's death. But he couldn't wait for it and didn't have time to write to his sister for more details.

Pike had attempted to hide his acquaintance with Mrs. Hobbs. So, why risk coming to Redcliffe Hall and being seen with her in the gardens? It was reckless and made Dominic suspicious. Was it to arrange another break-in? Had he become impatient or nervous of discovery?

Dominic was sure as he could be that it was Pike who struck Jack down. Might it be he who shot him? A far more attractive assumption than that of George wanting him dead.

Only a marksman could pick Dominic off from among the trees. That shot was aimed at his head with chilling accuracy. Pike was a clerk, hardly the type to be so handy with a rifle. And why kill him? It hardly fitted with what he'd worked out about the man. The fear of discovery, plus the resulting uproar when the magistrate investigated, would not suit his plans.

They approached the outskirts of the village.

Dominic's pulse raced and his shoulders tightened. He checked his pistol and tucked it into his waistband. If he had to, he would fire to protect Samuels but didn't want Pike dead. He needed to have a serious talk with the fellow.

He reined in and dismounted. "We'll leave the horses here. Pike's house is in the next street, two houses down."

Securing the reins to tree branches, they continued on foot.

Around the next corner, on the quiet street, the row of cottages was all dark. Country people retired early to save on candles and fuel.

Dominic slipped into the deep purple shadows beneath the trees. "We'll wait for word from Jack. I sent him to the tavern to keep an eye on Pike."

As he spoke, his footman loomed up beside him, his voice a dramatic whisper. "Our quarry is in the taproom, milord."

"Go back. As soon as he prepares to leave, alert us as quietly and quickly as you can."

"I'm good at bird calls, milord. Owls especially."

Dominic smiled into the dark. "Good. Stay out of Pike's way. He mustn't see you."

"Right, milord." Jack crept away as Dominic placed a cautious hand on the garden gate. Well-oiled, it swung soundlessly open.

Samuels followed him along the path to the front door of the small, half-timbered cottage. Dominic went to check all the windows. Circumnavigating the building, he found them securely locked, the curtains drawn. He returned to the front of the house, where Samuels had opened the door.

They slipped in and closed the door behind them. They were in a small parlor. Dominic took a taper from his pocket and lit it. The faint acrid odor of smoke drifted over the room. Its faint light hidden from outside with the curtains drawn.

Samuels gazed around. "What are we looking for, milord?"

"Money. A lot of it."

They moved about the simply furnished rooms. A cabinet displayed a humble array of china and a bookshelf with a few books. The bedchamber was as spartan as a monk's cell. A narrow bed, a candlestick on a table, and some clothes neatly folded on shelves. A woman's dressing gown smelling of lavender hung on a hook. Mrs. Hobbs?

Dominic checked the mattress, finding rusty springs beneath. He left everything as he found it.

Samuels roamed around, tapping the walls.

As he grew conscious of time running short, Dominic opened the last cupboard. The remains of a meal in a china bowl, bread, a jug of milk, a rind of cheese, and a tub of butter.

As he moved about, a heavy sense of disappointment weighed him down. Had he accused an innocent man? They'd found nothing of interest. No decorative items, only the rug. In the poor light, he had taken little notice of it. He crouched down and ran his hands over it. Silk, woven with rich blues and golds, and completely out of place here. Pike's one concession to luxury?

He flipped up a corner. The floor beneath was of wooden planks. "Help me with this, Samuels."

Together, they rolled up the rug.

Dominic's gaze swept over the floor. Mr. Pike was a neat fellow. Not a speck of dust or dirt. "Bring the taper closer." Samuels pointed. "There."

Pike had cut a square out of the timber.

"Allow me, milord."

Samuels bent down with his burglar's tool and jimmied up a plank. "Milord, have a gander at this!"

His hand on Samuels's shoulder, his pulse racing, Dominic peered into the dark space. A large box filled most of it. A pistol and a large blade tucked beside it.

Samuels pulled out the box. It appeared weighty as he set it on the floor.

Dominic held the taper over it, the light revealing several large sacks. He lifted one out and untied it. Coins, some of them gold sovereigns.

Samuels grunted. "That's a lot of blunt."

"He must have been pilfering from my uncle for years. We'll leave this undisturbed," Dominic said. "Pike would be in the habit of checking it." To do so fit the character of the man.

"Found this at the bottom, milord." Samuels held it out.

His heart skittered. It was a Bank of England banknote, made out for one thousand pounds, signed by his uncle. On the back, Alberic had written Jenner's name, but Pike had crossed it out. "Foolish, Mister Pike," Dominic murmured, fighting the rage flowing through him.

He pocketed the banknote while Samuels tidied everything else away and replaced the lid.

An owl hooted. Twice. Then hooted again.

Dominic grinned. "Jack."

Someone scratched at the door.

Dominic strode across and opened it a crack. "Pike's just left," Jack whispered.

"Right. Go home, Jack."

The rug replaced, they checked everything was as they found it, and left through the back door.

"A good night's work, milord," Samuels said after they'd turned the corner.

"Most satisfying, Samuels," Dominic replied as they mounted. "Thank you for your invaluable help. Your services will be rewarded."

Samuels chuckled. "Enjoyed it, milord. Anytime you want to do it again, I'm your fellow."

Dominic laughed. "I don't foresee it happening again, but I'll certainly bear it in mind."

As the horses cantered toward home, Dominic faced the worry still nagging at him. Unless Pike hid it somewhere else, he did not own a rifle.

⇛⤜⇚

BREAKFAST OVER, THE staff had gone about their duties.

Michael came in with a message as Olivia lingered over her cup of tea in the servants' hall. Redcliffe wished to see her. Now. She put down her teacup. What prompted such urgency and this surprising change in routine? Redcliffe always rode before breakfast.

"Where is Jack?"

"He went on an errand for his lordship."

It was barely eight o'clock. "An errand this early?"

"Jack said he'd be gone for several hours, Miss Jenner."

Olivia entered her office and tidied her hair before the small mirror she kept in the drawer of her desk. She pinched her cheeks before hurrying to the library. She already suspected something was up. Sam had been annoyingly smug this morning. Grinning as he cooked the eggs. And he refused to tell her why.

She knocked and was told to enter.

Redcliffe stood by the window, gazing out, his stance emphasizing his long, lean body. As he turned toward her, her pulse throbbed. She cleared her throat. "You wished to see me?"

His gaze warmed. "Sit down, Olivia."

She took the chair opposite the desk and waited, trying not to reveal her curiosity.

He strolled over to her. "Samuels and I rode into the village last night."

She stared at him. "You and the cook?" Had he lost his mind? She assessed his color for a sign of fever. "Your wound hasn't become infected?"

He cocked an eyebrow. "Ye of little faith." He hitched a hip on the corner of the desk and smiled down at her.

"I thought Sam looked pleased with himself this morning," she said with a perplexed frown. "Are you going to tell me? Why the village? And why in the dead of night?"

Redcliffe laughed. He turned to pick up a piece of paper from the desk and handed it to her.

She stilled. Could it be? It was. Stunned, she turned the banknote over in her trembling fingers. "Where did you find this?"

"In a box hidden beneath Pike's floor."

Her eyes widened. "You broke into his house?"

"Samuels assisted me."

Several emotions flooded through her. Relief, justification for her father, and the end of something which had long held her captive. She might cry if she wasn't so angry, "I can't begin to thank you, Redcliffe. You know how important this is to me." She stared down at the slip of paper in her hands, which meant so much. "I always knew Papa told the truth. He appealed to Sir Frederick Buckley for help, but by the time the magistrate responded, your uncle had died, and Pike denied he knew about it."

He leaned forward and placed a finger beneath her chin, raising her face and searching her eyes. "I expected you to be happy, Olivia."

"I am." She put a hand to her ribcage to still the pounding of her heart. "But I'm angry. And sad."

Sympathy softened his gaze. "Of course, you must be."

She wrapped her arms around herself, trying to rid herself of the painful knot of anger in her stomach. "I want to see Pike pay."

"He will. I've sent for the magistrate."

"I'm sure he'll obey your summons more swiftly than he did my father's."

"The thousand pounds is rightfully yours." He held out his hand for it. "I must show this to the magistrate." His somber green eyes appealed to her. "Am I to lose you now?"

As she handed it back, her breath caught in her throat. "I shall remain here as long as you need me."

"And after that?"

"I hope to buy the haberdashery. And I have a cottage in mind."

"The haberdashery?" His thoughtful gaze held hers until she had to look away. "I doubt you'll be content with that, Olivia. You are a passionate woman. You'll want a man in your life. One who can satisfy all your desires. I want to be that man."

Olivia trembled. Would he ask her to become his mistress? She feared if he continued, the words spoken could never be taken back. She wanted to put her hands over her ears, to not hear their relationship sullied in that manner. She could never agree. If she turned away from her sense of what was right, she would destroy her life. She shoved back the chair. "I must go."

He slid off the desk and put a hand on her arm, his voice low and urgent. "No. Olivia, hear me out."

She pulled away. "There is nothing more to say."

How she longed to give herself to him, to be with him. She would never want another man. Her chest hurt as she hurried to the door and turned to him, her hand on the door latch. "I'll send the magistrate to you when he arrives."

Redcliffe watched her, determination in his eyes. "We must talk about us, Olivia. But I agree, this isn't the right time."

She slowly shook her head and left him. It would never be the right time.

In the corridor, she cast a weak smile at Michael and hurried away. Her stomach churned at the inevitability of her departure, and tears gathered behind her eyes. Reaching the sanctity of her office, she sat down to go over in her mind what had just happened. She'd suspected Redcliffe might take matters out of her hands and act, but never to do this. Such a remarkable man, so brave, resourceful, and endearing. The man of her dreams. But they could never be together, and she must focus on her future. Although the thought of leaving him threatened to break her heart.

She sat shakily down. Her long-held wish for independence was about to come true. She dug in her drawer for her handkerchief and wiped her eyes. As the owner of the haberdashery, Mr. Mockford planned to sell when he retired. A good life awaited her, safe, quiet, and steady. She would purchase the pretty cottage on Ivy Street, which had been empty for two years and needed loving care. How different her life would be. No longer would her emotions soar and plunge at every turn. It would be easier when she didn't see him every day. Then surely, she would cease to long for a man she could not have. Really, she should be excited. She put her hands to her face. But she wasn't. Oh, dear God, she wasn't.

Her emotions were in turmoil, she had to get away from the house for a few hours. She would walk into the village. There was someone she wished to see.

CHAPTER NINETEEN

AFTER OLIVIA LEFT the library, Dominic swore under his breath. His damn impatience. He hadn't intended to raise the question of their future together now. He wandered over to the window and stared sightlessly out. Olivia wasn't ready to hear it. But this wasn't the end. He couldn't give her up. They were meant to be together. He wouldn't feel whole without her.

He'd arrogantly sought her as his mistress, but fortunately for them both, she wouldn't agree to those terms. And he'd cheat himself, too, when he wanted her with him every day and every night. To share his life and bear his children.

But would she agree to marry him? Olivia faced the truth more bravely and honestly than anyone he had known. And he could hear her reasons for refusing him before she uttered the words. Sound ones, too. She must trust him. Believe him to be sincere and not a licentious rake. He didn't believe for a moment that she wished for that half-lived life she sought. It was a compromise fate had forced on her.

Marriage to him would not be peaceful. Some in society wouldn't welcome Olivia as his wife. He'd hate for her to suffer their cool indifference and criticism. He'd been the brunt of a scandal after the print shop window displayed the caricature of him cavorting in a bed with three women. Not everyone would have forgotten the scandal. He'd received the sobriquet of the rakehell earl and had not been society's favorite son when he left London. Marriage to Olivia would stir it all up again. He didn't give a damn about himself. But to see her suffer when the *ton* turned their backs would anger him because it was so unfair.

Not because she lacked refinement, which she possessed in abundance, but because she hadn't been born into an aristocratic family. It was an undeniable fact.

Olivia's grandfather, Judge Alistair Jenner, was a highly regarded, erudite man. The *beau monde* flocked to hear him speak. And not all lords of the realm had impressive histories, many were granted lands and a title by the reigning monarch for political expediency, including a Redcliffe centuries ago. That didn't make them superior to the judge or his granddaughter, although Dominic knew many would disagree.

Thank God for good friends. Charles and Nicholas would stand by him, and he was sure their wonderful, fair-minded spouses would take Olivia under their wing.

He would make Olivia happy. He wanted to see her treated as she deserved. Dressed like the lady she was. All that remained was for her to say yes. They could be married quietly here before facing the uproar in London.

Dominic frowned. As keen as he was to ask her to be his wife, he couldn't. Not while someone conspired to kill him. He would never bring Olivia to the attention of this villain, whoever he is.

Jack knocked on the door, disturbing his thoughts.

"Sir Frederick Buckley said to expect him this afternoon, milord."

Time enough to ride over to see how the Graveses fared. Olivia probably hadn't called on them as she intended. He doubted she'd left the house since he'd been shot.

One day, she would ride beside him. He'd purchase a good mount for her. But how could he make plans when it all seemed so uncertain? He pushed his hair back with agitated fingers, wishing he could be sure of her. But he never gave up on what he wanted and gained confidence in knowing what she could not hide; she wanted him, too.

Was the gunman lurking in the woods waiting for another chance to shoot him? Dominic took his pistol from the drawer and loaded it. He hadn't taken that bridle path since he was shot. Riding alone, if the man lurked there, he would draw him out. He'd be ready for an ambush this time. Tucking the pistol into the waistband of his breeches, he strode to the stables.

In a benevolent mood, Onyx cantered along the path. As Dominic entered the wood, the familiar smells of leaf mold and sun-warmed greenery engulfed him. Birds twittered above, swooping under the forest's lush canopy. The sky had clouded over, but rain seemed far off as the path took him deeper into the densely forested woodland.

The deep potholes which had caused Onyx to stumble had dried up since the last deluge. The horse's rhythmic gait allowed Dominic to search for a sign he wasn't alone.

Nothing but a deer darting away. He clamped down his jaw, impatient to see an end to the threat that hung over his head like the sword of Damocles.

A few hundred yards ahead, a flock of birds erupted into the sky. A fox? He drew his pistol. Had it been overconfident of him to ride alone? The rifleman might wait somewhere ahead, well hidden among the trees. He should retreat and order Fellows to round up a few of the men to flush the devil out, but he might be wrong. And he wasn't about to put anyone at risk. Nor would he run away.

He heard a rustling in the bushes and turned the horse off the bridle path and onto a narrow, less-used path, which gave him more cover.

A flash of movement caught his eye ahead of him. It wasn't a fox. He swung his legs over the saddle and slipped to the ground, then slapped Onyx on the rump.

The horse galloped away.

Dominic's experiences of war guided him. Alert to every sound, he crept forward, eager to face his enemy. "Come out and show yourself."

The answer came swiftly; the shot biting off a piece of tree trunk a few feet above his head. Cursing, Dominic hunched over and changed direction, running toward the attacker.

He kept his head down but must have gotten too close for the gunman's comfort. His assailant gave up his hiding place and sprinted away through the trees. With only one shot left, no doubt he wished to be sure of his mark.

Dominic ran after him, tearing through the bushes and zig-zagging among the tree trunks to make himself less of a target. He had the man in his sights now. A short figure, his hat pulled down over his face. Dominic couldn't see him well enough to identify him. Was it Pike? "Stop! Or I'll shoot."

Partly obscured behind a bush, the gunman swiveled and took aim.

Dominic dropped to one knee and fired.

The man's ball hurtled past Dominic's ear, but his pistol found its mark. With a cry, the gunman slumped to the ground.

Dominic was up and running to where the man lay unmoving among the dead leaves. He fell to his knees beside the prone figure. He'd known. Oh, dear lord, he'd known. Gazing into George's eyes, he saw death approaching. His voice cracked. "Why, George?"

George gasped, fighting for air. "I owe…a lot more than I confessed, Dom. Criminals want their pound of flesh. I needed to disappear. It's this…or something far worse at their hands. Been waiting for you. Knew you rode this way. Didn't want to shoot you…fond of you. Might have known…I couldn't pull it off." He gave a breathy chuckle, and blood trickled down his chin. "Put up at an abysmal inn in the next town," he rasped. "Lice in the sheets. See to my horse, will you, Dom?"

"I will. Don't worry." Dominic untied George's creased neck-cloth and unbuttoned his soiled shirt. No longer the meticulous dandy he prided himself on being. His lifeblood ebbed away from the wound in his chest. "I wish you'd told me the whole truth."

"You wouldn't have wanted to hear how I hired a footpad to kill you...in Grosvenor Square."

A chill ran down Dominic's spine. "Dear God, George, you were behind that?"

"I'm a weak fellow, Dom. ...wanted to live like a king on a pauper's income."

"Did you kill Alberic?"

George clutched his bloody chest and groaned. "Did someone kill old Alberic? Not a bad idea... Too late..."

Dominic watched George's eyes grow blank.

He sat blinking tears away. Then he rose and slowly walked into the trees in search of Onyx and George's horse.

OLIVIA WALKED BACK from the village, mulling over her conversation with her old friend, Meg Turner, at her cottage. Lady Lowry's former housekeeper was yet to take another position, and if his lordship required a housekeeper, she would certainly apply.

She explained how Lady Lowry put her off because she'd stepped in when her employer abused a young footman. "Hateful woman," she said. "In a bad mood, since Lord Redcliffe refused her dinner invitation. Apparently, she had grand plans for him. But you know her, Olivia, how you endured her, I don't know. Needs must, I suppose. I don't regret leaving her employment. As you know, Turner wasn't rich, but he left me enough money to get by. If I live simply, I don't need to work. But I get lonely. And I enjoy the position of housekeeper in a big house. Never a dull moment."

Olivia smiled, so pleased to see her again. "Then I have something to ask of you."

Meg raised her reddish eyebrows. "Certainly. Anything."

⇥⟫⟩⟨⟨⇤

WHEN OLIVIA REACHED the end of the avenue of trees, she gazed at the old house, the stone walls bathed in golden, honeyed light. She wished she could embrace the future with joy and certainty, but her limbs were lead-like. As she walked along the drive to enter through the servants' door, Redcliffe emerged from the trees on horseback. As he rode closer, she saw the splash of crimson blood on his gloves and coat. Panic gripped her like a steel trap. She shouted out his name and broke into a run, her breath shortening with fear.

His shoulders drooped as he reined in beside her.

She studied his face for signs of pain and only saw sorrow. "Are you hurt?"

He shook his head as he dismounted. "Walk with me a little way, Olivia. I have something to tell you."

He led Onyx by the rein while they continued to the stables. Something awful had happened. She waited for him to speak.

"George Yardley was the gunman. He's dead."

"Mr. Yardley?" She caught her breath, not sure what to say. Yardley had been a relative. Redcliffe's good friend. How that must hurt him. "But why?"

"My death would give him the earldom. He was in desperate straits."

Growing increasingly horrified, she listened as he explained what had occurred in a flat, emotionless tone. Weak with relief that Redcliffe wasn't hurt, she longed to put her arms around him and hug him to her. She held herself back. He was shocked and saddened by Yardley's betrayal and needed time to himself.

She felt no sympathy for George Yardley. She hadn't liked him. And what he'd tried to do was unforgivable. It could have been Redcliffe lying dead in the woods. The thought made her tremble. Tears sprang to her eyes.

Redcliffe's sad eyes met hers. "I didn't have a clear view. After his first shot came so close, I couldn't let him have another crack at me. Hoped to wing him." He glanced at her and saw the tears in his eyes. "I didn't want to believe it could be George. Wouldn't have shot him had I known." Redcliffe dragged in a shuddering breath. "After the war, I was determined never to kill another soul."

She understood. Men had returned to the village after the war, carrying wounds in their hearts and minds apart from bodily injuries. Redcliffe's experience of conflict would be no different. "You didn't have a choice," she said passionately.

"Didn't I?" he asked bitterly.

"I'm sorry," she whispered. She moved closer and slipped her arms around his waist.

When he pulled her against him, she rested her head against his chest with a soft sob.

They stood silently as she tried to convey her sorrow for him without words.

Onyx's snuffling nose nudged her hair.

She started, then with a half-laugh moved away.

"He's impatient for his feed bag," Redcliffe said. Did the pain in his eyes ease a little? Or did she merely wish it had?

They walked silently on.

After a moment, she turned to him, sensing he wished to be alone. "Shall I leave you, Redcliffe?"

His shoulders lifted in a deep sigh. "I must see to the body and George's horse. The magistrate will arrive soon. I'll inform him about George, as well as Pike and Mrs. Hobbs. Go to the house, Olivia. I'll be along shortly."

He sounded so desperately sad. Not at all like the man she knew. Her eyes blurred with tears as she watched him walk away, then she turned back toward the house.

CHAPTER TWENTY

O N HIS WAY back to the house, having sent a groom for George's horse, Dominic thought about Olivia. How her eyes filled with compassion. How good it felt to hold her in his arms. He could feel the warmth of her tears through his shirt and was humbled that she shared his grief.

Walking through the door, he steeled himself to meet the magistrate, Sir Frederick Buckley.

Buckley arrived not long after Dominic returned to the library. Over a glass of wine, Dominic told him about George as calmly as he could.

Dominic doubted much shocked Buckley, but this clearly had.

"What a devil! I'm relieved it's all over, my lord. It's hard to believe, a cousin, you say?"

Dominic tightened his jaw and handed him the banknote.

The magistrate turned it over in his hands, noted the writing on the back, then placed it on the table. "We have Pike in custody. The constable is arresting Mrs. Hobbs as we speak. Acting on the letter your footman brought me, we broke into Pike's house and had no trouble discovering the box beneath the floor." Sir Frederick raised his bushy, fair eyebrows and shook his head. "Several thousand were stashed there. A tidy sum if you include this." He nodded toward the banknote. "I am deeply sorry I failed the old earl."

"It's possible Pike murdered him and has been searching for my uncle's money ever since," Dominic said. "But you'll never get him to admit it."

Sir Frederick's gray eyes hardened. "We'll get to the truth. We'll hold him and Mrs. Hobbs in the jail at Gateshead. If you and Mr. Samuels can ride over and make a statement, I'd appreciate it."

"I'll come tomorrow. I want to question them."

"Certainly. And an inquest into Mr. Yardley's death will be held in the inn forecourt in the next few weeks. But I don't foresee any problems."

"I want George to have a decent burial," Dominic said. "I'll arrange it with the vicar."

The magistrate's eyes widened, then he nodded. "Very good, my lord."

After Sir Frederick left, Dominic walked through the house to the rear and watched the constable push Mrs. Hobbs into his wagon. The woman screeched and punched at him with her fists. She managed to kick him hard in the shin before he bundled her inside. The wagon trundled away.

She could prove Pike's weakness, Dominic thought, as he entered the kitchen to speak to Samuels.

"Well, we did it, Samuels," he said when the cook greeted him.

"Yes, milord. Saw the constable drag the harridan away," Samuels said, chuckling. "A pretty sight indeed. She demanded to know what they'd done with her husband."

"She and Pike are married?"

"Not in a church of Our Lord, is my guess."

Dominic agreed. He doubted it would suit Pike's plans to have a wife, for there was little sign of Mrs. Hobbs inhabiting his cottage, only her dressing gown. "She let Pike into the house. Good thing we got him before he broke in again. He is a violent man."

Samuels rubbed his bristly chin. "Yes, that was a vicious blow to poor Jack's head."

"I'll drive to Gateshead tomorrow to give them a statement. We'll leave after breakfast."

"Right, my lord."

Dominic went in search of Olivia, but she wasn't in the housekeeper's room. As he returned upstairs, he thought about what Samuels had said. Pike was certainly capable of striking Alberic down, as he did Jack. The question returned to plague him. What was Uncle Alberic doing on the kitchen stairs? Had he hidden something somewhere on the upper floors? Olivia and he had searched the attic, but perhaps not as thoroughly as they should have. Being alone with her was distracting. Where was she? Now it was done and George's body taken to the church, he desperately wished for the comfort of her arms.

Returning to his desk, he sifted through his neglected mail. Alberic's letter, addressed to Dominic's mother, had arrived from Evelyn at last. With his heart thudding, he tore it open.

To my future heir, Alberic wrote. *I understand that if the fates decree, in this uncertain world, it will be you, Dominic, my brother's son. I'm sorry we never met. My culpability and guilt kept me away from my brother and his family, for which I am deeply sorry. But you are Michael's son, and I'm sure of sterling character.*

Welcome to Redcliffe Hall.

My health declines and therefore when you read this, I'll likely be dead. If that doesn't kill me, the man who stalks me will. I could bring in men to guard me, but I have no stomach for it. And no will to live.

The one thing that sustains me is the hope you will restore Redcliffe Hall to its former glory. Impossible for me, now. Since my accident, I fear I'm losing my wits. But not so much that I don't know I'm shadowed by a villain intent on robbing me. Since my steward left, I've heard noises in the house. Someone searches for my money. I've hidden it well. He'll never find it.

Even if he threatens to kill me, I'll never give up my secret. But I have to be careful. The magistrate came to see me, but I knew he thought I was out of my mind. Perhaps I am. I know I paid Jenner for the horses, and yet he swears I didn't. I liked the man. Could he be lying? I can't remember. My memory lets me down these days. Pike assured me I did.

Matters have worsened. Most of my servants have left. But I don't care. I no longer need people fussing around me.

You have lost your father, Dominic. It saddened me when the news of Michael's death reached me. You are in the army somewhere, so I've addressed this letter to your mother. I'm confident you will receive it. Know that long ago, I fell in love with a woman I had no right to. My peerless wife, Elizabeth. And using my position as earl, I married her, robbing your father of her love. She came willingly but never loved me as she had him. As I never stopped loving her, it is my penance for committing such a cruel act.

I may die before we meet, so must note down where I've hidden my valuables. I fear I will forget. There's a false section behind a drawer in a desk in the attic. The heavily carved oak with the damaged leg. You'll find what earthly goods I have to offer you there. Your father would know of it, of course, but he is gone.

I wish you well and hope that you will come to love Redcliffe Hall and appreciate its beauty. This is God's own earth, the loveliest county in England, and I wish you peace here, a good marriage, children, and great prosperity.

Alberic.

Dominic sat with his head in his hands as the past washed over him. If only the brothers had mended their rift. Alberic had never known how happy his mother and father were.

The letter left him heavy-hearted. He wanted to tell Olivia. They could discover whatever was hidden inside the desk together. He finally shook his head to clear his thoughts and rang for Jack.

"Where is Miss Jenner?" he asked when the footman came in.

"She has taken the trap to the Graves' farm."

"The Graves'?" A gnawing physical ache filled his chest. "Why now?"

"She wishes to give some books to Mrs. Graves."

Why the urgency? Didn't she know he needed her? After Jack left, Dominic prowled the library carpet, rubbing the back of his neck. Was he wrong to think she loved him? Damn it, he wouldn't run after her like a besotted puppy.

MARY HAD BEEN glad of the books and voiced the hope Olivia would return soon to discuss them. Olivia held their sweet baby in her arms and kissed the smooth cheek, then said her goodbyes. She didn't know when she would see Mary again but wanted her to have the books in case it was not for a long time.

She drove the trap home in the gathering dusk. How upset Redcliffe had been by Yardley's betrayal and death. And how desperately she longed to hold him and ease his suffering. She entered through the kitchen, where Sam gave her a colorful description of what had occurred when the parish constable took Mrs. Hobbs away.

"I never trusted that woman."

"She was a one, all right," Sam said. "His lordship and I will be off to Gateshead tomorrow to give our statements."

"You have missed your calling, Sam," she said with a smile. "You should have been a spy for the crown."

His chuckle followed her into the corridor.

It was difficult, but Olivia resisted going to the library to see Redcliffe. She kept busy until supper and retired early to her bedchamber. Her decision made, she tried to still the nerves fluttering in her stomach as she poured the water Jack had brought up for her into the hip bath.

Hours later, when the moon was high in the sky, she emerged from her room in her apricot gown. The house was quiet, the servants all in bed, except for the footman who would be on duty at the door. Holding her candlestick, she crept past the maids' bedchambers and made her way to the family wing.

Had Redcliffe retired or would he still be in the library? Jack had told her he sometimes stayed there until very late.

She hesitated at his bedchamber door. Could she leave him after this? She knocked.

"Enter."

Her heart fluttering, she stepped into the room.

Dressed in a banyan, shirt, and breeches, Redcliffe sat in a wing chair to one side of the fireplace, a candelabra beside him on the table. He held a letter in his hand. His eyes widened, and he came to his feet. "Olivia."

She closed the door. "Redcliffe." Her voice was a mere whisper, her throat tight with nerves. While she didn't doubt he wanted her, she was unsure of his mood, studying his expression. His seductive smile weakened her knees as he crossed the sumptuous bedchamber to her. Her candlestick wobbled violently in her hands.

He took it from her and placed it on the table, then pulled her gently against him, curving his arm around her waist. "My love."

She leaned her head against his chest and sighed. How could something which seemed so right be wrong? She would carry the memory of this night with him for the rest of her life. It would sustain her through her loneliness, for she would never marry.

They stood together, her body pressed against his, tucked beneath his chin. No explanation was necessary. Not now. Not ever. She would not tell him what she planned, because he would try to prevent her. His will would envelop her, impel her, and he'd never let her go. She was as weak as rushes in a flooded river where Redcliffe was concerned.

Her heart beating fast, she gazed up at him. "Kiss me, Redcliffe. Make love to me."

His breath stirred the hair near her ear. *"Darling,"* he murmured, his voice a long sigh. A finger beneath her chin, he claimed her mouth in a searing kiss. His hand low on her back settled her against him, and she could feel his desire for her as he angled his head and kissed her again. With a low groan, he pressed his tongue past her lips to touch hers.

Giddy, her senses filled with him, Olivia grasped the silk of his banyan as he trailed kisses down her neck. His quick fingers undid the hooks on her gown, and the material pooled at her feet, leaving her in her chemise and stockings.

Shaky with desire, she stepped out of it.

His hands cupped her breasts, and he bent and touched a nipple with his tongue through the thin cotton, sending a sharp urgency to her nether regions, making her warm and damp. Her hands swept over the expanse of his back, longing to touch his naked skin beneath the clothes. She had never expected to feel like this. Unquenched desire welled up inside her. Wanting him.

"Are you sure, darling?" His voice was low and urgent.

Bereft of words, she nodded.

He lifted her into his arms and carried her to the bed.

CHAPTER TWENTY-ONE

S TRETCHED OUT BESIDE Olivia, Dominic eased away a damp curl from her cheek. She slept deeply and didn't stir. In repose, her firm jaw softened, her mouth tender and vulnerable. He remembered her passionate, deep kisses. Her soft breasts were perfect in his hands, and he wanted to press his mouth there. How difficult to be so close and not rouse her with a kiss. But observing the dark shadows beneath her eyes, and her face, finely drawn, which hinted at strain, he resisted.

She murmured something and her dark lashes fluttered against her cheeks. His body stirred, wanting her. He wouldn't wake her, although he must before dawn. Sated and drowsy, they had talked late into the night. He'd told her how he had earned the title of the rakehell earl in London. He smiled. Outraged on his behalf, she showed no inclination to disbelieve his version of events, whereas some women might question it. But she'd come to know him, which few women had a chance to do. He'd never allowed them to get close enough.

When he confessed his love for her and his intention for them to marry, she'd fallen silent. She'd touched his cheek, he remembered, and her eyes became shadowed. She didn't argue, but nor did she agree. He would convince her.

Olivia fell asleep in his arms before he told her about his uncle's letter. But no matter, he would when she woke. They would search together for the money and make their plans. Right now, the only thing that did matter was the two of them, here, together. He felt as if his life had only just begun. More confident in their future, he didn't want to dwell on anything else. Not now. Only the two of them cocooned in his bed, rain pattering against the window. He closed his eyes.

DOMINIC WOKE. HE'D fallen into the deepest sleep he'd had for weeks. He turned in bed. She had gone. Smiling, he breathed in Olivia's perfume, blended with the heady scent of sex, then threw back the covers and rose to open the curtains. The sun's fragile early morning rays appeared over a band of distant trees. He rang for his valet to bring hot water. He would tell Olivia the news before he left for Gateshead.

When he came downstairs, she was busy in the servants' hall. He smiled a welcome and received a polite smile in return. In her office, he tucked a check for one thousand pounds beneath the inkpot on her desk, then went to eat his breakfast.

When he returned, she'd gone somewhere. Frustrated, he realized his news would have to keep until he returned from Gateshead.

Samuels awaited him at the stables. Dominic drove the phaeton through the gates and out onto the road. He intended to return by midafternoon, which would give him and Olivia an hour to search for Alberic's stash before her duties claimed her.

He and Samuels reached the Gateshead jail at midday. Inside, a sour-looking Pike sat beside the scowling Mrs. Hobbs.

While the constable stood, arms folded, Dominic took a seat opposite them at the table. He observed the couple, wondering how best to provoke one of them into an admission of guilt. Mrs. Hobbs seemed the best choice. He directed his question to her.

"You are married to Mr. Pike?"

Hilda Hobbs's shrill assertion trumped Pike's emphatic denial.

Pike stared coldly ahead. "As if I would marry a laundry maid. My father was a vicar. She is beneath me."

"Ow!" She turned to him, her hands forming fists. If she hadn't been shackled, she would have hit him. "We've been as man and wife since Hobbs died. I should never have agreed to your demands to keep it secret."

Pike glared at her. "She's lying."

Dominic nodded to Pike. "Why did you meet Mrs. Hobbs in the gardens at Redcliffe Hall?"

Pike's eyes narrowed. It transformed his face, reminding Dominic of a trapped animal. "Who says I did?"

"My gardener."

"I don't know the gardener. So how would he know me? And why would I come to see this woman?"

"You let Pike into the house that night, didn't you Mrs. Hobbs?" Not waiting for her answer, Dominic's gaze swiveled to Pike. "And you planned to try again. You struck my footman."

He shrugged. "Not I."

"It was him." Fury darkened Mrs. Hobbs's eyes. "Forced me to help him. I didn't want to. Don't accuse me of nothing else. It's the truth. I'll swear on the Bible. I won't swing at the end of a gallows rope for murder. Not for such as him."

Pike turned on her. "Be quiet, you fool."

"Call me a fool, do you? I'll not go down with you." Her panicked gaze caught Dominic's. "Pike killed the old earl. Hit him on the head when he refused to tell him where he'd hidden his money. Pike's been trying to find it ever since."

"That's an outrageous lie!" Pike said. "You'd best shut your mouth."

Mrs. Hobbs would not be silenced. She gathered herself together, eager to tell all. "Pike found the earl in his bed in the butler's pantry. He dragged him out and forced him to take him to the hiding place. He told me the old man broke free and ran up the stairs. Pike went after him and struck him down."

Dominic felt rage rise like gall in his throat. It was all he could do not to lean across the table and seize the smug killer by his collar and throttle him.

Before he gave in to the impulse, he rose and left the room.

He joined Sir Frederick for coffee in the office. "That was nicely done, my lord."

Dominic put down his cup. The result gave him no pleasure. To think of Alberic suffering the way he had. "Samuels and I will be on our way. I shall be here for the trial if you consider it necessary."

"With Mrs. Hobbs as a witness, I shouldn't think so."

When Dominic arrived back at Redcliffe Hall, he still couldn't find Olivia. Apart from the vase of delphiniums, her office looked oddly impersonal. Then he realized everything of hers had gone. The desk cleared, the shelves tidied. Uneasy, he searched the house for her. Then, his apprehension increasing, he ventured up to her chamber. In the small room, the wardrobe and drawers were empty. The bed was stripped. There was nothing left. She had gone.

He dropped onto the narrow mattress as distress warred with anger and then became a grim realization. Olivia had always intended to do this. She didn't trust him to take care of her. She still believed he wanted her as his mistress. He should have forced her to listen. But he thought they had all the time in the world.

When he rushed downstairs intending to ask Samuels if she had told him where she was going, Jack advised him of a visitor.

"Who is it?" he asked abstractedly.

"A Mrs. Turner."

He scowled. He didn't know the woman. "What does she want?"

"Said she is applying for the position of housekeeper, milord. Worked for Lord Willowbrook and has excellent references. She would have spoken first to Mr. Williams, but he's away."

"Housekeeper? What has brought her here?" Ah. He knew.

Of course. Olivia's plan. He drew in a sharp breath to ease his tight chest. Where was she?

He strode out to Mrs. Turner, hoping that if she knew, she would tell him.

A red-haired woman in her mid-forties with a broad, pleasant face rose from the chair in the entry and curtsied. "My lord."

"Come to the library, please, Mrs. Turner."

She handed him her references, then at his invitation, seated herself on the sofa, her gloved hands together in her lap.

He gave the letters a cursory glance. Olivia had chosen her, so he knew the woman would be efficient. She certainly had that look about her. "Miss Jenner arranged this," he said flatly.

"Yes, my lord."

"Where is she?"

"I am not at liberty to say. Please forgive me. I gave my word."

"You are a friend of Miss Jenner's?"

"I am, sir."

"Is she all right?"

"I believe so."

He sighed and sat back in his chair, observing her. "You seem well qualified. I expect my estate manager, Mr. Williams, to return tomorrow. See him. He'll introduce you to the staff and show you how things are done."

She beamed. "Thank you for your faith in me."

"You have yet to earn it, Mrs. Turner." He strode to the door and opened it. "But if Miss Jenner thought you'd do, I expect you will."

After she left, he turned back into the room. If Olivia expected him to let her go without giving him a chance to explain himself, she was mistaken. Their night together had only deepened his desire for them to marry, because he was in no doubt she loved him despite his faults. And marry her, he would.

First, he had to find her. She would not have gone far. She had told him she intended to remain in the village. But devil take it, he didn't know any of her friends. Olivia had no relatives. But he expected in this small community, he would find her soon enough. Although that was only part of the problem. To persuade her to marry him would require some finesse. Something that was inclined to desert him when impatience got the better of him.

BEYOND THE WINDOW, mist drifted through trees, some branches bare of leaves, turning what would ordinarily be a pleasing view into one bleached of color.

In the comfortable parlor, a fire burned in the grate. Olivia sipped her tea. Opposite her, Helen Caldicott, Meg Turner's sister, smiled warmly at her. They were good friends before Olivia's father died. When she had time for such friendships. And good friends remained so, even if one didn't see them for a while. It was wonderful to see her again. She wished she were better company.

Helen's eyes softened. "I will not ask you what happened, but if you wish to tell me, I'm here."

"Thank you, Helen. I'm grateful you understand. You and Meg have been so very kind." Would she ever feel herself again? It felt as if her soul had been ripped away and left her hollow. Redcliffe! What was he doing, thinking now? Did he hate her? She would rather that than for him to be miserable. Her heart ached for him. She longed to be in his arms. He might understand her reasons. She hoped he did. Would he come after her? She hoped not. If he did, she must remain strong.

How hard it had been to leave him after their night together. He'd been a passionate and skillful lover. When he brought up the subject of their marriage, her heart almost stopped beating. To marry him was an impossible dream. As his wife, she would cause him too much distress. She'd damage him in society's eyes.

And she saw how the lies spread about him in London had hurt him. Impossible! Her shoulders lifted in a deep sigh.

"What happened has left you bereft. I am sorry," Helen said sincerely.

Olivia nodded and bowed her head over her teacup.

"I hope the earl didn't mistreat you," Helen ventured.

Olivia shook her head. "I fell in love with him."

"Oh no. It would not be difficult to do, I grant you. I saw him in the village. But you were wise to leave Redcliffe Hall." Helen reached across and patted her hand. "Once you have your life in order, Olivia, all will be well."

"Yes. All will be well," Olivia echoed. Now she had the money, she must begin her new life. Buy the cottage and speak to Mr. Mockford about the haberdashery.

When Helen left the room, Olivia stared into the distance beyond the window. Exhausted, she wanted to curl up and sleep and push the world away, but impossible to banish Redcliffe from her mind. Was there nothing in his nature she disapproved of? She even liked his restless energy. The way he frowned and strode about and wanted to change the world. The soldier in him, the little boy. His vulnerability. He'd been hurt. Could still be hurt, although he tried to hide it. His body, tall and lean, his skin, the scars telling a story of his life, the one on his arm she knew was a war wound, the crescent-shaped one from the recent gunshot. A few others he declined to explain. A body well used.

She closed her eyes, remembering. How he'd made her feel. He'd gazed down at her after their breathing slowed, and lightly stroked her flushed breast, toying with a nipple, sending another flurry of sensations through her and drawing a mew of pleasure. "Did I hurt you?"

"No."

He lifted the damp strands of her hair away from her cheek. "No?"

"A little," she confessed. But it had vanished all too quickly in love's heady dance.

"Have you ever been in love?" she'd asked him. Thirsting to know all about him while she had a chance.

He'd kissed her lips to silence her. "The past doesn't matter. Only the future. You are my first and my only love."

Enough! Olivia closed her eyes as a tear escaped. "Goodbye, my love," she whispered into the quiet room.

CHAPTER TWENTY-TWO

DOMINIC GLANCED AT the mail spread across his desk. Joseph Grant, the new secretary, would arrive today. He gave up his attempt to create order and pushed himself away from his desk. The urge to go to Olivia made it difficult to concentrate on anything else. But he considered it wise to leave her alone for a day or so. Not to rush her. While he thought of the right way to approach her. Not go off half-cocked as he was wont to do, but remain calm. But the way to appeal to her so far eluded him. Declaring his love wouldn't work. Olivia knew how he felt.

Did the prospect of becoming a countess frighten her? Any woman not brought up for such a position in society would be understandably nervous. But they would not intimidate someone as determined as Olivia for long. Not once the hue and cry settled down. What concerned her most was how it would affect him. He groaned. Didn't she know he no longer gave a tinker's damn what society thought? His staunch friends would stick by him. And they would come to love her. He folded his arms, a little easier in his mind. This would form the substance of his argument.

Through the library window, Dominic spied a man walking up the path. Grant had arrived. Casting a relieved glance at the demanding correspondence awaiting his new secretary, Dominic rose to welcome him.

In the library, Grant hurried to shake his hand. "My lord. It is a pleasure to meet you."

"You walked from the village?" Dominic motioned to a chair.

"Yes, I came by the stage."

"Coffee? We have much to discuss. Or would you prefer to settle in first?"

A slender man with a pale, scholarly face, Grant keenly eyed the library. "Coffee, thank you. I am eager to begin."

"Excellent." Dominic went to pull the bell.

When he finally escaped from the library, leaving Grant to settle in, he rode out along the river to see the Johnsons' new barn. Mist rose off the water to drift through the trees, and the birds chirped around him. The beauty of this land tugged at his heart, but his spirits failed to rise. Where was she? Tomorrow, he would leave Grant to deal with a few matters while he searched for Olivia. He wouldn't face another sunset without knowing where she was and if she was safe and well.

An hour later, he returned from the Johnsons' to find Grant wading through correspondence with commendable speed.

Williams joined Dominic for luncheon in the dining room. They sat together at one end of the polished cedar table, long enough to seat over three dozen people.

"Are you pleased with Grant?"

"I am. A sober man, but personable. We'll get on."

"Excellent." Williams eyed him. "I hear I've missed quite a lot while I was in London."

Dominic carved off a slice from the joint of cold beef. "Yes, you have. I shall tell you all about it after we've eaten. Otherwise, it will spoil your appetite."

OLIVIA WOKE, HER temples throbbing. She attempted to sit up to leave her bed but fell back woozily. Laying her head gratefully on the pillow, she closed her eyes.

A cool hand lay on her forehead. "Olivia."

She opened her eyes. "Helen, I'm sorry. I must have drifted off."

"You aren't well. You've been asleep for most of the day. I've been worried. I called Dr. Manners."

Olivia gasped. "Oh, no, Helen. What a dreadful nuisance I am."

"Don't be silly. Of course, you aren't. It is lovely to have you here. Ever since Mother died, I long for good company. But we must get you well."

A tap on the door and the maid showed Dr. Manners in.

"Well, Miss Jenner. It is not like you to be ill." He checked the rate of her pulse. "Mm. Open your mouth."

"I'm only a little tired, Doctor," she said when she could speak. "I don't need to stay in bed." Tears gathered behind her eyes. *She must see about the haberdashery. Mr. Mockford might sell it. And she couldn't be a burden on Helen.*

"A slight fever, nothing too concerning." The doctor shut his bag. "Give Miss Jenner feverfew for her headache and any aches and pains, and plenty of liquids, Miss Caldicot. I don't expect Miss Jenner's condition to worsen, but should it do so, send for me."

He bent over Olivia. "You'll be all right after a few days of rest, Miss Jenner."

"Thank you, Doctor Manners." Olivia felt so feeble. *She must get up. She would tomorrow.*

The door shut behind them. Grateful to be alone, she closed her eyes.

Long fingers of the setting sun crept across the carpet, alighting on a dainty, chintz-covered chair as dusk approached. Had she slept for hours? Olivia remembered sipping a hot drink and falling asleep again soon after. Helen attended her assiduously. She would always be grateful to her friend. How tired she was still. But she must get up tomorrow.

⫸⫷

THE DOOR OPENED and Helen came in. She drew up the chair beside her. "Good morning. Would you like some breakfast?"

"Yes, please. I'm quite hungry."

"I can see the rest has done you some good, especially if you can eat a little breakfast. Perhaps some porridge and a coddled egg? I'll bring books and periodicals for you to read. You shall have to rest quietly in bed for today."

"I thought about getting up."

"But the doctor said you need rest."

"I'm feeling better. I don't like to be a nuisance."

Helen shook her head. "None of that. I'll fetch your breakfast. Meg will come to see you when she has a free moment and bring you news. She's taken up her position at Redcliffe Hall. Meg was concerned about you yesterday. She believes you suffer from exhaustion and a broken heart."

Olivia smiled. "Dear Meg." She thirsted for news of Redcliffe.

"I hope she doesn't mention your illness to his lordship," Helen said.

Olivia gasped. "Oh, no. She mustn't!"

"Meg is very levelheaded. I expect she'll wait to hear how you are."

"I hope so." Olivia's throat grew tight. Redcliffe would come here prepared to argue. And she wasn't herself. How could she resist him?

Helen rose. "Now, some breakfast."

After they brought a tray, Olivia picked at her food, trying to make a good meal of it, but at the thought of Redcliffe storming in and demanding to see her, her appetite fled. She flicked through the reading material Helen gave her, but nothing held her attention. By luncheon, she felt a little better but still tired. What was wrong with her? She'd always been so strong, facing adversity full-on and not letting anything bear her down. She wiped a tear from her cheek. The malaise had made her weak, but she would return to her old self soon.

The front doorbell rang with an imperious clang. Olivia tensed. Below, a deep voice. Helen's light voice in reply. A few minutes later, a heavy tread came fast up the stairs.

The door opened, and Redcliffe strode in, his face creased with worry. He strode to the bed. "My love. You are ill."

She tried to frown but was so happy to see him she couldn't hide a smile. "You must not call me that. It is entirely improper. I am not ill. I was merely overtired. I'm much better today." She noticed the strain in his eyes. "How did you find me?"

"I questioned Mrs. Turner."

"I hope you didn't interrogate her, Redcliffe. Poor Meg."

He smiled. "You are coming home with me."

"It is not my home. You have a housekeeper."

"As my fiancée, and soon to be my wife."

"I cannot marry you. Please, let's not argue."

He moved onto the side of the bed and enveloped her hand in his. "I never argue."

"You do. And you keep on until you get your way," she reminded him with an unashamedly fond smile. His proximity affected her so deeply, she feared she'd lose her resolve. She tried to remove her hand, but he threaded his fingers through hers. "It cannot be. You must go. Maids gossip. This will spread all over the village. I shan't be able to hold my head up. Or buy the haberdashery."

"Damn the haberdashery."

"And now you are cursing. Can it get any worse?"

"A good deal worse if you were not ill." His heated, demanding green gaze held hers, reminding her of their last night together and robbing her of breath. "Has Manners been to see you?"

"Yes. He said it's nothing. I'm only a little tired. Really, Redcliffe, you should not be here. It can do no good."

"Am I to list all the reasons we should marry? Some would

make a maid's hair curl. Should she be listening."

Distracted by the image he presented, she flushed and glanced at the door. "You might call them reasons. I am familiar with your forceful arguments."

He arched an amused eyebrow. "Arguments or reasoning are of no use now, Olivia. It's a fait accompli. We need each other. I am certainly no good without you."

How she loved him. Her lips trembled as she tried to hide her need for him. She shook her head. "It's because I care about you I must refuse you. I am not a gently reared young woman." She frowned. "I might have had a dozen lovers before we met."

He laughed, then he sobered and raised her hand, kissing her fingers. "I was your first lover, Olivia. And I intend to be your last."

She met his passionate gaze, remembering, and sagged against him. "One might hope for civility and good manners from local society, but it will not be so in London. The slights you would receive! I will not see you hurt because of me."

"You're wrong, darling. Together, we are strong. Nothing can hurt us."

"You won't feel comfortable there. And you should. It is your right. You are an earl."

His lips lifted in an ironic smile. "Even ramshackle earls like me have a certain standing in the *ton*, my love. My friends move in royal circles. What they say and do is aped by many. And they will support us."

She reached up and tidied away a lock of his hair, which had boyishly fallen onto his forehead when he leaned toward her. "Are you so sure, Redcliffe? I've been a housekeeper. *Your* housekeeper."

"You are a squire's daughter. A chief landowner in the county. And what of it? My friends will love you."

"The beau monde will not."

"In time, they will."

"No... Redcliffe... I cannot fit in with your world. I'm not sure I'd even want to."

"Darling, I'll be there with you. We'll spend most of the year here if you wish."

"The villagers..."

"Hang the villagers. I want you, Olivia. I've decided you shall be my wife."

Olivia smiled weakly. "And you always get what you want, is that not so?" She was losing the argument. She had known she would when he walked through the door with that determined stride. Heaven help them. She had no fight left in her.

"Not always," he said, feigning hurt. "But in this, I am determined to succeed."

"Redcliffe, when you decide on something..."

He cupped her head between his hands. "You love me. Don't deny it."

"I do." Olivia drew a shaky breath before his mouth came down on hers, warming her to her toes. She broke away quickly and pushed him back. "Enough. You must go. What will everyone think?"

"Their thoughts will be far more interesting than what has occurred. I intend to rectify that when you are well."

She frowned, despite the thrill of his promise. "Not until we are married."

Redcliffe's gaze swept over her face. "Then it must be as soon as you are well." He sobered. "You promise to marry me, Olivia?"

She sighed. "Yes, Redcliffe. Now, will you please go?"

He smiled and kissed her nose. "I'll return this afternoon to see how you are after I've spoken to the vicar."

When he'd gone, she realized she hadn't asked him about Pike and Mrs. Hobbs, and Sam, in whom she hadn't confided, because she didn't want to burden him with a secret, and oh, everything she'd left at Redcliffe Hall. It had felt like cutting off a limb. The house was so much a part of her now. Although Meg would see to the servants' welfare, she couldn't easily relinquish her role. She lay back on the pillow, fatigued, but more pleasantly so, as Helen came in.

"Well. His lordship is indeed a force to be reckoned with."

"He is," Olivia said weakly.

"I gather you resolved your differences?"

"Helen." She laughed. "I've agreed to marry him."

Helen's brown eyes widened as she slipped into the chair beside the bed. "You have?" She buried her surprise with a delighted smile. "He obviously adores you, Olivia. I confess to being a little envious. I can see you'll be happy together."

"Lord only knows what will happen once our marriage has been announced in the London newspapers," Olivia said.

"People get over things quickly, I find."

"I hope you're right. A countess has many duties to perform. I fear I'll be out of my depth."

Helen shook her head. "In that, my dear? I am confident you will excel at the role."

"You are such a good friend. I am blessed to have you and Meg."

"We have missed seeing you since...well, working for Lady Lowry made it impossible. I wonder what the horrible woman will have to say."

"I can imagine." Olivia's spirits drooped. Then she told herself nothing would spoil her wedding day. "Will you be my attendant? I shall also ask Meg."

"We'd love to. Will you have time to have a gown made?"

"Knowing Redcliffe, I doubt it." Olivia bit her lip and put a hand to her spinning head. "I shall have to purchase a ready-made gown."

"Oh, what a shame. I might have something in my wardrobe. When Papa lived, we attended many functions. You and I are about the same size, although I'm shorter. My seamstress can let down the hem. I recall a lovely blue silk. Shall I fetch it?"

"Oh, please do, Helen. It would be perfect."

After Helen left the room, Olivia pushed back the covers and left the bed. She felt so much better as she walked to the window.

The sky was the color of delphiniums. How poetic of Redcliffe. Her eyes weren't that shade of blue. She smiled and shook her head, then she thought of what lay ahead and covered her face with her hands.

Helen came in. "Are you all right?" She smiled. "Oh, you're up. That is a good sign."

"Yes, I feel so much better. I'm eager to get on with things."

Ready to tackle the world? She shivered with excitement and a heavy dose of trepidation.

CHAPTER TWENTY-THREE

I N THE MORNING, Dominic spent an hour with his secretary, dealing with urgent matters, then rode to Miss Caldicot's home, a stone country mansion on fifty acres, several miles beyond the outskirts of the village. Did Miss Caldicot live here alone? A place this size, it would not be easy. She must be the capable sort.

Leaving Onyx with a groom at the stables, he strolled through the gardens to the front porch, flanked by Doric columns.

Miss Caldicot greeted him in the entry hall.

His fingers curled around the brim of his beaver. "How is the patient today?"

"Olivia improves daily, my lord. She awaits you in the parlor."

Relief washed over him when he found Olivia dressed and seated on the sofa. Her face was a better color. Her irresistible welcoming smile teased a dimple from her cheek.

"Should you be out of bed?"

"I'm much better. And I can hardly receive you again in my bedchamber."

Dominic chuckled at her look of reproof and sat on the sofa beside her. "I've spoken to the vicar. We can be married in a sennight. I can get a special license from the bishop in York, but I must go to London to attend to a few matters. It will give you time to regain your health."

Her gaze searched his. "My goodness. There is a lot to organize."

"It must be a simple wedding, my love. Unless you'd prefer to wait and be married in London?"

Her eyes widened.

⇶⇇

OLIVIA FROZE AT the frightening possibility of a grand wedding in St. Paul's with royalty in attendance. She drew in a relieved breath when Redcliffe appeared as reluctant as she was. "A wedding in the village church will be perfect," she said. "Helen and Meg have promised to be my attendants."

"I've written to invite Charles and Nicholas. Although I doubt it will be possible for them to accept at this late stage. They lead busy lives." He smiled reassuringly. "I know they will want to come. Nellie and Carrie will be eager to meet you."

A duchess and a marchioness. Another surge of anxiety tightened her chest. What would they make of her? Would they think her a parvenu, after money and a title? Surely they would realize such a person could not fool Redcliffe. But there would be those among the *ton* who would believe it. She drew her bottom lip through her teeth.

He moved closer and put his arm around her. "I want you to enjoy your life with me, Olivia. I don't have the family rings, although they might be in the bank. If not, I'll purchase one in London." He smiled. "I hope you will approve of my taste."

"I'll love it because you gave it to me." She gave him an indulgent smile, a little frustrated. Wasn't it always like a man to disregard the most important things? "Redcliffe, I have no suitable clothes to wear."

He looked surprised. "Can you have some made here? A

London dressmaker will outfit you later. My sister or the duchess can recommend a good one."

His words made her starkly aware of the challenges ahead. But Redcliffe would see her through the worst, while it was all new to her. She was determined he would never regret his decision to marry her. "Who will give me away?"

"I thought of Williams."

"Oh, yes. Do you think he will agree?"

"Yes. I'll ask him."

"Redcliffe, please don't order him." She raised her eyebrows.

"You have such a poor opinion of me, my love." He bent down to kiss her cheek, not in the least affronted.

"What is the news from the hall? Has your secretary arrived?"

"Yes. Grant has proved to be an asset. Oh, with everything happening, I forgot to tell you about Pike."

She listened as he described his confrontation with Pike in Gateshead jail and how Mrs. Hobbs gave the game away.

"I'm relieved. They are villainous."

He drew a letter from his waistcoat pocket. "Evelyn sent me this."

His sister. Another bridge to cross. She would love them to be friends, but would it be possible? She took the missive from him and read it. When she finished, she sighed. "Oh, how your uncle must have suffered. But he wasn't averse to you inheriting the earldom. He welcomed you and wished you to restore the family fortunes and standing in society. I wonder if the money is still there? Obviously, Pike couldn't find it."

"I want you with me when I open the desk."

Excitement skittered through her. "I should like that, but I don't see how…"

"Tomorrow. I will take you back to the house. Move into one of the guest chambers until the wedding."

She glanced at the door and moved slightly away from him. "Redcliffe, it is better for me to remain here with Helen. The gossip will be bad enough without stirring up more."

He sighed. "If you must."

It would be impossible to resist the force of his will and her own desires should she stay there. "I consider it wise." She smiled at his annoyed expression. Everything went full steam ahead with Redcliffe. He was like one of those new locomotives she'd heard about.

"You do want children?" she asked shyly. She remembered how supportive he'd been when Mrs. Graves gave birth.

"I do. But first I would prefer time with my wife before the nursery claims all your attention."

Could she give him an heir? Another thing to worry her. Oh, to hold their baby in her arms! How much she had longed for a child, and not just one—a nursery full. She smiled. This was one argument she wouldn't engage in. Let nature take its course.

He stood. "I'll return in the morning, and if you are well enough, we'll hunt for Alberic's pot of money. Shouldn't be too difficult to find." He shrugged. "If it is where he says he put it."

"Do you think he might have been confused?"

"He seemed quite certain. I imagine we'll find something. But I doubt it will be much." He bent and briefly kissed her lips. "Tomorrow, my love."

Left alone, before Helen came in to hear the news, Olivia sat quietly, considering the extraordinary events since she came to Redcliffe Hall. She had fallen in love and was about to become a countess, which she could still hardly believe. It thrilled and terrified her in equal measure.

The door opened, and Helen slipped inside. "He didn't stay long."

"I'll return with him to the hall tomorrow for a few hours. I prefer to remain here with you until my wedding night if you'll have me."

"Of course I will," Helen smiled broadly. "We have much to do to prepare."

Olivia smiled back at her. How wonderful it was to see her good friends again, lost to her during that awful time. When she and Redcliffe returned from London, he had told her he planned to hold a hunt ball. Helen, an attractive blonde approaching thirty, had never married, instead, remaining at home to care for her invalid parents. Might there be a suitable bachelor among Redcliffe's acquaintances whom they could invite?

"You appear deep in thought," Helen observed.

"I must confess I get nervous when I think of what lies ahead of me in London."

"Be yourself. People will take to you. You will make a wonderful countess. You've read widely, speak French, and can converse on many subjects. And you are generous."

"I intend to use my position to help the less fortunate."

"I am certain you will make your mark on society. The way you've taken some of those poor unfortunate servants under your wing at Lady Lowry's and at Redcliffe Hall," Helen said fondly.

"Redcliffe has received a letter from his sister, Lady Trelawny. The village gossip concerning lost treasure at Redcliffe Hall could prove true. And it may not remain a mystery for long."

Helen leaned forward, her eyes alight. "Do tell."

"Well, the ghostly candlelight sighted moving through the house was Pike searching for the old earl's money. And the earl's letter may have revealed its hiding place."

"My goodness. I can't wait to hear what you find."

Olivia laughed. "I can't wait to tell you."

MIDMORNING ON THE next day, Olivia wore her blue pelisse over her lemon muslin gown and tied the blue ribbons of her straw bonnet beneath her chin. In the mirror, her cheeks were pink, and her eyes sparkled with anticipation. What would they find today?

Redcliffe had eyed her approvingly as he assisted her into the phaeton which bowled along the country road.

She glanced down at the passing road. "This seat is far from the ground."

He skillfully guided the horses around a sharp turn. "Nervous?"

"No. You handle your horses very well. You know, I used to drive Papa's curricle." She could refer to the past now with only a little sadness. She knew her father would rest easier if he could see how well things had turned out for her.

"Then you shall have your own vehicle."

When they approached the house, she gazed at it with fresh eyes. No longer her place of employment, it would soon be her home. A magnificent one with the windows sparkling, the paths swept, the early drift of autumn leaves raked into piles and burned by the gardeners, smoke spiraling into the sky. She shivered. There was a distinct chill in the air.

Redcliffe assisted her down and tossed the reins to Jack, who had hurried out to greet them.

In the entrance hall, she took off her bonnet and pelisse, then she and Redcliffe climbed the stairs to the attic.

Once the door closed behind them, Redcliffe pulled her into his embrace. "Remember when we first came here?"

Resting against his chest, she listened to the rumble of his voice. "How could I not?"

"It was difficult to keep my mind on our search. I could think of nothing but you."

She pulled away and attempted to frown, but smiled. "It was bad of you to bring me here without another servant to chaperone us."

"You might have said no."

She laughed. "How could I?"

"Did you want to refuse?"

"No. And you knew it."

His thumb traced her bottom lip. "I believe I did." He lowered his head and kissed her. With a soft moan, he drew her close again.

She pushed away from his arms. "Shall we examine the desk?

The staff are waiting for us to come down. If we are gone too long, they will guess the reason."

With a resigned nod, he gently put her aside and turned to the desk. "It must be this one. There's nothing else here that fits Alberic's description." He knelt before the oak desk with the damaged leg. "But before, I found no evidence of a secret panel."

He prodded the ornamentation along the top of the desk. "Nothing there."

Olivia had found a small round protuberance among the carvings. "What's this?" She pressed it. A panel fell open.

It revealed a locked door. "Well, look at that," Redcliffe said. "No key. Give me a hairpin."

Olivia pulled one from her hair and handed it to him.

He jiggled it in the lock. Minutes passed as she held her breath. Finally, a click. The door swung open. Three small document drawers occupied the space. They were too small to hold much of value. Redcliffe pulled each of them out. All of them were empty. "Nothing here. It's not looking hopeful, is it?"

Disappointed, Olivia stepped closer. "What's behind them?"

Redcliffe drew the three drawers out in one piece, revealing a large space behind.

Olivia gasped.

A cloth bag had been tucked inside.

Redcliffe drew it out. He untied the drawstring and upended the contents onto the desk. Jewelry, coins, and banknotes spilled over the surface.

He picked up a large ruby brooch, and she selected a long rope of beautiful gray pearls. A magnificent diamond tiara had lost its luster.

"I wish I could apologize for doubting my uncle. These are impressive."

"No wonder Pike was so keen to find them."

"He must have had some idea of their value." He opened a jewelry box. "My aunt's wedding ring." He held it out for her to see. "It needs to be cleaned."

She took the gold band from him.

"Would you rather have a new one?"

"Of course not." She handed it back to him. "It's a family heirloom."

He replaced the ring in the box and put it in his pocket. "The money will go into the bank, but the jewels are yours, Olivia. Take whatever you wish to wear. They are old-fashioned. I'll commission a London jeweler to reset them."

"The sapphire earrings." She admired the dainty setting of fine stones surrounded by diamonds. They would go perfectly with her wedding gown. "And the pearls." They were the finest she had ever seen.

"Take them, my love, with Alberic's compliments. And you must wear the diamond parure and my aunt's tiara when you attend London balls." He leaned back against the desk and drew her against him. "The money will go toward improving my tenant farmers' cottages, building fences, irrigation, and stocking the home farm." He kissed her nose. "Quite a find, eh?"

She took his hand. "Let's go downstairs."

"I'll put these in a safe place," he said as they left the attic.

"I'll speak to the staff. I want to invite Sam to the wedding."

"They will all attend the wedding."

"I know. And they will have their own celebration belowstairs. But I'd like Sam to be an usher. Do you agree?"

"If you wish." He paused, a hand on the banister. "You seem fond of the fellow."

"He is my friend, Redcliffe. That won't change."

He smiled. "I didn't expect it would, sweetheart."

Sam and the housemaids clustered around her when she entered the servants' hall. "It's like a fairytale." Emily's eyes sparkled with tears.

Sam greeted her in a formal, unfamiliar manner. "It shall be my pleasure to serve you."

"I am still the same person, Sam." Olivia smiled, realizing it would take time for the staff to come to accept her in her new role. "And I have something, in particular, to ask of you."

CHAPTER TWENTY-FOUR

D OMINIC KNEW ONLY a few of the guests who filled the pews of the small church. The Graveses were there, the Johnsons, too, and all of his staff. Samuels performed the job required of him with quiet dignity. Dominic had to look at him twice. The cook had cut his hair and was dressed in a dark coat. Dominic was unsure if he was pleased or sorry Samuels no longer thumbed his nose at the world.

Dominic was about to enter when a grand carriage swept around the bend, driven by six matched bays. A murmur rose from the crowd gathered around the church door. People stared at the duke's crest on the glossy black door panel.

A liveried footman jumped down and put down the steps as Dominic hurried over to greet his friends.

Four elegantly dressed people alighted.

Charles greeted him, and Nicholas slapped him on the back while Nellie and Carrie jostled to hug and kiss him.

"I just know I'm going to love her," Nellie said.

"We didn't think we'd arrive in time." Nicholas grinned. "Couldn't let you get married without your groomsmen."

"It's a wonderful surprise. I never hoped..." Emotion tugged at Dominic's throat. He swallowed. "Olivia will be thrilled, as I am."

"You have been missed in London, Dom," Charles said. "We

actually came to ensure you made it to the altar and secure your promise not to rusticate forever."

"Pleased you're entering the blissful state of matrimony, Dom," Nicholas said. "You could have knocked us over with a feather when we received your invitation. No way we'd miss it! We are all eager to meet the bride. Ah, and this must be her, now."

Jack was perched up on the box with Grimsby as the coach arrived. Olivia was inside with her two attendants.

"Samuels? Show the duchess and countess to the front pews," Dominic ordered as he went into the church with his two groomsmen.

At the altar, Charles held out his hand. "The ring?"

In his brief visit to London, Dominic had the ring cleaned. He handed it to Charles. Then he checked the flower in his button-hole hadn't wilted. Cushing had taken special care of his appearance, and his sharp eye rested on Dominic from his seat.

In London, Dominic had spent a night at his Mayfair town-house. He'd conferred with his butler, who alerted the housekeeper and staff to prepare for their arrival in a few weeks.

Evelyn sent a tear-stained missive to wish him and Olivia well. He supposed it would take time for her to accept that he'd chosen his bride and not the lady she dearly wished him to marry. But his sister had a big heart, and she loved him. And she'd promised to come to London to meet Olivia as soon as she was able, but not until Gerald had recovered from some malady. The doctor assured her it wasn't serious.

The organ music swelled.

Dominic turned.

Necks craned as Olivia walked down the aisle in a blue gown, her gloved hand resting on Williams's sleeve, a bouquet of white flowers in her hand. A floral wreath adorned her black hair. The gown and the earrings made her eyes very blue. She looked so lovely, she robbed him of breath. Her attendants, Miss Caldicot and Mrs. Turner followed, dressed in lemon and white.

With a loving glance, Olivia came to stand beside him.

Williams stepped away.

The vicar cleared his throat, and the atmosphere hushed.

Destiny, fate, or the stars had brought them together, while he'd had been busy avoiding falling in love. Had he always known that true happiness lay in loving and being loved? Perhaps he had. He'd just forgotten it along the way.

As the vicar's intone washed over him, Dominic gazed down at his bride, his heart full.

REDCLIFFE INTRODUCED HIS exquisitely dressed friends to Olivia when they stood outside the church: Charles, Duke of Shrewsbury, and his Duchess, Nellie, an elegant blonde; and Nicholas, Marquess of Pennington, and his marchioness, Carrie, a lovely redhead. Olivia saw in their faces the offer of true friendship, and any fears she might have had faded. She may not meet with such grace in London, but it was the people Dominic cared about that mattered most.

"As you did not expect us and wrote that you planned a simple affair, we would be delighted to host the wedding breakfast at the inn," Charles said. "I'll have them rustle up some musicians. But if you have made other arrangements, it's of no consequence."

"That's perfect, Charles!" Dominic turned to smile at Olivia.

"Musicians! We can dance the bridal waltz." Olivia smiled shyly at the duke. "Thank you, Your Grace."

"Charles, please. We stand on no ceremony with friends."

Olivia slipped away to tell Meg about the new arrangements.

"I must return to the house immediately," Meg said. Olivia quietly explained which bedchambers had been prepared and what needed to be done before the coachman drove Meg back to the hall.

When they arrived at the inn, the beaming proprietor stood at the door, awaiting them.

It seemed as if the entire village had gathered to watch them alight from the coaches. Olivia saw Lady Lowry among them. When she nodded politely, Lady Lowry returned a sour smile.

Musicians struck up as they entered the inn.

"Charles has drummed up a trio to play for us." Dominic grinned. "As I knew he would."

THE WEDDING BREAKFAST had been perfect. Mr. Bowls, the proprietor, put on a sumptuous spread, and Olivia waltzed with Redcliffe. "I love you, Lady Redcliffe," he'd whispered as he led her around the small dance floor.

His tender expression almost made her cry. "I love you, Redcliffe."

Charles made a wonderful, humorous speech, interspersed with interjections from Nicholas. Carrie promised to assist Olivia with her wardrobe when she came to London, and Nellie said she would hold a dinner in her honor. Olivia was stunned by how natural and friendly they both were.

When they came home, she went to change and found Meg had been busy. The countess's suite was restored to its former glory with lavender-scented sheets on the bed. Redcliffe must have ordered it done as soon as Olivia accepted him. Tonight, she would join her husband here, and their marriage would truly begin.

She went into the dressing room to change. Finding her few clothes hanging in the vast wardrobe caused a rueful smile.

As she pulled the gown over her head, she heard the door to the sitting room open. Moments later, Redcliffe walked in. She turned to him in her chemise, stays, and stockings, clutching the apricot sarsnet gown to her chest. "Redcliffe!"

He slipped an arm around her waist and pressed a kiss to her hair. "Am I not Dominic now?"

"Dominic," she murmured.

He ran his thumb along her bottom lip. "I enjoy hearing my name on your lips."

"A gentleman would knock."

He arched a brow. "And wait until you're dressed before I'm admitted, my lady wife?"

She gazed at him, helplessly drawn. "Our guests will await us in the salon," she said, her voice weakening.

"Let them wait," he said, his voice husky, his eyes dark with desire.

Olivia's body responded as passion like wildfire raged between them. She reached up to coil her hands around his neck.

He hefted her up in his arms and strode to the bed.

EPILOGUE

Marquess and Marchioness Powis's ball
Mayfair, August

OLIVIA'S GLOVED FINGERS trembled on Dominic's arm as they waited to be announced at the ballroom door.

"You outshine all the ladies here tonight," Dominic said in an undertone.

Of course, it wasn't true. "Hush, they'll hear you."

He chuckled softly and gave her the look that made her insides melt.

She smoothed down the skirts of the pale blue silk embroidered with silver thread the clever modiste Carrie had introduced her to had fashioned in an amazingly short time. Then put a hand to the diamond tiara. She wished her throat wasn't so dry. Would they all cut her?

Their regal host and hostess turned from welcoming another couple.

After the formal greetings, the marquess immediately engaged Dominic in conversation about the results of his horse at Ascot.

The marchioness, in gray lace with a magnificent diamond choker at her throat, smiled at Olivia. "You have the *ton* puzzled, my dear."

A spike of fear tightened Olivia's chest. "Puzzled, my lady?"

"You have tamed the Earl of Redcliffe, where many have tried and failed before you."

"I doubt I have tamed him." Olivia cast a smile at her tall handsome husband, who still talked to Powis. "I hope I have not. I rather liked him the way I found him."

"Indeed." Lady Powis laughed. "Ah, a love match. And the *ton* love nothing more than a romance."

It seemed to Olivia that the whole room grew hushed as she and Dominic descended the stairs into the beautiful ballroom lit by a thousand candles.

Charles and Nellie, Nicholas and Carrie came to greet them, and those around them followed suit. The moment's silence ended, and the noise rose to an insistent buzz as guests continued their conversations.

As a quadrille was announced, the exquisitely dressed guests gravitated to the dance floor. "May I have the pleasure of this dance, Lady Redcliffe?" Charles asked.

She smiled and gratefully took his arm while Dominic escorted Nellie.

It was some hours later when she and Dominic danced the waltz before they could exchange a few words. She had met so many people tonight, it made her head swim. "Our marriage seems to have barely caused a ripple," She smiled up at him, enjoying their closeness.

"The gossips talk of nothing but Lady Frencham," Dominic said. "It appears she has run away with her butler."

Olivia's eyes widened. "My goodness. Poor Lord Frencham."

"He is consoling himself with his mistress." He nodded to where a bald-headed gentleman danced with a woman in a purple gown.

"I see London shall take some getting used to," Olivia said breathlessly after he'd spun her around. "I've heard some gossip, too. Mrs. Marsham, a lady I am yet to meet, has apparently taken a new lover, but no one seems to mind."

"Least of all, Mr. Marsham," Dominic said with an ironic smile.

"If you took a lover, remember, what is good for the gander is also good for the goose," she said with a teasing smile.

"I have no intention of it, and neither will you, my lady," he said, narrowing his eyes. "For I would run the fellow through."

Thrilled by his passionate response, she met his intense green eyes. "Why would I, when I have the handsomest man in the *ton* at home?"

Redcliffe Hall two months later…

IN THE BALLROOM, the hunt ball was in full swing. Olivia sipped champagne as she wandered among the guests. The musicians played Beethoven, and dancers packed the floor for the quadrille.

Flushed and animated, Helen danced past with John Pembroke, a friend of Dominic's.

Might something come of it? How blessed she and Dominic were. Their dear friends would stay for several days. The men would take the guns out, while the women drank tea and chatted, roamed the gardens, and played whist, and in the evenings, there would be card play and dancing. A full contingent of staff was now employed. Sam had grown in confidence with a sous chef to assist him in the kitchen. He and Polly had just become engaged and planned to stay on at Redcliffe Hall once they were man and wife.

The guests laughed and enjoyed themselves. With Meg as housekeeper, they wanted for nothing.

Olivia's time in London had passed like a whirlwind. She'd curtsied before the Prince of Wales and other royals and met many dignitaries. Some she liked, some she didn't. Dominic told her she held her own admirably in any company, and while she was not blind to her shortcomings, she hoped it might be true.

Viscount and Lady Trelawny—Dominic's sister, Evelyn, and her husband Justin—were on the dancefloor. They'd warmly welcomed Olivia into the family. She looked forward to spending Christmas with them. Evelyn's choice of a bride for Dominic, Lady Marianne Gillingham, and her parents had come. Marianne was beautiful. In London, Olivia had worried that he should have married a lady from his world, but as the days passed into weeks and months, it no longer concerned her.

The orchestra struck up a waltz. Dominic made his way toward her, and her heart did that pitter-patter again. He was so handsome, so outrageous and determined, and so wonderful a lover. Her pulse skittered to think of what awaited them tonight.

"My dance, I believe, my love." They exchanged a look, and she flushed, sensing he was of the same thought as she. She'd become so bold in the bedchamber.

He spun her over the floor, and she breathed in his clean smell, uniquely him and very male, and thought how perfect this moment was.

Lady Marianne danced past them. She smiled boldly at Dominic.

Olivia ignored it. But during the evening, she drank two more glasses of champagne than she was wont to do.

After the ball ended and they retired, Olivia, in her lacy peignoir, dismissed Emily, who had become her lady's maid. She sat at the dressing table brushing her hair. It was down to her waist now. Dominic preferred it long. One hundred strokes every night until it shone.

A few minutes later, he entered in his blue and gold silk dressing gown. He bent to kiss her shoulder, then lay down on the velvet upholstered chaise. She watched him in the mirror, aware the wine made her bolder. She put down the brush and rose, then sashayed in her bare feet across the room to where he lay with one arm beneath his head watching her.

"Lady Marianne Gillingham is beautiful and very young," she said, pushing her curls back over her shoulder.

"She is." Dominic's gaze roamed over his lovely wife, remembering their sleepy early morning lovemaking, and wanting her again.

It was apparently not the right response. Olivia glared at him. She swung toward him, her filmy gown swirling around her elegant ankles. "Perhaps you should have married her. It would have delighted your sister."

"Evelyn is pleased to see me married. And happy with my choice."

She put her hands on her hips. "Do I make you happy?"

"Oh, you do, my darling. Very much."

"Marianne lacks a sense of humor. So perhaps it was just as well that you didn't marry her, Redcliffe."

His lips quirked. "No sense of humor, eh?"

"Not a shred."

He arched an eyebrow. "Take that off."

She fingered the silk. "This? You don't like it?" She untied the sash and let it fall open, then shrugged it off her shoulders.

She stepped out of it.

"That, too."

She pulled her nightgown over her head and stood before him, naked.

He lost his breath. His gaze heated, and he shrugged the dressing gown off his shoulders, revealing his nakedness and need for her. "Come here."

Shivering with desire, Olivia climbed onto the chaise and into his arms. Nuzzling her chin against his neck, she murmured. "I love you."

"I am mad for you." His hands roamed over her back and cupped her bottom, settling her against him.

His erection nudged her most sensitive part.

"Mmm."

"I'm no longer Dominic?" he asked softly.

She raised her head to kiss his jaw. "You will always be my Redcliffe."

With a gruff laugh, he crushed his mouth to hers.

His hands on her hips, he pushed into her.

Her fingers raked through his hair, tugging hard. She murmured his name and moaned, loving it, loving him.

With a deep groan, he stilled and drew her down to him. "I'll hear no more of this nonsense, Olivia," he gasped as his breath eased. "I never doubted you were right for me. And I was not such a fool as to let you go. I love you and want you by my side, always."

"And I, you, my love," she murmured as her fingers toyed with the curls of dark hair on his chest. For now, she was content not to argue. Content to bend like a reed in the river. But she wanted more. There was so much a countess could do to help the less fortunate in society, and she'd make him proud he'd chosen her as his wife. Soon, she would begin, but right now, just being with him was enough.

She took his dear face in her hands and pressed her lips to his.

About the Author

A USA TODAY bestselling author of Regency romances, with over 35 books published, Maggi's Regency series are International bestsellers. Stay tuned for Maggi's latest Regency series out next year. Her novels include Victorian mysteries, contemporary romantic suspense and young adult. Maggi holds a BA in English and Master of Arts Degree in Creative Writing. She supports the RSPCA and animals often feature in her books.

Like to keep abreast of my latest news? Join my newsletter.
http://bit.ly/1m70lJJ

Blog: http://bit.ly/1t7B5dx
Find excerpts and reviews on my website: http://bit.ly/1m70lJJ
Twitter: @maggiandersen: http://bit.ly/1Aq8eHg
Facebook: Maggi Andersen Author: http://on.fb.me/1KiyP9g
Goodreads: http://bit.ly/1TApe0A
Pinterest: https://www.pinterest.com.au/maggiandersen

Maggi's Amazon page for her books with Dragonblade Publishing.
https://tinyurl.com/y34dmquj

CPSIA information can be obtained
at www.ICGtesting.com
Printed in the USA
BVHW032316100622
639494BV00010B/216